Victory *for the* Sewing Factory Girls

Victory *for the* Sewing Factory Girls

Posy Lovell

First published in Great Britain in 2024 by Orion Fiction,
an imprint of The Orion Publishing Group Ltd.,
Carmelite House, 50 Victoria Embankment
London EC4Y 0DZ

An Hachette UK Company

3 5 7 9 10 8 6 4 2

A CIP catalogue record for this book is
available from the British Library.

ISBN (Paperback) 978 1 3987 1885 2
ISBN (eBook) 978 1 3987 1456 4

Typeset by Input Data Services Ltd, Bridgwater, Somerset

Printed and bound in Great Britain by Clays Ltd, Elcograf S.p.A.

www.orionbooks.co.uk

For my grandad, who would have loved me writing about football. There were so many times when I wished I could ring him and have a chat while I was writing this story.

Chapter One

Clydebank, Scotland, 1916

Ellen looked out of the window and sighed heavily.

'It's so quiet,' she said. 'The streets are empty.'

Her sister Bridget rolled her eyes.

'Och, Ellen, don't be so dramatic.'

'All the men have gone.' Ellen rested her head against the glass and watched as her breath made it steam up.

'They have not.' Bridget sounded amused. 'Some men have gone recently, some had gone already, and some are staying put because – as you well know – the lads who work at the shipyard won't be conscripted. Nor married men. And anyway, they've passed the conscription law now, but it doesn't come into effect until March.'

Ellen ignored her. She hated when Bridget spoke sense.

'There's no one out there.'

'It's raining and it's freezing cold.'

Ellen wiped the window with her hand. 'I can't see a single soul.'

Bridget put down her pen and tutted.

'Ellen,' she said, 'stop looking out of the window and come and make yourself useful. Because the streets may be empty, but the shop is not.'

With exaggerated effort, Ellen dragged herself away from the window and instead leaned against the counter.

'Everyone looks worn out,' she said, watching one customer pick up a skirt and hold it against her daughter to see if it would fit. 'Tired.'

'So do you.' Bridget was adding up a column of numbers in a ledger. 'Now would you please stop talking for a second and let me concentrate.'

'Everyone's so sad.'

'Fifty-five,' said Bridget, scribbling in the book. 'And sixty. Everyone is a bit sad, yes. But that's not surprising, is it?'

'I suppose not,' Ellen replied. She pulled the stool from behind the counter closer to her and hauled herself up on it because her feet hurt and she needed to sit down. 'But . . .'

Bridget shut the ledger with a thud and waved goodbye to the woman and her daughter, who'd decided the skirt wouldn't fit. 'Ellen,' she said, sounding more than a little exasperated. 'Everyone is sad because there is a war on.' Her expression softened as Ellen looked at her. 'And you are tired because your James is on a ship somewhere in the middle of the ocean, goodness knows where, and you are pregnant and decidedly green around the gills all the time, and my darling niece, as much as I adore her, is quite the handful.'

Ellen tried to smile at the mention of her daughter, but found it was quite an effort to shift her morose mood now she had let it take over. 'She's definitely that.'

She looked over at the shop floor. Mrs McGinty from the next street was rubbing the hem of a pair of trousers between her thumb and forefinger, looking disdainful.

'That's good work,' Ellen called. 'Hand-stitched.'

Mrs McGinty frowned. 'Fabric's thin.'

'We've lined the knees and the rear. Won't wear through.'

Ellen caught her sister's eye and made a face. Mrs McGinty was, as their friend Sadie always said, 'a fusspot'.

'Price is a wee bit steep,' said the fusspot. 'It's second-hand after all.'

Ellen shot her a fierce look. 'Those trousers came from one of Sadie's posh friends in Glasgow,' she said. 'They'd barely been worn because the wee lad who owned them grew three inches in as many weeks. And I fixed the hem myself, and I lined the inside, and they're worth the money we're asking.' She held McGinty's gaze. 'If you had tokens, they'd be cheaper.'

Ellen, Bridget and Sadie ran the shop together. It was called the Clydebank Clothing Exchange because they took donations from local people in exchange for tokens, then mended the clothes, or adapted them, and then sold them. The folk who'd donated worn-out or too-small clothes could spend the tokens they'd earned in the shop.

It had been a labour of love when they first started but now they were so busy they'd had to employ another seamstress – Sadie's sister Rachel – and Ellen was proud that they were keeping their heads above water. And goodness, the money was certainly coming in handy now James had joined the navy.

'We're closing,' she said, suddenly feeling a rush of anger as McGinty peered at her stitching. 'Sorry. Time to go.'

She slid off her stool slightly awkwardly, and bustled the other woman out of the shop, ignoring her protests that it was only three o'clock in the afternoon.

'Early closing today,' she said, giving her a nudge to get her out of the door and shutting it behind her.

'It's Tuesday,' Mrs McGinty called through the glass.

Ellen turned over the sign in the window so it read 'closed' and leaned against the door.

'I can't stand that woman.'

Bridget raised an eyebrow. 'So I gathered.'

Ellen snorted.

'Her husband's flat-footed apparently.' She marched back to the stool and sat down again with a sigh. 'Flat-footed my eye.'

'Missing James?' asked Bridget, astutely. It annoyed Ellen how well her sister could read her moods. 'He's been gone a while, now, eh?'

'Do you remember when Da fixed the wall above our bedroom door?' Ellen said thoughtfully.

'Yes.'

'And it made our door a wee bit shorter, so we kept banging our heads? And then we got used to it, so we ducked, but sometimes we'd forget and we'd hit our heads and it would hurt?'

'Yes,' said Bridget again, with a little less certainty this time.

'It's like that.' Ellen nodded. 'Just the same.'

'Right,' Bridget said with a small frown. 'The same as our bedroom door?'

'I'm getting used to him being away,' Ellen said. She swallowed because she felt a lump in her throat, and she didn't want to cry. Not again. She cried all the time just now. Yesterday she'd cried while sorting some tiny wee baby booties because they were just so sweet and small. And this morning she'd cried because Annie wouldn't eat her porridge and said she wanted her da.

She lifted her chin. 'I don't want to get used to him being away,' she said.

Bridget looked like she was going to ask a question but instead she put her hand on Ellen's. 'It's all right to be sad, you know.'

'Don't,' said Ellen with a grimace. 'Don't be nice. Because when I start crying, I don't tend to stop.'

'Then buck up,' said Bridget mildly. 'We just need to grit our teeth and get on with it.'

The rattling of the door handle made them look up.

'It's Sadie,' said Ellen, in a rush. 'Don't tell her.'

'Don't tell her what?'

'About the baby.'

Bridget looked surprised. 'She doesn't know?'

Ellen looked at the door of the shop, and then at her sister. 'Not yet,' she said in a low voice.

'You'll have to tell her soon enough.'

Ellen adjusted her apron over her thickening waist. 'I'm just not sure . . .' she began, as Sadie rattled the door handle again.

'Ellen?' she called. 'Ellen?'

'Answer it,' Ellen said to Bridget. 'But shhhh.'

'Bossy,' said Bridget, but she went to the door just the same and unlocked it. Ellen knew she'd not say anything – Bridget could always be relied on. She wasn't sure why she didn't want Sadie to know about her new baby yet. It was just that there was something in Sadie's eyes recently that made her reluctant to share the news. And there seemed to be a distance between them that hadn't been there before.

'Why are we closed?' said Sadie, coming inside. 'It's Tuesday.'

'McGinty was here,' Ellen began.

Sadie rolled her eyes. 'Fusspot.'

'Aye.' Ellen managed a small smile. 'I threw her out and shut the shop.'

'Don't blame you.' Sadie unwrapped her scarf and took her hat off. 'Missing James, are you?'

'A little,' said Ellen. She saw Sadie and Bridget exchange a concerned glance and it irritated her. 'I'm fine,' she said firmly to Sadie.

'Are you?'

'Yes.' She looked at her friend. 'Are you?'

'Aye. All fine.' Sadie dropped her gaze which made Ellen think she might be lying. But she didn't understand what was wrong because as far as Ellen could see, nothing had changed for Sadie. Her husband Noah had not joined up, and even though conscription had happened, he wouldn't be called up because he was a teacher. James wouldn't have been called up either because he worked at the shipyard, but he had joined the navy anyway. Ellen shook her head gently, wanting to dislodge the sadness. Wasn't she known for being cheerful? Wasn't she the one her da always said was like a ray of sunshine?

She forced herself to smile, though it felt a little odd. 'I've had an idea.'

'Oh no.' Bridget looked alarmed. 'What now?'

Sadie leaned against the counter, pretending to be faint. 'It's not a strike, is it?' she said, fanning herself.

This time Ellen did manage a genuine smile.

'It's not a strike,' she said. 'Though as far as I remember, Sadie, you were the one who came up with that idea.'

Sadie shrugged, looking rather happy about it, and Ellen felt her mood lift, a tiny bit, surrounded by her two favourite women.

'Remember how in the strike we thought we were stronger together?' she began.

'Of course.' Sadie nodded.

'Well, I thought, there are lots of women like me, aren't there? Women whose husbands are off at sea, or at the Front. And maybe we'd be stronger together too.'

Bridget, who was a passionate suffragette, stood up straighter. 'Keep talking.'

Ellen reached under the counter and pulled out a banner she'd been stitching, whenever she'd found a minute. She unfolded it and stood back to let Bridget and Sadie see.

'Join the Clydebank Clothing Exchange,' Sadie read aloud.

'Everyone welcome,' Ellen added. 'But I've not had time to stitch that bit yet.'

Bridget leaned over and examined the stitching. 'Nice work,' she said.

Ellen rolled her eyes. 'Of course.'

'What does it mean?' Sadie asked.

'Remember when we started?' Ellen said. 'In the strike. When everyone was desperate and we all came together to help with clothes and food and . . .' She ducked her head, suddenly feeling a little silly. 'And, well, friendship?'

'We did,' said Sadie. She put her hand on the banner and rubbed the fabric gently. 'We really did.'

'I thought perhaps we could just throw open the doors – once a week, maybe? More if we need to. We can collect donations for folk, and for the troops, and perhaps knit socks? And just, you know, be there for one another.' There was a pause. 'Maybe it's a silly idea,' she said quickly. 'Everyone's busy . . .'

She reached out to roll up the banner again but Bridget caught her hand. 'I think it's a good idea.'

Sadie took her other hand. 'Me too,' she said. 'I think it might be just what everyone needs.'

'Really?' said Ellen.

'Really.' Sadie smiled. 'We'll help of course, won't we, Bridget? We'll all work together.'

Ellen felt an overwhelming sense of relief. 'I was hoping you'd say that. Because I have absolutely no idea how I'd do it without you.'

Chapter Two

'It's going to be more like the Clothing Exchange we organised during the strike,' Ellen told Bridget's friend Ida later that day. 'Everyone will be welcome to come along and do their bit and make new friends.'

'Ellen's got it all worked out,' Bridget added.

Ida, who loved nothing more than bringing people together, looked pleased. 'Tell me more about it,' she said.

They were in Bridget's flat above the Clothing Exchange. It was two flats really – the other one was above the shop next door – McKinley's General Store, which Ida owned. Ida, who was rather clever with a hacksaw and a pot of paint, had made a door in between the two. Ellen thought it was very handy how the two women – who were very close friends – could come and go between their flats. The arrangement seemed to suit them well.

Bridget was still married, of course, but her husband Malcolm had moved to Manchester after the strike. He and Bridget had given up the single-end flat they'd shared and Malcolm rarely came back to Clydebank now. In fact, Bridget hardly ever mentioned him, though Ellen knew they wrote to one another.

'I just thought it would be nice to bring people together,' Ellen said. 'Don't set a place for Annie, she'll be asleep in two minutes.'

She looked over to where her daughter lay curled up on a chair.

Bridget followed her gaze and smiled fondly as she put cutlery on the table and began to slice the bread.

'We're going to get together and talk, and knit socks, and collect donations.'

'Sounds wonderful.' Ida had cooked dinner and now she ladled the soup into bowls and brought it to the table, while Bridget put the bread down and pulled out the chairs. Ellen sat down. 'I'm very happy to help.'

'The more the merrier,' said Ellen.

Bridget took a sip of soup and nodded. 'This is delicious, Ida.'

Ida smiled, appreciating the compliment, and Ellen thought – not for the first time – how content her sister was nowadays. She'd never been so calm when she lived with Malcolm. Not that he was an unpleasant man. On the contrary, he was a good, kind chap, though Ellen hadn't been overly fond of him at first. But Bridget had seemed so prickly almost as soon as they'd married. Tightly wound.

She looked at her sister while they ate. Bridget was listening to Ida chatting about the Clothing Exchange and watching her closely.

'Are you missing the suffragettes?' Bridget said.

Ida paused in her stream of conversation. 'Is it that obvious?'

Bridget put her spoon in her empty soup bowl and got up from the table. 'It's obvious, but understandable,' she said. She went to Ida's side and put her hand on her shoulder. 'I feel it too.'

Ida tilted her head towards Bridget for a second.

'Do you?' she said. 'Honestly?'

Ellen watched Ida with curiosity. She was always so confident, Ida. Sure of herself. Yet suddenly she seemed to need Bridget's reassurance, just like she – Ellen – turned to James for reassurance. It was nice to see. She was glad Bridget had a friend like Ida.

'Of course I do, you silly goose,' said Bridget with affection. 'The fight for women's suffrage has been such a large part of our lives for so long.'

'And now it's gone,' said Ida.

'Not gone,' Bridget said. 'Paused, for a while.'

'And aren't we seeing everyone this very evening?' said Ellen, keen to make Ida feel better. She thought Ida was marvellous, and didn't like to see her gloomy.

'To roll bandages for the Red Cross,' said Ida.

Ellen opened her mouth to say that rolling bandages was a worthy task, but Ida jumped in again before she could speak. 'It feels like the fight has gone out of us.'

'Tea?' Bridget took the plates to the sink and filled the kettle. 'Well, perhaps Ellen expanding the Clothing Exchange will give us another cause to focus on,' she said. 'Like knitting socks for soldiers.'

'Mrs Pankhurst would approve.' Ida's voice held an edge that Ellen was surprised – and a little irritated – by.

'You don't think we should be supporting the men who are fighting? Men like James?'

'I do, of course.' Ida sighed. 'Goodness knows they need our support.'

'But?' Ellen spoke sharply.

'But I think there has to be a better way.'

Ida's words played on Ellen's mind as they went to meet their friends later. Was there a better way?

She tugged her sister's sleeve as Ida marched on ahead. They'd dropped little Annie off at their parents' house and they were heading to the church where the bandages were being rolled.

'Do you think Ida's right?' Ellen asked now. 'Is there a better way? What did she mean?'

Bridget shrugged. 'The very idea of war makes me feel sort of bleak and hopeless,' she said in a low voice. 'Those boys – your sweet James, or Sadie's brother Daniel, being given weapons and taught to kill other men just like them? It makes me want to cry.'

'James isn't fighting in the trenches,' Ellen said. 'He's on a ship.'

'A battleship,' Bridget said.

Ellen shuddered.

'I don't like to think about it.'

'But what's the alternative?' Bridget said helplessly. 'I'm not sure.'

The bandage rolling was taking place in the hall at St Andrew's Church – the very place where the Clydebank Clothing Exchange had started.

They walked up the path and through the wide door. The hall was full of women, bustling around collecting baskets of rolled bandages, or sitting rolling them, or knitting socks. Bridget looked very tired all of a sudden, and Ellen wished she'd suggested staying at home and letting Ida come on her own. But Ida put her hand on Bridget's back and steered her towards the corner. 'Come on,' she said. 'Chin up. Helen's over there.' And Bridget smiled, and Ellen thought that bringing women together to do something purposeful was a very good idea indeed.

She followed Bridget and Ida to the corner where Helen and a few of the other suffragettes were busy rolling bandages.

'It's funny being back here, isn't it?' said Helen after a while. 'Back where we spent census night to avoid being counted.'

'It feels like a very long time ago, and yet hardly any time at all,' said Ida.

'So much has happened since then,' Ellen agreed.

Bridget looked down at the bandage in her lap. 'Was it worth it?' she asked. 'All the fighting we did? It all came to nothing in the end.'

'Ah but you see, Bridget . . .' Helen dropped a finished bandage into her basket with a flourish. 'It's not the end.'

'Really?'

'We're not done yet. Trust me.'

Bridget smiled at her, and Ellen smiled at Bridget, and felt the same little shiver of excitement she'd felt back in the days of the strike, when she was part of something important. And then a voice made her wince.

'Evening, ladies.'

Ellen closed her eyes briefly, and when she opened them, Bridget was screwing her face up in a way that made Ellen want to laugh.

'Christina,' said Ida, coldly. 'We've not seen much of you, lately.'

'I've been busy,' Christina said. 'There are battles still to be won.'

Bridget narrowed her eyes. Ellen couldn't blame her. It was Christina whose actions had once landed her sister in jail, if only briefly. And, Ellen recalled with a little smile, alongside herself.

'That's what I was just telling Bridget,' said Helen. 'The fight for women's suffrage goes on.'

Christina looked at Helen as though she'd grown an extra head.

'Not that fight,' she said, sounding like a disapproving schoolmistress. 'Not now, Helen.'

Helen made a face at Bridget and Ellen. Bridget made no effort to hide her smile.

'Mrs Pankhurst is leading a campaign to distribute white feathers to those men who have not joined up,' Christina said.

'What for?' Ida frowned. 'For what purpose is she distributing white feathers?'

'To let them know they are cowards.'

'Or unfit to serve,' Ida pointed out. 'Or working in a reserved occupation.' She lifted her head and looked straight at Christina. 'Like shipbuilding.'

Ellen laughed but quickly turned it into a cough. Half the men in Clydebank worked at the shipyard. Bridget snorted loudly, again making no attempt to hide her disdain.

Christina did have the grace to look slightly sheepish. 'Well quite,' she said. 'White feathers would not be well received in Clydebank.'

'I'm not sure they'd be well received anywhere,' Ida said. 'I have nothing but respect for Mrs Pankhurst, but I do not like this idea.'

'Nor do I,' said Bridget. She curled her lip. 'I'm not surprised you're in favour, Christina. Some people would think it a little . . .' She paused. 'What's the word I'm looking for, Ida?'

Ida gave Bridget an amused glance. 'Hypocritical?' she suggested.

'That's the one.' Bridget turned back to Christina. 'Some folk might think it's a little hypocritical for you to label others a coward.'

Christina glared at Bridget with such venom that Ellen shivered. But Bridget wasn't backing down. Ellen knew her sister better than she knew herself and she understood that Bridget didn't dislike many people, but those she did dislike, she disliked with absolute fervour. Ellen almost admired it.

Christina eventually dropped her gaze and Bridget looked mildly triumphant.

But Christina wasn't finished. 'I have turned my attentions elsewhere,' she said. She pulled up a chair and sat down, addressing the suffragettes as though she was telling them a secret.

'As you know, women are being paid to work in munitions factories. Many of them young. Many of them never having earned their own money before.'

There was a murmur of agreement from the women.

'In fact, they are being paid rather well,' Christina added.

'I'm not sure that's strictly true,' Bridget began, then stopped talking suddenly. Ellen knew it was because Christina liked to remind her sister that she was one of the few former workers at the Wentworth sewing machine factory who'd not gone out on strike, and Bridget didn't like to be reminded of that.

'Consequently, there are worries about morality and drunkenness,' Christina went on. She stood up. 'So women like me – and like all of you, should you be interested – have been recruited to patrol the areas around the munitions factories and keep things in check.' She began unbuttoning her coat and slipped it off to reveal a rather smart uniform. 'We are the Women's Police Service.'

Ellen saw Ida sit up a bit straighter.

'Are you working at Wentworth?' Bridget asked.

'Not at Wentworth, no,' Christina said. 'Not directly.'

Ellen exchanged a look with her sister, who sighed and went on: 'Are you working in association with Wentworth?'

'Indeed I am.'

'The same Wentworth that sacked my sister . . .' Bridget gestured towards Ellen. 'And my friends and, in fact, me, when we all stood up for what was right?' Bridget said.

Christina looked at her. 'That was a long time ago, Bridget.'

'Was it?'

Ellen put her hand on top of her sister's, wanting to support her but also to calm her. She felt the same about Wentworth, but the strike and everything they'd done back then seemed small in comparison to the war. And James being so far away. And all the death and the worries.

'Things have changed,' Christina said. The people running the factory have changed. And Wentworth is making munitions now. Doing its bit, as we all must.' She looked around at the suffragettes. 'Would anyone like to join me?'

There was a moment of quiet, and then to Ellen's dismay, and from the expression on Bridget's face, hers too, Ida stood up.

'I'll join you,' she said.

Chapter Three

Clydebank

7 Feb 1916

My dear James,

The weather has been dreadful. Just rain every day. Annie loves it of course. She begs to go outside and splash in the puddles – you know what she's like, never happier than when she's covered in mud.

James, you'll see such a difference in her now, even though it's only a few weeks since you were home. She's talking all the time and she's very strong-willed. She may only be wee, but if she doesn't want to do something, I can't make her. Ma says she's a proper Kelly, but I always say she's half Kelly and half McCallum, thank goodness.

What's the weather like where you are? I know you can't tell me where you are but maybe you can tell me that? I hope you're looking after yourself and getting enough to eat. And be careful, James, won't you? I need you to come home to me and Annie and the new baby. I think it's a boy, you know, because remember when I was expecting Annie how sick I was all the time – well, this time I'm still a bit queasy, but nothing like as bad. And my hair's looking much better this time round. So I think it's a boy.

I know you said in your last letter that I wasn't to do too much and to take things easy, but you know me better than that, James. And I've come up with a plan.

We – me, Bridget and Sadie – we're expanding the Clothing Exchange again. Making it more like it was when we started, back in the strike. We're going to open it up to anyone who wants to come along and get folk to work together to help each other. I think it'll really benefit the women whose men are away, and those who are struggling or – God forbid – widowed. Ida's helping too. And I think some of Bridget's suffragette pals are going to come as well.

Speaking of which, remember that awful woman Christina? She was always so rude to Bridget? She's turned up again like a bad penny and guess what, James? She's joined the police! I know! There's a women's police force now, because apparently the munitionettes are all getting out of hand now they've got money in their pocket. I find that hard to believe, because I know some of the folk who are working at the factories and they look dead on their feet half the time and not as though they're about to cause havoc. And sure, don't most of them have weans at home, and husbands away, and a house to look after? When are they going to have time to get out of hand?

But anyway, that's what Christina says. And Bridget says she thinks the people who want to have power over others are absolutely the last people who should have it, and Christina is the perfect example of that. And I think she's right, actually. Because Christina is far too bossy for her own good, and she thinks she's the only one who knows how the world works, and the rest of us are idiots. I find her very annoying.

Look at me, I've written half a page about Christina without even getting to the point. Which is that she is working with Wentworth to keep their munitionettes from getting into trouble, so obviously, we were all a bit put out about that.

And then she asked if any of us wanted to join her. And who do you think said yes? Ida!

Now Bridget's up to high-doh about it all, and she and Ida seem to be hardly speaking. Bridget's furious. Ida's not remotely sorry – she's marching about in her uniform, looking splendid and loving every minute. And do you know, James? I don't know how I feel. Because of course Wentworth let us down. I understand they were the enemy back then. But now . . . well, we're all just getting on as best we can, aren't we? And if that means working at Wentworth, then maybe that's all right.

What do you think?

Anyway, I want to get this in the post today, so I'll stop now. Write back soon, my darling. Annie and I miss you so much.

Your Ellen X

Chapter Four

Rachel was walking home, trying to decide how best to tell Sadie her big news. She was absolutely convinced that Sadie wouldn't mind. In fact, she thought her sister could even be pleased. Because since Daniel had joined up and their ma had moved out to the coast with their other brother, there was no denying that money was a little tight.

But now Rachel would be contributing properly. Proving to Sadie that Rachel coming to live with her and Noah wasn't a total disaster.

She'd be delighted, Rachel thought now. Over the moon.

But her steps slowed as she drew closer to the stairs and she sat down on the wall, looking up at the window of their flat.

'Sadie will be absolutely furious,' she muttered to herself with a sigh. 'She'll be raging.'

Because Rachel had got a job at Wentworth. Not making sewing machines – not like Sadie had done back before the strike. Making munitions, as well as stretchers to be sent to the Front for injured soldiers. And horseshoes, apparently, which sounded far less exciting but necessary all the same. Rachel was going to Do Her Bit, and she knew her sister would hate it.

And to add to Rachel's worries, there was definitely something the matter with Sadie. She was so out of sorts all the time. Short-tempered and snappy, or simply sad – which was worse, actually.

Rachel wanted to ask if she was all right, but she was scared about what Sadie might say. What if she said she'd changed her mind and Rachel had to leave Glasgow and go to live in Largs with Ma?

Or what if Sadie was sick? Rachel knew all about that, because she'd been ill for a lot of her childhood. She'd been wrapped up in cotton wool and cared for with so much love that she'd not noticed all the things she was missing out on until it was too late. She didn't want that for Sadie. Not one bit.

'What are you doing out here?' Sadie had walked along the road without Rachel noticing. She looked tired and thin, which made Rachel worry again.

'Just thinking,' she said.

'What about?'

Rachel took a deep breath. 'I've got something to tell you.'

Sadie sat down on the wall next to her. 'You know Mr Anderson won't be happy about you sitting on his wall?'

Rachel looked at her sister and smiled. 'About *us* sitting on his wall.'

Sadie shrugged. 'He likes me.' Her eyes held a flash of mischief that Rachel hadn't seen for a while. And so, feeling bolder, she blurted: 'What's the matter, Sadie?'

'The matter?'

'You seem so sad,' Rachel said. She stretched her legs out and looked at the toes of her battered boots, so she didn't have to meet Sadie's eyes. 'Always.'

Sadie was quiet for so long that Rachel thought she wasn't going to answer, but then she took Rachel's hand.

'Noah and I . . .' she began.

Rachel closed her eyes. Was this going to be when Sadie told her that she and Noah didn't want her living with them anymore? But then Sadie made a funny sound, like a half-sob, half-wail, and she realised her sister was crying. Properly crying, with tears running down her cheeks and her shoulders heaving.

'Oh good lord,' said Rachel in horror, throwing her arm round her sister, 'Oh, Sadie, what's wrong?'

'I thought I was pregnant,' Sadie gasped, struggling to get the words out in between sobs. 'I thought this was finally it, but then I started bleeding. And I don't know how to tell Noah. Not again. He's going to be so sad.'

'It's happened before?' Rachel asked, suddenly realising why Sadie had been so sad for so long.

Sadie nodded, her face buried against Rachel's shoulder. 'This is the second time,' she whispered.

Appalled that her sister had been going through all this without saying a word, Rachel held her and stroked her hair, like their mother had done when they were wee, and murmured that everything was going to be all right, Sadie just had to wait and see. Eventually she stopped crying and sniffed instead, and Rachel let go so she could find her handkerchief in her pocket.

'Here,' she said, passing it to Sadie.

'Thank you.' Sadie wiped her eyes and dabbed her nose, then looked at Rachel. 'I'm so sorry. I don't know where that came from.'

'Don't be sorry,' Rachel said, a little fiercely. 'Don't be sorry for being sad.'

Sadie nodded, looking more like herself.

'Shall we go inside?' Rachel asked, as two women from down the street walked past and looked at them curiously. 'I'll make tea and we can have another chat.'

She looped her arm through Sadie's and they went in.

Noah wasn't home. Rachel remembered him saying he was staying late at school for something – she'd not been listening properly – and she was quite glad. She adored her brother-in-law but she wanted some time with Sadie. Just the two of them.

Sadie sat down and Rachel made tea and when they were both settled, she said: 'Tell me everything.'

'Noah and I have been married for four years,' Sadie said. 'And we want a baby more than anything.' She took a deep breath. 'When we'd been married for two years, it happened and I was so pleased. But then I started bleeding. And we tried to be positive. Tried to think that it wasn't meant to be this time and it would happen again. But it didn't, not for another two years. And now . . .'

Sadie looked so stricken and sad that Rachel wished she'd put sugar in her tea.

'Have you been to see the doctor?'

Sadie made a face. 'Yes, and it was awful.'

'Dr Cohen?'

'I can't even talk about it,' Sadie said, burying her face in her hands. 'I've known him my whole life. It was mortifying.'

'He couldn't help?'

'He just said what would be would be.'

Rachel rolled her eyes. 'Right.'

'I'm fine with it,' Sadie said. 'Most of the time I don't even think about it. I just go along pretending everything's all right. But then I thought we'd done it this time, and I had that wee bit of hope and it's just knocked me for six.'

'I'm sorry,' Rachel said. 'I wish there was something I could do to help.'

Sadie gave her a small, stoic smile. 'I'll be fine,' she said. 'I will. I'll keep busy and keep going. You know I love spending time with wee Annie, and the Clothing Exchange is so busy that it's a good distraction . . .'

She trailed off and with a lurch of horror, Rachel remembered that she'd not yet told Sadie about her new job. She was still planning on helping out at the Clothing Exchange when she could, but she'd have to cut her hours. Ellen's plan to open up to new volunteers had come at the right time for Rachel, which made her feel a little guilty. But now wasn't the time to share her news.

'But?' she said.

'But what?' Sadie looked puzzled.

'You said you were fine most of the time,' Rachel explained. 'And it sounded like you were going to say "but . . .".'

Sadie nodded slowly. 'But I think Ellen's expecting again.' She breathed in a juddery breath. 'And I think she's hiding it from me, which means she must know that something's wrong, which means I've not been coping as well as I thought.'

'Just talk to her,' Rachel suggested. 'She's not coping either.'

Privately she thought that Ellen was more nervy than she'd ever seen her before. She'd always been so cheerful and positive, but now her smiles were forced and Rachel often caught her staring into space, chewing her lip.

'She's missing James,' Sadie said. 'It must be so frightening to have him off doing goodness knows what and not knowing if he'll ever come home again.'

'Expanding the Clothing Exchange will help.'

'I hope so,' said Sadie. 'I've got to give it to Ellen. It's a grand idea. And it won't just benefit her, it'll be good for lots of women around here.'

'You too,' said Rachel. 'Ellen will need your help, and getting involved will help you.'

Sadie nodded. 'You're right, of course. I just wish I didn't feel so awkward around her at the moment.'

'Talk to her,' Rachel said. 'You're such good pals, and you've been through a lot together. You can help each other now.'

Sadie looked at Rachel with such affection that Rachel felt a little squirmy inside. 'You're so wise for someone so young,' she said.

'I'm seventeen.' Rachel was a bit affronted. 'I'm a grown woman.'

'Ach, you'll always be my wee sister.' Sadie reached over and patted Rachel's leg. 'But thank you.'

They grinned at one another.

'Oh,' said Sadie suddenly. 'What was it you wanted to tell me?'

Rachel looked at her, wondering what to say.

'Nothing.'

'You said you had something to tell me.'

'I did, but it's fine,' Rachel said. 'Honestly, it can wait.'

'Rach, tell me.' Sadie looked at her with a piercing stare that made Rachel cave immediately.

'Don't be cross,' she said, which was completely the wrong way to start because now Sadie was sitting still, waiting to be annoyed.

'Go on,' Sadie prompted. 'Why would I be cross?'

Rachel screwed her face up. 'I'm going to carry on sewing at the Clothing Exchange,' she began, choosing her words carefully. 'But I've also decided to do something for the war.' She took a breath, then spoke quickly. 'So I've got a job in a factory. A munitions factory.'

Sadie narrowed her eyes. 'A munitions factory?'

'Aye.' Rachel swallowed, knowing there was only really one to speak of. 'That's right.'

'Wentworth?'

There was a pause.

'Aye,' Rachel said eventually. 'Wentworth.'

Sadie held her gaze for a long moment, and then she got up.

'I'm going to bed,' she said. She walked out of the room without saying anything else, leaving Rachel looking out of the window, where it was still light outside.

Chapter Five

Ellen was feeling sick again. It seemed to creep up on her in the evening, which was when Annie was at her most boisterous and in need of attention, and when Ellen was bone tired.

This evening the nausea had come over her just as she'd been trying to count up the money she had left for the rest of the month, wondering if it would stretch far enough. Of course James was getting a wage from the navy now he had joined up, but it was much less than he got at the shipyard, where he had been made a supervisor. And the Clothing Exchange was always busy, but Ellen had to admit it wasn't going to make any of them rich, especially now they were paying Rachel too. In fact, she was thinking that expanding the Clothing Exchange back to how it was when they were striking – when everyone had pitched in and they'd made huge pots of soup and loaves of bread – would help her as well. Because goodness me, everything was just so expensive.

She rubbed her forehead, holding on to the chamber pot she'd grabbed when the nausea had overwhelmed her. Her skin felt clammy, but the sickness had passed now. She was all right.

She took a long breath and then let it out slowly. Yes, she was definitely less shaky. She tucked the pot under the bed and went back into the kitchen where Annie was sitting on the floor, with her back to her, being suspiciously quiet.

'What are you up to?' Ellen asked, pausing for a moment in the doorway to admire her daughter's sweet curls.

Annie turned and gave her mother the most heavenly smile.

'I is posting,' she said. Ellen looked at her proudly. She thought Annie was very clever with her talking because she wasn't much past two years old, and she was already chatting away in proper sentences.

'What are you posting, doll?' she said. She crouched down next to her daughter and went cold as she realised Annie was clutching her purse in her tiny hand. 'Annie? What are you posting?'

Annie held out her fist and opened it with a flourish to show a coin. And before Ellen could stop her, she'd popped it through a gap in the floorboards.

'Annie, no,' gasped Ellen. She took the purse and looked in despair at the empty void inside. Annie poked her little fingers towards the floor and Ellen squinted through the gap to see, down under the floorboards, the rest of the coins twinkling at her, out of reach.

She sat down on her behind with a thump wondering what to do. Could she pull up the floorboards somehow and reach down? For the thousandth time she wished James was here to help her. Her da would know what to do, but he'd been ill recently and she didn't want to worry him.

Annie clambered to her feet, pushing her face against Ellen's for a kiss. Ellen hugged her daughter tightly.

'Mama cross?' asked Annie, wanting reassurance.

Ellen twirled one of Annie's curls round her finger. 'Mama's not cross,' she said. 'Shall we go for a walk? Go and see Auntie Ida?'

'Tida,' said Annie, nodding. She loved Ida's shop, which was a treasure trove of exciting things to look at. 'Tida and Biscuit.'

'That's right, doll,' said Ellen. 'Auntie Ida and Auntie Bridget.' She just hoped the frosty atmosphere between her sister and Ida had thawed a bit.

It wasn't far from Ellen's flat to the shop, so they walked over, Annie chattering all the way. Ida was just shutting up as they arrived, so Ellen scooped up her daughter and dashed across the street.

'Ida!' she called. 'Ida, I need your help!'

Of course, Ida was more than willing to lend a hand. She gathered up various things from the store, then pulled down the shutters and followed Annie and Ellen home.

'You get this one ready for bed and I'll get cracking,' she said, and Ellen thought that the sheer comfort of having someone there to lend a hand might overwhelm her.

When Annie had gone to sleep and Ellen came back into the kitchen, Ida was lying flat on the floor, her arm stuck down the floorboards and a pile of coins glistening next to her. Ellen felt almost dizzy with relief.

'There you go,' Ida said. 'I think that's all of it. The wee tinker, putting all those coins down there.'

Ellen sat down on the floor next to her friend and took her hand. 'Ida, you're a treasure. I'm not sure what I would have done without you.'

Ida looked pleased. 'Ach,' she said. 'You'd have worked something out eventually. But it's nice to feel useful again.'

'Do you have to get back, or can you stay for a cup of tea?' Ellen asked, getting to her feet and holding out her hand to help Ida up. 'I might put the rug from the bedroom in here, you know. It would cover the gaps in the floorboards and it would make it warmer in winter.'

'That's a good idea,' Ida said, getting to her feet too. 'Tea would be lovely.'

The women sat by the window, watching the world go by as they drank their tea. Ellen wanted to ask if Ida and Bridget were still not speaking but she wasn't sure how to bring it up, until she remembered what Ida had said earlier.

'Is that why you wanted to join Christina's police force,' she asked, 'to feel useful again?'

Ida frowned. 'It's not Christina's police force. I've joined despite her, not because of her.'

Ellen hid her smile. That was her told.

Ida looked out of the window. 'I have been feeling a little lost,' she said. 'Since the suffragettes paused their activities.'

'I'm not surprised.' Ellen had always loved the vim and vigour with which Ida approached her fight for women's rights, and how it had changed Bridget's life. And now it had all been taken away. She sighed. This war was affecting people's lives in so many ways. 'And you're enjoying being part of the police?'

'So very much,' Ida said, looking more cheerful. 'I like feeling part of something. An organisation. Everyone working together for the greater good.'

Ellen nodded. 'I understand that.'

'And the best thing about it is, I've hardly seen Christina.'

Ellen laughed out loud this time. 'That's a relief.'

'Gosh, I know. Your sister's already annoyed with me. If I started spending all day with Christina she'd really be in a stushie.'

'You don't want that,' Ellen said. 'I know what it's like to be in Bridget's bad books.' She looked at Ida. 'Is she softening a bit?'

'Aye,' Ida said with a nod. 'She tuts every time I put my uniform on, mind.'

'But she's speaking to you again?'

'She is.'

Ellen felt a rush of relief. Things were awkward enough between her and Sadie just now, without her having to deal with Ida and Bridget falling out, too.

'Will you help with the Clothing Exchange?' she said. 'If you've got time, that is, with your shop and the police force. I think the more people that are involved, the more everyone would benefit.'

Ida smiled. Her face was marked with a scar from an accident when she was younger, and her smile was lopsided, but Ellen always thought she smiled with her eyes instead. 'I was already planning to,' she replied.

'Excellent.' Ellen sighed. 'I think everyone needs something to keep us going.'

'Finding it hard without James, eh?' Ida said.

Ellen always found that kind words made the tears come, so she squeezed her eyes shut. 'Aye,' she said gruffly. 'And I'm expecting again.'

Ida patted her hand in a way that suggested the news wasn't a surprise. 'Aye,' she said. 'It's tough.'

Ellen opened her eyes. 'I've got no money,' she said. It was such a relief to say the words. 'It feels a bit like it was during the strike – I had money, and now it's all changed. And I'm scrabbling around for enough each week, remembering how it was for Sadie back then.' She rubbed her head. 'And I'm one of the lucky ones, Ida. I've just got Annie to feed. There are folk around here with men in the army and three or four or five weans to keep fed and warm.'

Ida nodded. 'We can help with that,' she said. 'Bringing the Clothing Exchange back to how it was can help with that.'

Ellen felt that relief again. Ida understood perfectly what she wanted to do.

'I need to spread the word,' she said. 'Make sure everyone knows.'

'I have a rather good deal with the advertising department at the newspaper,' Ida said. 'How about I swap out the ad for McKinley's this week and replace it with something about the Clothing Exchange?'

'Would you do that?'

'Of course.'

Ellen grinned, feeling cheerier. 'I'm making a banner,' she said. 'I've been sewing every night when Annie's in bed. I thought we could hang it outside the shop so everyone who walks past will see it.'

'Wonderful,' Ida said. 'I think this idea will be an enormous success.'

Chapter Six

Clydebank

29 Feb 1916

My dear James,

Are you safe? We all heard the dreadful news about HMS King Edward VII. *They say she hit a mine. And it was so close to home – not far from Scapa Flow. Thank goodness there were no lives lost. But it made me worry about you even more than I already do. I keep wondering how the ships know where the mines are. And I know there are minesweepers, but they can't be everywhere all at once. I can't even decide it if would be better to know you were somewhere close – in the North Sea perhaps – or far away in the Atlantic. Perhaps it's better I don't know. Just keep safe, my love. And write back as soon as you can.*

It's so strange here now. Of course, lots of the men are still around, working at the shipyard, but the streets are quieter – and conscription comes into force next week so things will change again. Those of us left behind are finding things hard. But our plan to extend the Clothing Exchange is coming on. I'm just worried we won't have the space for everyone who needs us. And we will be needed. Remember how difficult it was during the strike? Well, it's like that. So many weans going hungry and the women all doing the best they can. We need to work together to help everyone.

So that's keeping me busy, of course. And Sadie's running about here, there and everywhere. She's got friendly with a woman in Glasgow who's helping refugees and Sadie's giving her a hand. I think she's avoiding me, to be honest. And I think she's avoiding me because she's realised I'm expecting. Oh James, my heart aches for her because I know she wants a baby and she doesn't have one. But I don't know what to say to her to make it better. Perhaps I can't make it better. What do you think? I wish you were here so we could lie in bed at night, my head on your chest, and you could tell me what you think I should do.

Anyway, that's not the half of it. Sadie's annoyed at Rachel too, though I don't know why. And Ida and Bridget are still being prickly with one another because of Ida joining the police service, though Bridget's not as cross as she was. It's a bit like when you have a stone in your shoe and it's a constant irritation all day. We're all just like stones in each other's shoes. It never used to be like that.

That's one of the reasons I really want this idea about extending the Clothing Exchange to work. I need it, James. I need something to hold on to. Something to focus on. Something to distract me from worries about you and Sadie and Annie and the new baby.

Anyway, I have droned on long enough, so I will stop now so I can catch the post. Please write back as soon as you can. I miss you.

Your Ellen X

Chapter Seven

Sadie was enjoying having a project. She was pleased to have something else to think about that wasn't babies, or Rachel joining Wentworth. She still hadn't spoken to her sister, not properly, since she'd announced she was going to work at the factory. Sadie felt Rachel's betrayal like a dagger in her heart and for the first time she really understood why Ellen had been so upset when they'd gone out on strike and Bridget, Ellen's beloved big sister, had stayed at work.

In fact, Bridget was upset too, according to Ellen. Because Ida had joined the Women's Police Service and was working at Wentworth. Or alongside Wentworth, as Bridget put it. Sadie felt like everyone was disappointing everyone else. And the worst of it all was that she felt she'd disappointed Ellen too, by not telling her she knew she was pregnant. And not letting her see how sad she really was about her lost babies.

So Sadie had thrown herself into the preparations for expanding the Clothing Exchange once more, hoping it would help her deal with all the sadness and hurt that was swilling around inside her, and so far it was working.

They really were very busy. They'd decided to do what they could for the forces, so Bridget and Ida had collected skeins of wool from the Red Cross for the women to knit into socks for the soldiers. Ellen had cleared a space in the storeroom for donations

– they were asking for books for the military hospital in Glasgow, where convalescing soldiers were being treated, and cigarettes and tobacco to send to the troops with their socks.

Sadie, though, was keen to focus her own efforts on helping the women left behind. Not that the soldiers and sailors didn't need their concern – of course they did – but all around her she saw signs of the same hardship that they'd seen during the strike. Sadie knew just how hard it had been back then. The terror of not knowing if they'd be able to put food on the table the next day. And that had been a few weeks – this war had already been raging for more than a year and goodness only knew how much longer it would carry on. She had been following with some interest what Sylvia Pankhurst was doing in London, employing mothers to make toys, and caring for their children while they worked. Sadie wasn't sure they could do something as big in Clydebank, but she was pretty convinced they could come up with an idea that would help mothers on a smaller scale.

'Sadie?' Ellen said, jolting her out of her thoughts. 'Could you help put up the banner?'

'Of course.'

She followed Ellen outside the Clothing Exchange. 'Show me?' she said.

Ellen handed over the banner and Sadie spread it out on the ground. 'That's great,' she said. 'You've done a good job there.'

Ellen smiled. 'Thank you. I thought it would stretch right across the front of the shop. I've got the step ladder out.'

'I think it'll fit perfectly,' Sadie said.

Ellen arranged the ladder at one end of the shop window, picked up the banner, and went to climb up.

'No!' Sadie said, tugging at her friend's arm. 'Don't you get up there.' Ellen turned to look at Sadie and Sadie added faintly: 'In your condition.'

The two women looked at one another for a long moment and then eventually Sadie spoke.

'Are you pregnant, Ellen?'

Ellen screwed her face up. 'I am. How did you know?'

'Just a feeling.'

Ellen nodded, hugging the banner to her chest.

'Why didn't you tell me?' asked Sadie, wanting to know but afraid of the answer.

'Because . . .' Ellen began. 'Because you don't have a baby and I think you want one, and I think it's been hard for you, and I was worried I might upset you.'

Her explanation was so precisely what Sadie had thought it would be that for a moment she couldn't speak. Then she nodded. 'That's right.'

Ellen reached out and took Sadie's hand in hers. 'Do you want to talk about it?'

Sadie shook her head. 'Not right now,' she said. 'But maybe one day soon.'

'I'll be here,' said Ellen. 'I'm sorry if me expecting has upset you.'

'It hasn't,' Sadie said honestly, surprising herself. 'Not really. Not more than everything else.'

'How is Noah?'

'Same as always,' Sadie said with a shrug. 'Putting on a brave face.'

'Good old Noah,' Ellen said fondly.

'Aye.' Sadie squeezed Ellen's hand. 'I feel better now you know that I know.'

'I feel better too,' Ellen said. 'Secrets are never the answer.'

Sadie lifted her chin, thinking about Rachel and half wishing she'd never said that she was going to work at Wentworth. What was that expression? Blissful ignorance? There was some truth in that. 'I suppose not.'

Ellen looked down at the banner in her arms. 'Are we going to get this up, then?'

'Give it here.' Sadie took the fabric and clambered up the ladder.

'No one's going to miss this, are they? It's enormous. It must have taken you ages.'

'It's given me something to do when Annie's in bed,' Ellen said. 'It's been nice, actually.'

Sadie felt a rush of sympathy for her friend. It must be lonely for her at night without James. Ellen was usually so cheerful and there was no doubting that she was more subdued now than Sadie had ever known her to be.

'About here?' she asked, fixing one end of the banner to a nail on the shop front wall.

'Perfect,' said Ellen.

Sadie came back down and moved the ladder along so she could do the other end.

With a bit of effort she got the banner attached.

'Is that straight?'

'Up a bit,' said Ellen. Sadie moved it slightly. 'That's it.'

She climbed down and the women stood back to look at the banner.

'It's still a bit squint,' said Sadie.

'Och, it's fine as it is,' Ellen assured her. 'The important thing is everyone sees it when they go by.'

'They'll definitely see it,' said Sadie. 'In fact, I'm worried we won't have enough space for all the people who'll want to come to the Clothing Exchange now. Remember how we filled the church hall last time? That was much bigger than the shop is. But it's full of bandages now so we couldn't move there even if we wanted to.'

'We'll make it work,' Ellen said. 'Though that worry did cross my mind, too. Especially with Ida's advert in the newspaper. That was nice of her to do that, wasn't it?'

'Ida's one of the good ones,' Sadie said.

'So are you,' said Ellen, her eyes filling with tears. 'A really good one.'

Sadie gave her friend a hard stare. 'Those are pregnancy tears,' she said.

'They are,' Ellen said, sniffing. 'But it doesn't mean I'm not right.'

Softening, Sadie gave her a hug. 'You're a good one too, Ellen McCallum. The new-look Clothing Exchange is going to help so many women – you'll see.'

'I hope so,' Ellen said. 'I really need this.'

As it turned out, Sadie was right about them running out of space. Sadie tried to count the women who turned up when they opened the doors but everyone kept moving so it was tricky. She was pretty sure there were more than twenty women there though, and some of them had brought their children with them, so it was all a bit of a squeeze and really rather chaotic. Fortunately it was a fine day, so they could spill onto the pavement outside. Ida brought some chairs and stools from her shop and the flat upstairs and somehow – just as Ellen had said – they muddled it all together.

Sadie stood behind the counter, watching the women knitting and chatting and planning and felt so proud of Ellen that she thought she might burst.

'I think we need to be a bit more organised this time round,' Ellen said, appearing at Sadie's side. 'Less of a drop-in centre and more specific times. I thought we could try to meet twice a week. Might help control the numbers a bit.'

'Good idea.' Sadie nodded. 'It's great, though, eh? Shows how much it's needed.' She bit her lip, not wanting to interfere in what she very much thought of as Ellen's initiative, but also knowing she had an idea to share. 'I wondered if perhaps some of the women who live further away might want to set up their own versions of the Clothing Exchange close to where they stay? Spread them all across Clydebank. I could mention it to folk in Glasgow too. Maybe one day there will be clubs all over Scotland.'

Ellen stared at her. 'That's the most wonderful idea, Sadie.'

Sadie was pleased.

'Winnie lives *way* out past the shipyard,' said Ellen. 'She'd do a great job. And Agnes is off the other side of Wentworth.'

'Perfect,' said Sadie. 'Spread the word.'

Ellen hurried off and Sadie's attention was caught by a nicely dressed woman hovering in the doorway, looking a little out of place. Her dress was clearly expensive – Sadie's expert eye could appreciate how well cut it was – and Sadie wondered why she'd come.

She came out from behind the counter and went over to speak to her.

'Hello, welcome to the Clothing Exchange.'

The woman smiled at her hesitantly.

'My husband's in the army,' she said. 'I thought it would be all right to come?'

Her accent wasn't local.

Sadie nodded. 'Everyone's welcome,' she said. 'I'm Sadie. Ellen's over there . . .' She pointed to where Ellen was deep in conversation with Agnes. 'This was her idea.'

'It's a grand idea,' said the woman, taking her hat off to reveal gleaming blond hair. 'I'm Lucinda Henderson.'

'Hello, Lucinda,' Sadie said, smiling. 'Come on in.'

Lucinda looked around at the hustle and bustle in the small shop and breathed out. 'This is perfect,' she said.

'It's going well,' Sadie agreed. 'Come and meet some people. Can you knit?'

'I can.'

'This way.'

She led Lucinda to the corner where a small group of women were busy producing socks. 'Everyone, this is Lucinda,' she said. 'Lucinda, this is Susie and Isabel, and that there is my wee sister, Rachel.'

Rachel stood up, her ball of wool dropping to the floor and unravelling as it rolled under Susie's chair.

'Mrs Henderson,' she said. 'Goodness me. I didn't expect . . . I didn't know . . .' She paused and then she smiled. 'Hello.'

'Hello,' Lucinda said. 'Rachel, is it?'

Rachel nodded, looking a little flustered. Sadie watched in confusion. 'I work at Wentworth,' she said. 'I just started.'

'Good for you,' Lucinda said. 'Now, who's got some wool so I can get cracking on these socks?'

Rachel looked at Lucinda for a moment, and Sadie thought she saw an understanding pass between the two women. Then Rachel bent down to gather up the wool she'd dropped and the moment passed. Susie found some knitting needles and Isabel produced some wool, and Lucinda was soon chatting away with the others like old friends, leaving Sadie wondering what on earth had just happened.

Chapter Eight

Sadie was making space for donations in the back room of McKinley's when Bridget came down from the flats above.

'Oh hello,' Sadie said. 'Are you two speaking again?'

Bridget looked a bit surprised to see her there, which was understandable really, as Sadie had let herself in – she and Ellen had a key to McKinley's just as Ida had a key to the Clothing Exchange.

'Oh,' Bridget said, glancing back up the stairs. 'Hello. What did you say?'

'I said are you and Ida are speaking again?' Sadie tilted her head in the direction of Ida's flat. 'You've been to visit?'

Bridget smiled. 'Yes,' she said. 'We are speaking again.'

Sadie thought she looked relieved, and she didn't blame her. It was horrible falling out with friends.

'I'm just making some space,' Sadie explained. 'For more donations.'

'Go ahead,' Bridget said. She made to walk away from the stairs, then she stopped, and tilted her head. 'Listen . . .'

Sadie listened. Upstairs, she could hear Ida singing. She wasn't the most tuneful musician and some of her high notes didn't quite hit the right spot but it made Sadie smile all the same.

'She's feeling more like herself again,' Bridget told Sadie.

'I'm so glad.'

'Me too, in fact,' Bridget said. 'It's lovely to be doing something useful again.'

'I can see that.' Sadie looked at her friend. 'The gleam has returned to your eyes.'

'Heavens,' said Bridget. 'Who knew my eyes had lost their gleam?' But she looked rather pleased about it.

'Bridget? Have you seen my boots?' Ida called down from upstairs.

Bridget rolled her eyes at Sadie. 'By the door,' she shouted. 'Where you left them.'

Ida laughed and in a moment she came downstairs too, looking rather smart and a little intimidating in her police uniform and stockinged feet, holding her boots in her hand.

She too looked a little surprised to see Sadie.

'Hello.'

'Sadie's just making room for donations,' Bridget said rather hurriedly, Sadie thought. 'I said that I'd been visiting.'

'Aye,' said Ida. She sat down on the bottom step and started pulling her boots on and lacing them up.

'Are you going to work?' Sadie asked. 'Police work?'

'I am.' Ida sat up a bit straighter. 'I think I might get to do some proper patrolling today.'

Bridget sighed and Ida looked over at her.

'You know that if this really bothers you, I won't do it,' she said. She looked at Sadie. 'The same goes for you and Ellen.'

Sadie shook her head. Ida stood up and Bridget went to her and straightened her tie.

'We heard you singing,' she said, patting Ida's chest quickly and then standing back. 'Go. Do your bit.'

'Christina says there are patrols within the Wentworth grounds,' Ida said. Sadie pulled a face. 'But,' Ida added quickly, seeing Sadie's expression, 'she also said there were patrols outside. I thought I'd request to work those and then it's not the same as working at the factory.'

Bridget nodded. 'It's fine,' she said. 'It's fine. Everyone will understand.'

'She's right,' Sadie said. She glanced out of the window where she could see the Wentworth clock tower in the distance. 'These are trying times for everyone. We just do what we have to do.'

'Go on,' said Bridget. 'Scoot.'

'You're a good woman, Kelly,' said Ida. 'And you, Franklin.'

'Spark,' Sadie said with a smile. 'I've been Spark for four years.'

Ida grinned. 'Right you are,' she said.

They smiled at one another and then Ida glanced out of the window at the clock tower.

'Oh my goodness, I'm late,' she said. 'I'll be in trouble.'

'Good luck!' Sadie said.

'All right.' Ida went to the door, then paused. 'What did you make of that Lucinda?'

'The posh one with the blond hair?' Bridget said. 'She seemed nice enough. Got stuck in straight away. She said her husband's in the army. He's an officer.'

'Aye,' said Ida thoughtfully. 'Right enough.'

'What?' Sadie was curious. 'What are you thinking?'

Ida shrugged. 'Didn't expect a woman like her to be hanging round a welfare centre in Clydebank, that's all.'

'Ida, that's not like you to judge someone by their background,' Bridget chastened. 'You know the suffragettes were all sorts of people. Helen's from a really well-to-do family, but many of the others aren't.'

'I know,' said Ida. 'I just got the impression she wasn't being completely honest about why she was there, that's all. I saw her when she arrived and she sort of hovered in the doorway like she was working out what to say.'

Sadie nodded thoughtfully. She'd noticed that, too. 'Nerves, perhaps.'

'Perhaps.'

'She certainly rolled her sleeves up and got stuck in, and I heard her chatting to Isabel about how much she missed her husband.'

'You're right, ignore me,' Ida said. 'I'm being horrible.'

'Never,' replied Bridget with a chuckle.

Ida slapped her forehead. 'Now you absolutely must stop talking to me, because I have to go. See you in a wee while!'

'Where's Ida?' Ellen asked as they set up for another meeting of the Clothing Exchange later on. 'I thought she'd be here.'

'No,' said Sadie, reluctant to lie but not wanting to bring up Ida's work with Wentworth either. 'She's got something on.'

'The police?'

Sadie paused. There really was no fooling Ellen.

'That's it.'

Ellen nodded. 'Right,' she said. 'She looks good in her uniform, eh? Like she was born to it.'

Sadie blinked in surprise. 'You don't mind?'

'Och, maybe a bit at first,' Ellen said, scrunching her nose up. 'But everything's different now, isn't it?'

'Is it?'

'You don't think so?'

Sadie thought about it. 'It is different,' she said slowly. 'But I don't think that necessarily means everything that went before has to be forgotten.'

Ellen bit her lip. 'No,' she said. 'I suppose not.'

There was an awkward pause.

'Did that Lucinda say she was coming again today?' Sadie asked eventually, more as a distraction than anything else.

Ellen nodded. 'I think so. She was nice, eh?'

Sadie grinned, pleased the tense moment had passed. 'Ida thinks she's up to something.'

'Does she?' Ellen frowned. 'Annie, sweetheart, don't play with those cigarette boxes, they're not nice for little girls. Up to what?'

'Maybe she's after the socks,' Sadie joked, gesturing to the corner, where there were already piles of donated cigarettes and finished pairs of socks for the soldiers and sailors.

'Well, I don't blame her,' Ellen said gravely. 'What woman wouldn't want a pair of thick woolly socks in this particular shade of muddy grey?'

'Indeed,' said Sadie, going along with Ellen's joke. 'I believe all the best-dressed ladies in Paris are wearing them.' She scooped up Annie and tickled her little feet, making her giggle. 'Like Miss Annie, here.'

'I heard the queen herself has a pair,' said Ellen, dissolving into laughter.

Sadie was pleased that Ellen seemed brighter. She thought that having the chance to speak to other women whose husbands and sweethearts were in the army or navy had really helped her – making her understand that her worries and sadness about James joining up were normal. Of course she had great support between Sadie herself and Bridget and Ida, but none of them had husbands who were serving, or wee ones growing up without their da.

'There's far too much fun going on in here,' Bridget said, coming through the back door of the shop and making Sadie and Ellen both jump. 'No Rachel?'

Sadie rolled her eyes. 'I don't know where she is, and frankly I'm not bothered.'

'Oh dear,' Bridget said mildly.

Sadie put Annie back down on her feet so she could run to her aunt for a cuddle.

'Is she in your bad books?' Ellen asked.

'A bit.'

'She is funny how she tests your patience,' Bridget said, giving Annie a tickle and making her laugh.

'Funny for you,' said Sadie, but she smiled despite herself.

'Och, I don't blame her for being lively,' Ellen said. 'She was so sick when she was wee and now she's healthy and she wants to grab life with both hands and make the most of it.'

'Maybe we could all do with taking a leaf out of Rachel's book,' Bridget pointed out, putting a squirming Annie back on her feet. 'Is she being a nuisance?'

'I can't even talk about it,' Sadie said, holding her hands out as if to ward off her irritation with Rachel. 'I can't even think about it.'

Bridget laughed, but Sadie suddenly found she couldn't smile. She was still very annoyed with Rachel.

'I think we'll be busy today,' Ellen said, jumping in to soothe things, as she always did.

'What do you have planned?' Sadie asked. 'Because I wondered if we might collect some toys or baby clothes, alongside the bits for the soldiers. Give the mammies left behind a bit of a hand as well.'

'That's a lovely idea,' Ellen said. 'We'll chat to everyone about that.'

'Sylvia Pankhurst is doing something similar down in London,' Sadie said, pleased when Bridget gave her an approving glance. 'The women are doing their bit and we need to support them.'

'Absolutely,' said Ellen. 'Here's everyone coming now. Goodness, I thought we might not have so many today but look, Agnes seems to have brought a crowd with her.'

There was a bustle of activity as the shop filled up with women, chattering and laughing. Sadie and Bridget went upstairs to make tea and brought it down on trays, and as they handed the mugs round, Sadie spotted Lucinda, chatting to Susie Montrose. Susie looked proud as punch and Lucinda was nodding earnestly.

She tried to edge closer to them so she could hear what they were talking about, but she was distracted as Ida arrived and came over to where Sadie and Bridget were standing.

'How did you get on?' Bridget asked – slightly grudgingly, Sadie thought.

'Training is over and I am officially a member of the Women's Police Service,' replied Ida, smiling broadly. 'And I asked not to be sent to Wentworth, and they said I could patrol elsewhere.' She adopted an official tone. 'We are to police the morals of the girls.'

Bridget raised an eyebrow. 'You?' she said, looking at her friend with an expression Sadie couldn't quite read. 'Policing morals?'

Ida's eyes twinkled. 'Well, I've to make sure no one breaks the curfew.'

'And will you have to wear a hat?' Sadie asked.

From behind her back, Ida produced a marvellous hat.

'Lovely,' said Sadie, genuinely impressed.

'Sounds wonderful,' Bridget agreed, and Sadie was pleased that they seemed to have put their difference of opinion aside. If only she could do the same with Rachel.

Ida grinned. 'Thanks,' she said, smiling at Bridget. 'Oh look, Lucinda's here.'

'She is.'

'Have you spoken to her?' Ida asked Sadie.

'Not yet.'

'Come on.' Ida tugged at her sleeve, and with Bridget behind them, they marched over to where Lucinda was still chatting with Susie.

'We've not been introduced,' said Ida, holding her hand out for Lucinda to shake. 'I'm Ida McKinley, I run the shop next door.'

'Lovely to meet you,' said Lucinda. She introduced herself. Bridget stepped closer to Sadie. 'See,' she said in a whisper, right into Sadie's ear. 'She's perfectly nice.'

'What brings you here?' Ida said, pulling up a chair next to Lucinda and sitting down.

'I've not long moved to Clydebank,' Lucinda said. 'I don't have many friends, and I miss my husband. It seemed the perfect place to meet people.' She smiled around at everyone. 'Women.'

Ida nodded. 'It's nice to have you here, doll,' she said. Sadie sat down next to Ellen, wondering if Ida was being nice because she really didn't think Lucinda was up to something, or because she did think she was up to something and she wanted to know what it was.

'Actually,' Lucinda said, raising her voice a little so everyone in the room could hear her. 'One of the reasons I wanted to come along to the Clothing Exchange was to speak to you all about an opportunity.'

'Oh, here we go,' Ida muttered.

Suddenly Sadie knew what Lucinda was about to say. She absolutely knew and she kicked herself for not working it out sooner.

'My father is a man called Hamilton Blyth,' Lucinda said. She stood up and put her half-knitted sock down on the chair behind her. 'He's the new manager at Wentworth sewing machine factory.'

There was a collective intake of breath from the gathered women. Heads swivelled in the direction of Ellen and Sadie, who were both staying very still.

'I'm sure you all know that Wentworth has swapped its sewing machine production for munitions,' Lucinda continued. 'We're very proud to have won several government contracts. But we need staff, desperately. My father asked me to come and meet you all and ask if any of you would be interested in joining us. Becoming a munitionette.' She said the word with a flourish. Bridget almost expected her to throw her arms out like she was introducing an act on a stage.

The room was silent. The women were looking from Lucinda to Sadie and Ellen and back again. 'We are doing our best to aid the war effort,' Lucinda carried on. 'Working for king and country to support the troops. Working on the front line, at home.'

Ellen looked at Sadie as if she expected her to speak up but Sadie simply folded her arms. 'Carry on,' she said, bullishly. 'Tell us more.'

'The money is good,' Lucinda said, faltering slightly in the face of such indifference. 'And we provide regular meals.'

'We provide meals,' said Bridget, who was leaning against the counter. She gestured at the soup pots at the side of the room. 'Or at least we're going to.'

Lucinda swallowed. 'Bridget, is it?'

'Aye.'

'You were a suffragette, I hear?'

Bridget glowered at her. 'I'm still a suffragette.'

Lucinda's shoulders slumped a little but she carried on. 'Sylvia Pankhurst says family life is impossible for munitionettes,' she said. 'We're going to provide a nursery on the factory site, so there's no need to worry about the children. And . . .' She hesitated, her voice wavering as the women all stared at her. 'And there will be social events. Maybe even a cinema. At the factory.'

She pinched her lips together, and looked around. 'Is anyone . . .' She took a breath. 'Is anyone interested?'

There was a long pause. Sadie looked at Bridget who looked furious, then at Ellen, whose face had gone quite red. All the anger she'd been feeling, about the baby, and Rachel working at Wentworth, and the unfairness of Ellen being pregnant, burned deep inside her. Quite slowly, but deliberately, she stood up and took a step towards Lucinda.

'Get out,' she said.

'But . . .' Lucinda said, her voice shaky. 'I just . . .'

'Get. Out.'

Chapter Nine

Sadie was shaking with rage. She looked down at her trembling hands with a certain amount of surprise. She'd never been an angry person as a rule. Not out-of-control anger, at least. When her father had dropped down dead one day she'd pushed all her feelings into caring for her family. When Wentworth reduced their pay and increased their working hours, she'd funnelled her annoyance into fighting for their rights. But now, as she stared at Lucinda, she felt pure, blinding, white-hot fury.

And she quite liked it.

'Get. Out,' she said. She looked at Lucinda's pretty blue eyes filling with tears, at her neat skirt, which wasn't faded from washing, or frayed at the hem from wear, and she wanted to scream.

So she did.

'Go!' she shrieked. Beside her she felt Ellen wince, but she didn't care.

Looking terrified, Lucinda hitched up her beautiful skirt, turned tail and hurried away, pushing through the women who stood watching. Sadie heard the shop's door bang shut, there was a moment of stunned silence, and then a hubbub of voices.

Sadie burst into tears.

'I didn't mean it,' she gasped. 'It's not her I'm angry with.'

Ellen put her arms round her and gathered her in close. Sadie could feel Ellen's abdomen, hard and tight against her own, and tried to pull away, but Ellen held on and after a second, Sadie relaxed, comforted by her friend.

'It's not her,' she said again.

'I know,' Ellen soothed. 'I know it's not.'

'It's everything. It's the war, and not having a baby, and it's Rachel . . .'

'Rachel?' said Ellen, but Sadie shook her head, not ready to get into that now.

'Come and have a sit down and a cup of tea.' Ellen stroked Sadie's hair. 'You'll feel better.'

But Sadie didn't want a cup of tea.

'You have to go after her,' she said, untangling her arms from Ellen's. 'Please, go after her and tell her I didn't mean it.'

'Really?' Ellen looked startled. 'You want me to go after Lucinda?'

Sadie gave Ellen a little shove. 'Go on, please.' She wiped her eyes with the heel of her hand. 'Please, Ellen. She's nice. I shouldn't have spoken to her like that.'

'Maybe you should go after her,' said Bridget, who was standing close by.

'She won't want to talk to me,' Sadie said. 'I shouted at her.'

Bridget shrugged. 'Go on, Ellen. Bring her back here and we can all apologise for not being as kind to her as we should have been.'

Sadie saw Ida and Bridget exchange a glance and then look at the door.

'Maybe we should all go?' said Ida.

'Jings, we don't want to scare the poor lassie,' said Ellen. 'I'll go.'

She took Sadie by the shoulders. 'Sit down, get yourself together, and I'll be back in a minute.'

'With Lucinda,' said Bridget.

'If she wants to come back,' Ellen said. 'Yes.'

She gave Sadie a quick kiss on the cheek, then she hurried out after Lucinda.

Sadie's legs were wobbling so she sat down. The women all fussed around her, bringing her tea and checking she was all right. Sadie felt she didn't deserve the care she was getting. Hadn't she been awful to Lucinda?

'Ellen will find her,' Bridget said. 'She'll find her and she'll explain.'

'I shouldn't have reacted that way,' Sadie said.

Bridget gave her a little smile. 'Och, haven't we all flown off the handle at one time or another?'

'I hope Ellen finds her.'

'She will.'

Annie climbed onto Sadie's knee.

'Let Auntie Sadie have a rest, Annie,' said Bridget, but Sadie put her arms round the little girl.

'She's fine,' she said. She put her face into Annie's curls, smelling her baby smell. 'She's lovely.'

'Want a wee brandy, doll?' asked Susie Montrose, producing a hip flask. Sadie shook her head, touched by the concern.

Agnes sat down next to her and put her hand on Sadie's knee briefly. 'I heard what you said about a baby,' she said. 'I don't want to presume but if you ever want to chat . . .' She took a deep breath. 'Well, I'm here, that's all.'

Sadie looked at her. She was an older woman – a similar age to Sadie's mother – and she didn't have any children. Understanding what she was saying, and appreciating the gesture, Sadie nodded. 'Thank you.'

Outside the shop, Ellen paused, trying to see where Lucinda had gone. It was a fine, dry day and there were people about, so it took a moment before she caught a glimpse of Lucinda's blond head rounding the corner and hurried after her.

After a few minutes of searching, she eventually found Lucinda sitting on a fallen tree on the green, not far from Wentworth. The factory gates were just up ahead, and the clock tower loomed over the street.

Ellen walked over to Lucinda and sat down next to her.

Lucinda looked at her with red-rimmed eyes. She didn't say anything, but she didn't get up and walk away either.

'You know,' Ellen began, 'this is where we all gathered on the first day of the strike.' She pointed up towards the factory. 'Me and Sadie, and the other cabinet polishers, we all stopped working and we walked out of the gates, right there, and we came here.' She laughed. 'We thought it would just be us, and just for a day or two. But then there were more of us, and then the whole factory just about went out on strike.' She gave Lucinda a small, conspiratorial smile. 'Not Bridget, mind.'

Lucinda was staring at her, understanding dawning on her pretty face. 'It was you?' she said. 'You started the strike?'

Ellen lifted her chin in pride. 'Aye,' she said. 'We did.'

'I didn't know.' Lucinda buried her face in her hands. 'It was really you?'

'Aye. That's why the Clothing Exchange exists, in fact. We started it when we weren't working – as a sort of welfare centre first, but then after the strike we kept it going.'

'Lord,' Lucinda said into her hands. She lifted her face. 'No wonder you all reacted as you did.'

'Sadie has a lot on her mind,' Ellen said. 'She's sorry she shouted at you. I know you don't know us very well, but it's really not like her to be that way.' She smiled again. 'She can be a wee bit frightening when she wants to be, mind you.'

Lucinda's shoulders relaxed just a little bit and Ellen was glad. 'I imagine she can be.'

'But we're all nice, really.'

'Everyone has been very kind.' Lucinda made a face. 'I can't believe I made such a fool of myself.'

'Not at all.'

'My father is the nicest man you could ever meet,' Lucinda said. Ellen thought that unlikely if he was the new man in charge of Wentworth, but she just nodded. 'He's so proud to have won these government contracts, and he's been having sleepless nights about how to fulfil them. And then I saw the advert in the newspaper . . .'

'Ida's advert,' said Ellen.

'Yes, I believe so. And I thought the Clothing Exchange would be the perfect place to recruit new staff for the factory.'

'Your father didn't ask you to come?'

'No, I just wanted to help.'

Ellen chuckled. 'Aye, well, perhaps you'll ask him next time. I imagine he knows all about the strike and how it started.'

'He does,' Lucinda said, bristling just enough to make Ellen think she could grow to like her. 'As do I. I just didn't know it was you who started it.'

'That was a nice thing to do,' Ellen said. 'Even if it didn't go to plan.'

'You know a couple of the women back there are already working at Wentworth?' Lucinda said. 'I recognised them.'

'Really?' Ellen was surprised. 'Who?'

'I don't know names.'

'It pays well, you said?'

'It does. Twenty shillings a week.'

Ellen almost fell backwards off the fallen tree, she was so startled.

'Twenty?'

'Yes. That's to begin with. Some of the women have taken on more responsibilities and duties so they're earning more.' Lucinda laughed and leaned towards Ellen as if she was letting her into a secret. 'You know some of the managers think women can't be trusted with money.'

Ellen snorted. 'Aye, that sounds right. When anyone who's walked by the shipyard on a Friday afternoon knows it's the wives who go to collect the pay packets in case their men drink it all away.'

'It was them who persuaded my father to employ the Women's Police Service to patrol. Keep the ladies in check.'

'Ida's joined them,' Ellen said. 'My sister's friend.'

'The one with the gimlet stare?' Lucinda smiled. 'Sounds about right.'

'She's a softie really,' Ellen said with a chuckle. 'But she can be intimidating. When she wants to be.'

'I find them all rather intimidating,' Lucinda admitted. 'Personally, I don't think a Women's Police Service is at all necessary. The women all seem a nice bunch. I often hear them laughing and chatting as they go by.'

Ellen felt a sudden jolt of memory, like a stab wound, of all the cabinet polishers working hard, but laughing together at a shared joke. Women she knew as well as she knew her sister. She felt light-headed for a second with nostalgia and regret. No, not regret. She didn't regret the strike – she would never regret that. It was more a sadness that things had to change.

'What's the work like?'

'Hot,' Lucinda admitted. 'Hard. The torpedoes are heavy.' She smiled. 'But the horseshoes aren't.'

'Torpedoes?' Ellen said. 'Is it dangerous?'

'It can be.'

'Hours?'

'Long. With an early start. But with breaks.' Lucinda rubbed her nose. 'Short breaks.'

'Twenty shillings a week?'

'Yes.'

Ellen thought about her empty purse and the knotted anxious feeling she had every time she had to pay for something.

'And there's a nursery you said? We . . .' Ellen swallowed. 'The women who work there can bring their children?'

Lucinda pulled her shoulders back. 'That was my idea,' she

said. 'If we want women to work, then we need to consider their children.'

'It's a good idea.'

Lucinda looked pleased. 'I hope so.'

There was a small silence.

'You know, my father told me that a lot of the changes that have taken place in Wentworth are because of the strikes.'

'Really?' Ellen was surprised, but proud to hear that. 'Like what?'

'Well, the breaks, for a start. My father says there is a move to treat workers as people and not trained monkeys.'

'When they changed our hours and our pay, before we went on strike, they said they could teach a gorilla to do our work,' Ellen said, feeling the old prickle of anger at the lack of understanding about their job. 'I was a cabinet polisher. It was skilled work.'

'I know,' Lucinda said. 'Munitions work is skilled, too.' She gave Ellen a quick sideways glance. 'And all the wives of sailors and soldiers are so proud to be doing their bit. Getting stuck in. Just as their husbands are doing.'

Ellen imagined James at sea, firing a torpedo that she'd made.

'Twenty shillings?' she said again.

'Every week.'

'Is your husband really in the army?' Ellen said suddenly. 'Or did you make that up, just to make yourself seem part of the Clothing Exchange? Because you didn't need to. My sister's husband works in a factory in Manchester so he's not been conscripted, and Sadie's husband is a schoolteacher.'

Lucinda bit her lip. 'No, I didn't make that up. His name is Douglas and he's in the army. We've been married for seven months.'

'How long as he been gone?'

'Six months, three weeks and two days.'

Ellen put her hand out and touched Lucinda's, where it rested on the tree trunk. 'My husband's name is James,' she said. 'He works at the shipyard, so he wouldn't have been conscripted, but he wanted to go. He's in the navy.

'How long has he been away?'

'A year,' Ellen said. 'But he came home on leave before he shipped out.'

Lucinda leaned towards Ellen, touching her shoulder with her own. It was a little gesture of solidarity and Ellen realised that for all her fancy skirt and nice accent, Lucinda was in the same boat as she was.

Ellen lifted her chin. 'All right,' she said, making it sound as though she was doing Lucinda an enormous favour, when both of them knew it was really the other way round. 'I'll do it. I'll come back to Wentworth.'

Lucinda nodded.

'I was hoping you'd say that,' she said. 'You're going to love it.'

Chapter Ten

Sadie was worried that Ellen had been gone a long time.

'She might have had to go all the way to the factory before she caught her,' Bridget said, reading her mind. 'Don't fret.'

'I feel awful,' Sadie said. 'I hope she talks her into coming back.'

Bridget handed Sadie a mug of tea. 'It's a strange time for everyone,' she said. 'We just need to keep that in mind.'

'You're right.' Sadie blew on the hot tea to cool it down. 'But I was really annoyed that she had the cheek to come here and ask us – us – to go and work at Wentworth.'

'I wonder if Ellen's filled her in about the strike,' said Bridget with a smile. 'I bet Lucinda was horrified when she heard who you are.'

Sadie managed the ghost of a smile.

'I work at Wentworth,' said one of the younger women who had come along to the meeting that evening. 'Is that all right? Can I still be part of the Clothing Exchange?'

Sadie looked at the woman. She was about Rachel's age but at first glance looked older. She was very thin, with sallow skin and dark smudges under her eyes.

'Course you can, doll,' she said, feeling bad. 'Och, of course you can.'

The woman sighed in relief. 'My wee brothers could really do with some new breeks,' she said.

'What's your name?' Sadie asked.

'Bessie.'

'Bessie, I'm Sadie, and this is Bridget and over there's Ida.' Hearing her name, Ida looked up and nodded at Bessie.

'I know all about the strike,' Bessie said. 'My auntie worked at Wentworth back then and she was one of the ones on strike, like you.'

Sadie smiled. 'It was a long time ago.'

'Aye. My auntie, she's passed away now, but she always said the folk that ran Wentworth were miserable sods. That's what she called them. Miserable sods.'

'She's not wrong,' said Bridget. 'I'm just going to go and collect up the socks everyone's been knitting. Nice to meet you, Bessie.'

She wandered off and Sadie turned her attention back to Bessie.

'My auntie would be fair annoyed with me if she knew I was working at the factory,' Bessie said. Sadie thought of Rachel and felt a kinship with Bessie's poor dead auntie. 'But do you know what I'd tell her?' Bessie looked straight at Sadie. 'And what I tell you now?'

'What?' said Sadie.

'That some folk don't have a choice,' Bessie said. 'That some folk have to swallow their ideals and their annoyances and their anger and just go and do the work, for their money at the end of the week. Because the weans need food and shoes and clothes on their backs, and the roof's leaking again, and the wind is cold through the windows at night, and the men have gone for whatever reason – and it's up to the women to keep things going.'

Sadie nodded. She knew all about that.

'Aye,' she said. 'You're right about that.'

There was a short pause. Bessie looked at her feet and Sadie, wanting to make her feel better, gave her a nudge.

'Now, tell me about these brothers of yours and let's see what we can find for them, shall we?' she said. 'I've got two brothers myself and I remember they would grow like weeds when they were wee.'

'There are six of us and I'm the oldest,' Bessie said, following Sadie over to where the short trousers were piled in order of size. 'Then there's my sister, Frannie, then the four boys. Angus is the oldest – he's thirteen – and wee Petey is the baby. He's six.'

'Heavens,' said Sadie, sitting down on the floor and eyeing the pile of clothes. 'Your parents have their hands full.'

'Aye, well it's just Ma now,' said Bessie. 'Da's gone.'

'Joined up?'

'Christ no,' said Bessie with a snort, making Sadie laugh in surprise. 'That selfish sod would never join up. He went off somewhere just after Petey was born and never came back.'

'He's probably been conscripted now,' Sadie pointed out, but Bessie shook her head.

'He'd find a way to get out of it. Useless bugger.'

'Can't be easy for your ma, with six of you,' Sadie said, thinking about her own family after her father had died. 'Does she work?'

'Aye, she does, in the tobacconist on Kilbowie Street. But munitions pays more. And they feed me.'

'And your sister? Frannie?'

'She's going to be a nurse.' Bessie beamed with pride. 'So we're both doing our bit.'

'Good for you.' Sadie held up a pair of trousers. 'Would these do for your Petey?'

'I think so.'

Sadie put them to one side and carried on going through the pile. 'What's it like at Wentworth, then?'

'You used to work there?'

'I did. But not for long. And I expect it's very different now.'

Bessie sat back on her haunches. 'It's great,' she said. 'The other munitionettes are nice. We can have a laugh and I like being part of something. The food is good. The money's even better.'

She paused and Sadie looked at her. 'But?'

'I've never been so tired in my whole life,' admitted Bessie. 'My feet feel like they're bruised from standing. My fingers are swollen.' She held her hand out to show Sadie her misshapen knuckles and Sadie noticed the skin on her palm was tinged with yellow. 'It's really hard work.'

'I remember how hard it was at Wentworth when we were only making sewing machines,' Sadie said, holding up another pair of trousers. 'How about these ones?'

'Yes please,' Bessie said. 'Perfect. The boys will love these.'

'Are you making shells?' Sadie asked, putting the trousers on the pile with the others.

'Aye.'

'Is it dangerous?'

Bessie shrugged. 'They say it isn't. And they're careful, right enough. We're not allowed anything metal in case of sparks – not even hairpins. One girl got stopped trying to bring in her knitting needles.'

'They search you?'

'Aye. The policewomen do it.' She nodded towards Ida. 'Like your pal, there.'

Sadie was a little shocked by that, and she wondered how Ida would feel about that part of her new job.

'It sounds . . .' She searched for the right word and gave up. 'It just sounds really hard.'

'But the food's good,' Bessie said with a grin. 'And there's plenty of it.'

Sadie looked at Bessie's skinny wrist that looked like a chicken bone and her hollow cheeks and wondered how thin she'd been before.

'Right,' she said. 'Here are the trousers. Is there anything else they need?'

Bessie screwed her face up. 'A couple of jumpers wouldn't hurt. Ma knits but it takes a while to make one, let alone four.'

'I'll see what we've got,' Sadie said. She got to her feet and helped Bessie up too. She felt light as a feather in her grip, the bones in her hands like twigs.

'And let's see if we can find you some bread and cheese too, eh?' she said. 'Just to keep you going.'

Chapter Eleven

Several times a day, Rachel wished she'd never taken the job at Wentworth. She wished she'd never even heard the name Wentworth. It was so hard. Backbreaking work. The hours were long. And they were the lucky ones. Wentworth had a canteen where they gave the munitionettes proper meals. They had breaks and a washroom and toilets. And every time someone said how good it was that Wentworth looked after its workers so well, Rachel would give a little smile and think, that was because of Sadie and Ellen and all the folk who'd gone on strike.

She knew she was luckier than some of the women working in other factories. But she was still so tired that all she could do during their breaks was sit and gather herself before going back to the factory floor to carry on. And most exhausting of all was slapping on a smile when she got home each evening. Looking Sadie in the eye and saying 'aye, not bad' when she asked how her day had been, when really all she wanted to do was flop down on a chair and complain about how much her feet ached and her back creaked and her knees clicked.

Rachel was walking up to the factory for another shift, thinking again how lucky she was that Sadie and Noah had moved to Clydebank so she didn't have to get the train to work like Sadie had when she worked at Wentworth. It was early. So early the sun was only just coming up, even though it was summertime. But

Rachel was getting used to the early starts. More or less.

And she couldn't deny the money was good. She was giving Sadie a proper amount towards her keep at last – she handed over most of her weekly pay – and she still had enough left over for a wee treat every now and then. Or to squirrel away and keep for a rainy day, as Ma always said. So when the aching in her back became unbearable she would go and find her little money pouch and count up what was inside, and suddenly her joints didn't hurt quite so much.

Sadie was sort of speaking to her now. Almost. Not proper chats, but she wasn't ignoring her altogether like she had been. Rachel thought the money was probably helping there, too. Though she suspected Sadie would never admit that.

The other thing that Rachel was enjoying was being around so many other women. She'd grown up with women of course – Sadie, and Ma, and Ma's best friend Auntie Miriam, as well as Ellen and Bridget and Ida. There were women everywhere in Sadie's life. But she'd never really had friends. Not proper ones. She'd been in and out of school as a child, because she'd always been so ill, so often, that she'd never really had the chance to make a friend.

But now she had Bessie who worked next to her, and who popped into the Clothing Exchange whenever she could, and who was funny and clever and found everything 'an absolute hoot'. She had already taken Rachel to the cinema which had opened at Wentworth – though it was really just a room downstairs with thick curtains at the window and a projector but it was still fun. Tomorrow night they were going for a drink. Rachel shivered with the sheer excitement of just thinking about it. A drink! Imagine!

So it wasn't easy, working at Wentworth, but it was worth it.

Rachel turned the corner and joined the stream of women all walking up towards the factory gates, keeping an eye out for Bessie, who usually dashed in at the last minute, tearing her hat off as she went.

Up ahead, she thought she caught a glimpse of a familiar face. Was that Ellen, in among the throng? It certainly looked like her.

'Ellen?' she called, in confusion. The woman up ahead stopped walking, the crowd parting round her, but she didn't turn round. Rachel hurried towards her.

'Ellen?' she said again.

It was Ellen. She turned to Rachel, looking worried.

'What are you doing here?' she said urgently. 'Did Sadie send you?'

'What? No.' Rachel frowned. 'Why are you here?'

Understand was dawning on Ellen's face.

'Do you work here?'

Rachel bit her lip. 'Aye,' she said. Then she lifted her chin a little, mildly defiant. 'I do.'

Ellen didn't look angry, as Rachel expected. She just looked surprised. And a little relieved.

'Why are you here?' Rachel asked again.

Ellen looked around herself both ways, then spoke in a low voice. 'Because . . .' she began.

'Why?' Rachel demanded.

Ellen screwed her face up. 'I'm starting work at Wentworth today and I've not told anyone,' she said in a hurry.

'You're starting work at Wentworth?' Rachel was astonished. 'You? Ellen McCallum?'

'Yes, me, shhh!'

'Sadie's not here,' Rachel said mischievously. 'She won't hear.'

Ellen looked guilty and, Rachel thought, fairly wretched. 'Don't tell her.'

'She's barely speaking to me as it is.'

'That's what I'm worried about.'

Rachel reached out and touched Ellen's elbow. 'Listen, we all do what we have to do,' she said. 'We've all got our reasons for working here.'

'Aye,' said Ellen cautiously.

'Sadie will understand.'

'Will she?'

Rachel shrugged. 'She will eventually.'

'And Bridget?' Ellen rubbed her nose.

'Her too.'

'Are you sure?'

Rachel wasn't sure, but she nodded anyway. 'Want me to show you around?'

'I worked here for years. I should be the one to show you around.' Ellen laughed and Rachel was glad because Ellen hadn't been laughing much recently.

'It's changed,' Rachel said, starting to walk again. 'It's changed a lot.'

'All right, then,' Ellen said, walking alongside Rachel. 'You show me what's what.'

They strolled through the huge factory gates and Rachel felt Ellen stiffen beside her.

'Must be strange being back here, eh?' she said.

'So strange,' Ellen muttered. 'There are a lot of memories in these walls.'

She set off across the courtyard and Rachel had to jog to keep up.

'This was the timberyard,' Ellen said. 'I always loved the smell of the wood.' She sniffed loudly. 'It doesn't smell the same now.'

'Horseshoes,' said Rachel. 'It's all horseshoes here now.'

'Horseshoes?' Ellen said. 'My goodness.'

'They use the foundry,' Rachel explained. 'Like when they were making the metal parts of the sewing machines. But now it's making horseshoes.'

Ellen looked terribly sad.

'They're still making sewing machines,' Rachel said quickly. 'Just not many.'

'Right.' Ellen nodded. 'Shall we go this way?'

She marched off again, towards the main part of the factory and then stopped in amazement just inside the doors.

'Oh my,' she breathed.

'I know.'

The main room was filled with shells. Hundreds of bombs lined up neatly, each one as big as a cart, waiting to be filled and sealed – that was Rachel's job – and loaded up and sent to the Front.

'This was spindles and shuttles,' Ellen said quietly. 'And over there was needles.'

'And packing,' Rachel said, pointing to the doors at the far end. 'That's the same.'

'Aye,' said Ellen slowly. 'Come this way.'

She led Rachel round the edge of the room and into the wash-rooms and changing rooms and once more, stopped dead.

'This,' she said, looking around her in disbelief. 'This was cabinet polishing.'

'Where you worked?'

'Yes.' Ellen gave a small smile. 'Where the strike began.'

'Oh,' said Rachel, feeling the weight of Ellen's memories pressing down on her. 'Jings.'

Ellen laughed. 'Jings,' she repeated.

'Did they explain?' Rachel asked. 'All the rules?'

'Oh yes.' Ellen nodded. 'No hairpins. No jewellery.'

'Chance would be a fine thing, eh?'

'No gossip,' Ellen said.

'Gossip costs lives,' Rachel parroted. 'That's on all the posters.'

'All we did was gossip, back in the day.'

'Not anymore,' Rachel said mock sternly. 'Keep mum.'

Ellen laughed again and Rachel felt a rush of affection.

'I'm glad you're here,' she said.

'Me too.'

'Whistle's going to go,' Rachel said. 'I should get changed. Do you know where you have to be?'

'Yes,' Ellen said. 'I'll see you later. Oh, and Rachel?'

'Don't worry.' Rachel squeezed Ellen's hand. 'I won't say a word.'

Ellen nodded and then headed out of the changing room and vanished into the crowds of women arriving for work.

'Rachel?' Bessie appeared at her side, looking flustered. 'Goodness, I thought I was going to be late, and then there would have been trouble, but I've made it.'

'Just in the nick of time,' said Rachel, pleased to see her friend. 'Again.'

'Oh shush, we've got plenty of time. Well, we've got three minutes. Come on, let's get changed.'

Rachel and Bessie's job was finishing shells, dropping in the detonators, then screwing on the plates that sealed the explosive inside. Sometimes Rachel pictured the shell she was finishing exploding in a German trench, shattering into pieces and blowing the soldiers to smithereens. She wasn't sure how she felt about that, so she tried not to think about it. And she also tried not to think about quite how dangerous her job was, working with explosives. One misjudged hit with her hammer, and things could go very wrong.

To be honest, it was so hot and noisy inside the factory that it was quite hard to think anyway. She and Bessie could barely exchange a word while they were working, but they managed to swap smiles as they lugged the shells across to the pallets, and they could catch up in their breaks, brief though they were, and when they stopped to eat. Rachel caught a glimpse of Ellen every now and then. She was working at the far end of the room unloading the empty shells ready to be filled. Rachel was glad Ellen wasn't working with the explosives. She felt a bit protective of her, knowing she was expecting, and she wondered if she'd told Lucinda that. Or anyone in management. It was going to be hard to keep track of all these secrets, she thought. Perhaps she'd have to stop speaking altogether in case she let something slip out.

When the whistle sounded at the end of the day, the women went to change out of their boiler suits and rubber boots. The changing room was filled with babbling voices and laughter, Bessie and Rachel adding to the cacophony as they planned their night out later in the week.

'What about the Empire Pleasure Palace?' Rachel suggested. 'There's a variety show on.'

'That's a good idea,' Bessie said. 'I love watching the dancing.'

'Oh, me too.' Rachel swayed to invisible music, in a slightly clumsy fashion. 'Though I'm a terrible dancer myself.'

'Maybe you've just not met the right partner,' Bessie said, with a gleam in her eye.

Rachel pulled off her boot, and grinned at her new friend. 'I've got no time for partners,' she said. 'I'm too busy having fun.'

'Glad to hear it.'

They finished getting changed, folded their boiler suits up ready for tomorrow, then Bessie put her arm through Rachel's and together they strolled out of the changing rooms towards the gate.

As they walked, Rachel became aware of shouts and cheers coming from across the way. She tugged on Bessie's arm to stop her walking.

'What's that?' she said. 'What's going on?'

Bessie listened, her head tilted to one side. 'Don't know.'

'Shall we go and see?'

'Of course.'

Curious, they headed in the opposite direction to the gates, round the corner, and there, to Rachel's absolute astonishment, they found a group of other munitionettes, dashing about like mad things, their faces pink with exertion. Other women – and a couple of men – were standing to one side, watching and cheering.

'What on earth . . .' Bessie began, but Rachel – thanks to her brother Daniel's passion for sport – was one step ahead.

'It's football,' she said. 'They're playing football.'

'Football?' Bessie looked bewildered.

'Come on,' Rachel said, setting off towards the group of women watching. 'It's fun.' She glanced back at her friend. 'It's easier than dancing.'

'Hiya, girls,' said an older woman who was standing to one side, not taking her eye off the action. 'Ginny, for the love of God, would you at least try to kick the ball?'

A pretty woman with red curls and freckles stood still with her hands on her hips and glared.

'I'd like to see you do better, Hilda Scott.'

'Och,' said Hilda. 'You know I would, if it wasn't for my hip . . .'

The pretty woman – Ginny – stuck her tongue out, but she was smiling, and Rachel found she was smiling too.

'Are you here to play or watch?' Hilda said, still focused on the match.

'Oh, erm . . .' Rachel looked at Bessie, who shrugged, wide-eyed. 'Play?'

'Right you are, I'll swap you in a minute. Look at poor Katie over there, she needs a break. And Ginny can come off . . .' she raised her voice '. . . if she doesn't try to kick the blooming ball.'

'Rachel,' hissed Bessie. 'I don't know how.'

'It's not hard, Bess. You just have to kick the ball into the goal.'

'Really?'

'It's fun.' Rachel said, suddenly desperate to have a go. She'd often played in the street with her brothers growing up. All the children round their way would join in, playing enormous games up and down the road until one of the grown-ups would get fed up and tell them to stop.

'It's not very ladylike,' said Bessie.

Rachel grinned at her. 'Neither am I.'

Chapter Twelve

Ellen thought that it was strange how quickly she'd got back into the swing of factory work. So much had changed since the day she'd walked out of Wentworth. She'd got married, had Annie, made a success of the Clydebank Clothing Exchange; war had been declared. Everything was different, and yet in many ways, it felt just the same.

Walking to the factory each morning felt so normal – even though most days she was walking the route carrying Annie, or holding her little hand. In fact, all in all, the strangest thing about being back at Wentworth was the fact that it didn't feel strange at all.

It had been a little odd to be shown around by Rachel, who'd just been a wee girl when Ellen was last inside the factory. And she'd had mixed feelings when she heard Wentworth was still making sewing machines. She'd briefly worried that she might be put into one of the departments that were making the machines and was relieved to be given a job in munitions instead. She'd started off bringing in empty shells, but after a few days she was moved into filling them, which she actually preferred because it meant she was kept rather separate from the rest of the huge – and very noisy – factory floor.

'Come on, doll,' she said to Annie now, as they went into the factory. 'Let's go.'

It was the start of Ellen's second week at Wentworth and so far, no one had even questioned what she was up to each day. Sadie was spending most of her time in Glasgow, working with the Belgian refugees who'd arrived. Bridget had stepped in to keep McKinley's ticking over because Ida was working shifts with the Women's Police Service. And Rachel, of course, was at Wentworth too.

Ellen hadn't told anyone – except Rachel – where she was working. And her ma, because on the days Annie couldn't go to the nursery, Ma had to look after her. She'd pursed her lips when Ellen had told her where she was going to work.

'And what does your sister think about this?'

'I've not told her yet,' Ellen had admitted. 'But I will.'

'See you do,' Ma said. But Ellen hadn't. So now she was lying to Bridget and Ma. And crossing her fingers that soon Annie could go to the nursery every day because Ma was going away, up north. It didn't sit right with her, keeping all these secrets, but the feeling of her wages in her purse at the end of the week had made things a lot easier.

The nursery was in a part of the factory which had once been used to store wood for the cabinets, right at the edge of the building. Ellen could still smell sawdust in the air, which made her remember the pride she'd taken in her work. It was funny, she thought, how her father had worked here, and then she and Sadie, and now Annie was being cared for in the same place.

'Howareya today, Annie?' said Mrs Kennedy as they arrived. She was an older, very cheerful Irish woman. She'd told Ellen she'd not long moved to Clydebank when war broke out and Ellen was glad she was a newcomer to the town and not someone who'd bump into Bridget at the shops and say, 'I saw your Ellen at Wentworth . . .'.

'She's full of beans,' Ellen said. 'Good luck.'

Annie ran off inside the nursery without so much as a backwards glance, and Ellen gave Mrs Kennedy a rueful smile.

'She's grand,' Mrs Kennedy said soothingly. 'I'll see you later.'

Checking the time on the clock overhead, Ellen hurried away. She was so pleased there was a nursery at the factory. Lucinda had told her the government wanted more factories to open them so more women could work, and had given Wentworth extra money as a sort of experiment. Sylvia Pankhurst was doing the same down in London, apparently. Ellen thought Bridget would be impressed by that, and she wished she could tell her. Perhaps in a couple of weeks.

She went into the changing room and put on her boiler suit and rubber boots. She quite liked the outfit. Wearing trousers made things so much easier than swishing about in a skirt. She'd written to James about it and she'd drawn him a wee picture of herself in her overalls. She thought he'd think it was funny. She hoped so, anyway.

She tucked her hair into her cap, pulled on her face mask and then her gloves, and walked on through to start work, nodding hello at the other women who were doing the same. Ellen was a bit disappointed that there didn't seem to be camaraderie between the workers like there had been before the strike. She supposed it was harder to have a laugh and a joke when your face was covered over and you were doing work that was literally life or death. It was a shame, though. She missed the feeling of being part of something. One thread in a rope, as they always used to say.

Back in Ellen's day, this room had been the place where the designs were put onto the sewing machines. Now it was where the shells were filled. It was the only part of the process that was done separately – the rest of the time the shells were simply moved from place to place on the main factory floor.

But the shell-filling room was much smaller than the other parts of the factory, and it had its own changing room, and even its own canteen. Ellen was disappointed that it meant she wouldn't see much of Rachel but she liked that it was all a bit more manageable. When she'd first been moved on to shell filling she'd wondered why it was separate, but after just a few minutes, she understood why. Because the women who'd been working there a while were yellow – and everything they touched was yellow too.

The munitionettes in the rest of the factory had a yellow tinge, there was no doubt about it, but the ones who filled the shells were worst of all. Ellen had been alarmed on her first day when she realised, because she thought there would be no disguising that. She was hoping it would wash off, though so far she'd not noticed much yellowing of her skin and she was very careful about keeping her mask and gloves on. After all, she thought, putting her hand on her taut abdomen briefly, she didn't want anything to happen to the baby.

'They call us Canary Girls,' said a woman called Phyllis who had a broad smile and a shock of dark hair with a definite ochre hue to the ends.

'Is it poisonous?' Ellen had asked, worried about her baby, or cuddling little Annie.

'Och, no,' Phyllis had said. 'At least, I don't think so. My friend Elaine left the factory a while ago and she's completely back to normal now.'

'That's a relief.'

'They say it's as safe as railway travel,' Phyllis said. 'We get checked out by the doctor every two weeks anyway. They'd pick up on any problems.'

'We do?' Ellen was a little concerned about that. She'd not told anyone at Wentworth that she was expecting as she thought they might tell her to go home. Which was ironic, really, because being pregnant – and worried about having another mouth to feed – was the main reason she needed the work in the first place.

Today was the day of her medical check. Fortunately, her name was called straight away because her hands were shaking and she was worried about spilling the powder she was filling the shells with.

The doctor barely glanced up as she went into the room.

'McCallum?'

'Yes, sir.'

'Sit.'

Ellen sat down in front of him, taking off her mask and gloves.

'Open,' he said.

Ellen looked at him, not sure what he wanted her to open, and then took a chance on her mouth.

He checked her teeth and gums, like she was a horse at market, and wrote something down.

'Any coughing?'

'No.'

'Good. Off you go.'

Ellen got up, relieved not to have been asked any awkward questions, and went back to work.

Working in munitions was more physical than cabinet polishing had been, there was no doubt about that. The shells were enormous and Ellen wasn't a large woman. But it was similar in that she had to concentrate hard on what she was doing, and that meant the hours went by quickly and soon it was time to fetch Annie again.

Mrs Kennedy handed her over, sleepy and more than a little grumpy.

'It's a long day for her,' she said as Annie curled up against Ellen, resting her head on her shoulder.

'Aye,' said Ellen. 'For all of us.'

She heaved Annie up a bit higher and set off towards the gates.

'Ellen!'

Ellen turned to see Rachel running towards her, looking absolutely delighted.

'I've not seen you,' she said. 'Have you moved?'

'Shell filling,' Ellen said. 'In the bit to the side.'

Rachel frowned. 'Is that all right?'

'It's hard work.'

'No, I meant with . . .' She nodded towards Ellen's middle. 'You know?'

'I was a wee bit worried at first but they say it's as safe as railway travel and I get on the train without a second thought.'

'I suppose,' Rachel said. Then she gave Ellen a quick grin. 'Sadie still doesn't know, eh?'

'No,' Ellen admitted.

'You know she'll find out?'

'I know.' Ellen nodded with a smile. 'She always finds out. I just didn't want to add to her burden. Not yet.'

Rachel nodded. 'The money helps, eh?'

'It helps a lot.'

'And the women are so nice.'

Ellen shrugged. 'It's hard to chat.' She screwed her nose up. 'That's what I'm missing actually. The friendships I had in cabinet polishing.'

Rachel gripped Ellen's arm. 'Oh my god,' she said. 'You need to come and meet my girls.'

'Och, I'm dead on my feet, Rachel,' Ellen said. 'And I've got Annie.'

'There's a bit to the side where some of the weans sleep,' Rachel said. 'Annie can curl up there, no bother.'

'To the side of what?' Ellen was bewildered.

'Come on, you'll see.'

More than anything, Ellen wanted to go home, tuck Annie into bed, and then go to sleep. But something about Rachel's eager expression made her follow the younger woman round the corner to where the factory building opened out on to a patch of rough grass. There were twenty women there; no, there were more than that. Thirty, maybe? Many were in their boiler suits and they were running laps around the grass. In the middle of the women, an imposing-looking lass was standing with a whistle in her hand.

'Come on, girls,' she was shouting. 'It's football, not crawl ball.'

'Crawl ball's not a real thing,' Rachel murmured to Ellen.

'I know that, thank you,' Ellen muttered back, astonished at what she was seeing. 'What is this?'

'It started a while ago, apparently,' Rachel told her. 'But more and more women are joining in every time. And now others are coming to watch. Men too.' She nodded over to where a group of young men were standing together. One of them, who had blond hair and a chiselled jawline, winked at her and Ellen was amused to see Rachel blush.

'Do you play?' she asked.

'Aye.' Rachel ducked her head, looking pleased. 'Hilda there says I'm quite good.'

'Franklin!' Hilda bellowed, as if on cue. 'What on earth are you doing standing there?'

'Hiya, Hilda,' Rachel said cheerfully. 'Brought my friend along to play.'

'Not to play,' Ellen said in horror. 'I'm not playing.'

'That's what Bessie said, but she joins in now.' Rachel pointed to where two women were running rather half-heartedly around the grass. They were both in their normal clothes – not their boiler suits – and Ellen thought their heart wasn't in it. One of them looked like she was about to keel over. Rachel made a face. 'Well, sort of.'

At the edge of the grass, next to a wall, was a pile of coats and blankets. Curled up there was a little boy, just a bit bigger than Annie. Ellen, wondering what it was exactly she thought she was doing, took her daughter over and settled her next to the lad. Then she stood up and looked at the game. The women had stopped running now, and Hilda had thrown them a ball. One of them – a pretty girl with red hair – was kicking it up in the air, keeping it up as she bounced it from knee to knee and then on her foot, and then her knee again. Ellen was almost struck dumb with awe.

'My da would love this,' she breathed. Her father was a huge football fan, and had played a lot when he was a lad too.

'You'll love it,' Rachel said. 'It's so much fun, Ellen. Last time I could barely stand up, I was laughing so hard.'

'Franklin!' Hilda shouted again. 'C'mon!'

Obediently, Rachel ran across the grass to get into position. 'Just join in, Ellen,' she called. 'It's all a bit slapdash, but it's great.'

'Should I get changed again?' Ellen called. But before she could make a decision, Rachel kicked the ball towards her, and suddenly, Ellen had hitched up her skirt and she was running across the grass with the ball at her feet, her hair flying out behind her, and feeling for all the world like the old Ellen. Ellen from before the war. Ellen whom everyone called a ray of sunshine, who brought a whole factory out on strike and made the town stand still. And she loved it.

Chapter Thirteen

Clydebank

30 March 1916

My dear James,

How I wish I knew where you were. Sadie and Noah have a map of the world on their wall – you know what Noah's like. Every day is a chance to learn something. And the other day I was looking at it, and marvelling at the vastness of the oceans and thinking how very small your ship must be in comparison. And then Noah must have realised what I was thinking about because he came over and he said that even though there was all this water in the world, the chances were you were in the Atlantic. I think he was trying to make me feel better, but I'm not sure it did. Not really.

Anyway, Annie sends you big kisses and cuddles. She is chattering away all the time now. I think being with other children at the nursery at Wentworth has made her even more of a chatterbox than she was already. Honestly, she never stops talking. Ma thinks she's clever as clever, of course, and is telling everyone who'll listen about her wonderful granddaughter.

Working at Wentworth is hard work, James, like I said in my last letter. Did you get that letter? I always worry they will arrive in the wrong order and perhaps you're reading this, astonished to know that I am back at the factory. I hope not. But you've not replied to my last one, so perhaps it hasn't arrived?

Anyway, I wasn't really enjoying it, the work, not at first. Because it's so loud, James, and you can't afford to lose concentration for one second. So there isn't much time to chat and I wasn't finding the other women very friendly. But then something wonderful happened. If you were here, I'd make you guess, but that won't work in a letter so I will simply tell you right out. I have started playing football.

I know! Your wife, kicking a ball about. It's not very ladylike, is it? Rachel dragged me along one afternoon. You remember what she was like when she was wee? Always wanted to join in with the boys. And I wasn't sure at first, because what do I know about football? But Rachel talked me into it and oh, James, it makes me feel like myself again!

It's all women, of course. There is a woman called Hilda who's in charge. She didn't mean to be in charge – it just worked out that way. She used to play, apparently, but stopped more than ten years ago. Now she just teaches us everything she knows. She's quite the character, James. You'd love her. She must be fifty and she shouts and bawls at us while we're playing but she's got the loveliest way about her, and when she tells me I've done something well, I almost overflow with pride. She started everything off, so Rachel says. One breaktime, she got some of the girls running round this wee scrubby bit of grass to keep their energy up, and then it took off, and someone found a ball one day, and now we're practising all the time. Rachel says the football sessions are 'slapdash' and they were, they really were. But I've only been going a week or so and they're already getting more organised. There are about thirty of us now, and Hilda makes a plan each week of what we're going to practise and everyone gets stuck in. It's not easy for everyone though. Rachel's pal Bessie comes along but she's a skinny wee thing and she can't always catch her breath. And she's not the only one. Some of the munitionettes look wretched. Hilda says being fitter will help and she says management know all about it and they're pleased. They want us to keep going.

Because here's the thing, James. It turns out, munitionettes are playing football all over the place. Lots of them down in Lancashire, Hilda says. I wanted to ask Bridget if Malcolm knows about that, but I've still not told her I'm working at Wentworth, so I can't. I know, I know. I will tell her, I promise.

Anyway, because there's no men's football now, some of these women's games are being written up in the papers, and they're entering competitions and all sorts. Hilda says they're getting hundreds of folk coming to watch and they're raising money for the war effort, which is a good thing, eh? I think Hilda wants us to be like that one day. Though, I have to be honest, I'm not sure we're ready for that. Not yet, anyway!

Now I must go, because I have to get Annie ready for bed. We both send you a thousand kisses and all our love.

Your Ellen X

Chapter Fourteen

Bessie wasn't feeling well, so Rachel walked home with her after their shift, just to make sure she made it because she really didn't look good at all.

She'd seen her inside the tiny flat she shared with her ma and all her wee brothers and sisters. Bessie obviously hadn't wanted Rachel to come in, because she opened the door a crack and slid through the narrow gap, saying she'd be right as rain after a good night's sleep.

'If you're sure?' Rachel said.

'Aye. Goodnight.'

'Goodnight.' Rachel hoped Bessie was right that she just needed sleep, but she wasn't convinced. Bessie was very thin and the whites of her eyes were tinged yellow now, just like the rest of her.

She'd opened her mouth to say she'd come back in the morning before work, but Bessie had already shut the door. So now Rachel was hurrying back to Wentworth because she had football practice and Hilda was becoming rather tyrannical about everyone getting there on time.

She turned the corner by the Clothing Exchange and saw Bridget pulling down the shutters on McKinley's store.

'Hiya,' Rachel called.

Bridget whipped round, then looked disappointed as she saw Rachel.

'Oh Rachel, I thought you might be Ida.'

'Sorry,' Rachel said with a grin, crossing the street to her. 'Am I a disappointment?'

'Never,' said Bridget. 'I just thought she'd be back by now.'

'Is she off at work? With the police service?'

'She is.' Bridget fixed the shutter tight and stood up. 'She says she is simply patrolling the railway station and making sure the munitionettes behave themselves.'

Rachel raised an eyebrow. 'The munitionettes I know are too tired to do anything but behave themselves.'

'That's what Ida says. She says it's really quite dull.' Bridget sighed. 'But I still worry. Not everyone is pleased to see women in police uniform.'

'That's true enough.'

'I worry that some people – some men – will look on it as a challenge.'

'You sound like Noah,' Rachel said. 'He's always worrying about Sadie when she's late back.'

Bridget gave a little smile. 'He knows what Sadie's like.'

Rachel opened her mouth to say something else then shut it again, because she'd just had the most startling thought – well, more of a realisation actually. That the way Bridget and Ida were with one another . . . they were just like Sadie and Noah. Like a married couple. She blinked. But they were just good friends, surely? Companions?

'What?' said Bridget. 'What's the matter? Do I have dirt on my face?'

'Nothing,' Rachel said hurriedly. 'Nothing at all.' She took Bridget's arm. 'I'm going back to Wentworth,' she said. 'Walk with me and we might catch Ida on the way.'

'Aye, go on, then,' said Bridget. 'The walk will do me good.'

The women set off towards the factory, with Rachel telling Bridget about the football team. She'd been a bit worried that Bridget might be annoyed about her working at Wentworth, because she knew she'd not been happy about Ida even working close by. But the older woman seemed to have accepted that things were different now. Rachel made a mental note to tell Ellen that.

Just before the factory gates, Rachel spotted Ida up ahead, looking rather impressive in her police uniform, talking to a sour-faced woman.

'There she is.'

'Blast it,' Bridget murmured. 'She's with Christina.'

'You don't like her?'

Bridget made a face. 'I try to be civil but she doesn't make it easy.'

'Maybe Ida will see us and come over.'

But what actually happened was that both women turned at the same time, as if to walk in their direction, and saw them.

'Oh, Bridget!' Ida called, looking pleased. 'How nice to see you. And Rachel. Hello!'

'I thought I might catch you on your way home,' said Bridget. 'Are you finished for the day?'

Ida glanced at Christina.

'Ida has just agreed to accompany me into Wentworth,' Christina said. 'I want her to see some behaviour I'm rather concerned about.'

Next to Rachel, Bridget groaned, but quietly enough that Christina wouldn't hear.

'Is it important?' she asked. 'You must both be tired after your shift. Christina, could you not show Ida tomorrow?'

'It has to be now.' Christina looked bullish. 'They won't be there tomorrow.'

With a sinking feeling, Rachel realised this miserable-looking woman had to be talking about football.

'Surely it can wait?' she said.

'I did say I'd go . . .' Ida looked unsure, glancing from Bridget to Christina.

Bridget was softening. 'Well, I suppose if you said you'd go . . .?'

'Come with us, Bridget,' Ida suggested. 'We won't be long, will we Christina?'

Christina rolled her eyes, and Rachel thought that she was indeed rather annoying. 'I'm not sure . . .'

'Och, it's just a quick check and then we'll be done, surely?' Ida looped her arm through Bridget's, making it clear they came as a pair and Rachel was struck, again, by how they seemed like a married couple.

'Perhaps,' said Christina.

'Then Bridget can come too.'

Christina nodded reluctantly, and Rachel wondered if she could somehow run ahead, to warn Hilda that this over-zealous policewoman was on the warpath. And in fact, to warn Ellen, who she was fairly sure hadn't told Bridget she was working at Wentworth again. But the factory gates were right there, and there was no time.

Bridget looked as though she most definitely did not want to go to Wentworth, but Christina marched off with Ida following, so Rachel and Bridget exchanged a glance and went too.

'Is it strange to be going back after so long?' Rachel asked. She knew Bridget had worked at the factory too.

'It is,' Bridget said, glancing around as they went through the gates. 'Wentworth was part of our family forever, and part of Clydebank for even longer, and then it all changed when Ellen started the strike.'

'She's really something, your Ellen.'

Bridget nodded. 'She was full of enthusiasm and fire back then. Now she seems sad and quiet.'

'She's been brighter recently,' Rachel pointed out, thinking that if Bridget knew Ellen was happier now she was back at the factory, she might not mind that she hadn't told her.

'She's up to something,' said Bridget.

'Is she?' Rachel tried to look innocent.

'Whatever it is seems to involve a lot of sewing and knitting

– I've seen her with bits of fabric and balls of wool from the Clothing Exchange.'

Rachel was startled. That hadn't been what she thought Bridget was going to say. 'Oh, right.'

'I'll find out,' Bridget said with a grin.

Rachel closed her eyes briefly. That was exactly what she was worried about. 'Let's catch the others up.'

'I don't understand why you can't just tell me,' Ida was saying to Christina as the women walked across the courtyard.

'I want you to see it.'

'Christina, it sounds like you're getting yourself up to high doh about nothing,' Bridget said mildly. 'Is this like when Mr Churchill came to Clydebank?'

Christina fixed Bridget with a stern look. 'This is nothing like that,' she said.

'Well, I hope not,' Bridget carried on. 'Because that time your behaviour landed me in jail.'

Rachel couldn't believe her ears. Jail? Bridget?

Ida stifled a laugh and Bridget gave Christina a sweet smile. 'Remember?'

'I don't think your memory is entirely accurate,' Christina said frostily, leaving Rachel desperate to know what had really gone on. 'Now, here we are.'

They went through a gate and round the corner and to Rachel's absolute relief, it seemed they were too late. Hilda would give her a row tomorrow for missing practice, but Rachel wasn't worried about that now.

'Och, I think we might have missed them,' Christina said. 'Quickly.'

She hurried off and Rachel, Ida and Bridget followed at a more leisurely pace.

'What on earth is she so worried about?' Bridget asked in a low voice.

'Something going on that she thinks we should be stopping but that seems to be approved of by the factory bosses,' Ida said.

Rachel bit her lip as they walked across to where Christina was standing, hands on hips beside the rough whitewashed markings of the pitch.

'It's a football pitch,' Bridget said, not remotely interested. 'Why have you brought us to a football pitch?'

She turned to Ida. 'Ellen will be fuming. Do you remember she was so determined to get Wentworth organising sports teams and picnics, and it never happened while we worked here?'

'Oh aye, she was.' Ida grinned. 'She'd love this.'

She does, thought Rachel. She really does.

She looked at Christina, whose face was set in a grimace.

'It's the munitionettes,' she said. 'They're the ones playing football.'

'Marvellous,' said Ida cheerfully. 'Good for them to make friends, an excellent way to promote health, and I imagine it's enormous fun.'

'Yes,' said Rachel. 'Enormous fun.'

'Football is a sport for men,' Christina said. 'Brutish men at that.' She shuddered. 'It's not something respectable women should be doing.'

'Well, they're not doing it now, are they?' Bridget pointed out, gesturing to the empty field.

Christina grimaced. 'It's not for women. Not nice women.'

Bridget rolled her eyes.

'I'm not a football fan in any way,' she began. 'In fact, I have never managed to understand why my father takes it all so seriously.'

Rachel opened her mouth to tell Bridget she had it wrong, and football was something quite special, but the other woman hadn't finished.

'But I can see this is important,' Bridget went on. 'It's a game for everyone. Look, all you need is a wee patch of grass and a ball, and anyone can join in. Like Ida said, it's good for the mind and the body. We should be encouraging this, not criticising it.'

'I'm planning on speaking to management at Wentworth tomorrow and asking them to put a stop to it,' Christina said.

'No,' said Rachel urgently. 'Don't do that.'

Bridget looked at Rachel, understanding dawning. Then she took a step towards Christina. 'I really don't think that would be a good idea,' she said. Rachel thought she sounded quite fierce.

'Ida?' Christina said, looking round Bridget, which obviously annoyed Bridget greatly. 'What do you think?'

Rachel held her breath. What would Ida say?

'I think this uniform has gone to your head,' Ida said. 'And if you go to management, you'll make a laughing stock of yourself and the Women's Police Service.'

'How dare you?' Christina began.

Bridget looped one arm through Ida's and the other through Rachel's. 'Be quiet, Christina,' she said. 'No one's interested.'

And together, the women turned and walked away, leaving Christina gawping after them.

Chapter Fifteen

'And then Ida told her she was going to make a fool of herself and the police service,' Bridget said. 'And we walked off, leaving her opening and closing her mouth like a fish.'

Everyone laughed, and Bridget smiled broadly. Sadie watched her with interest, thinking how much she had changed since they'd first met. Back then, Bridget had been serious and sensible – or at least, that was what Sadie had thought of her at first. Perhaps even a little prickly. But joining the suffragettes and becoming friends with Ida had transformed Bridget, or perhaps it had just let everyone else see who she really was.

Now Sadie was the prickly one. Quick to anger, because she was almost always a little bit irritated about something, and prone to snapping at her friends and her lovely Noah, who was the kindest, sweetest and handsomest husband anyone could ask for. Sadie knew she was lucky to have him, and she knew she could be nicer to him, but she couldn't still her sharp tongue and barbed comments.

She was sitting on her own, slightly apart from the other women who'd come along to the Clothing Exchange today. She was sorting out toys that had been donated – which Sadie was very pleased about – but she had a niggling suspicion that no one wanted to help her because she wasn't very good company.

She'd forced herself to join in as Bridget told the story about

Christina being up to high doh about the munitionettes playing football, and she even managed to crack a smile at Bridget's impression of the other woman.

'You'd better watch it,' Ida said, nudging Bridget. 'That Christina holds a grudge. She'll be out to get you now.'

'Not at all,' Bridget said, looking at her friend with a mischievous glint in her eye. 'She'll not be out to get me – she'll be out to get us.'

Ida pretended to roll up her sleeves. 'Aye? Well, I'll be ready for her.'

All the women laughed again, and Sadie gave a small chuckle too, because it was actually quite funny, and Bridget and Ida together were like a double act you'd see on stage at the Gaiety Theatre. She felt her shoulders relax a little.

'Ellen, Ida and I were saying you'd be furious about the munitionettes playing football,' Bridget said.

Ellen, who was sitting rolling balls of wool with Rachel, looked alarmed. Sadie saw her glance at Rachel, who dropped the end of the yarn and had to get up to find it under her seat.

'Why would I be furious?' Ellen asked. She sounded worried.

Bridget laughed. 'Just because you always wanted sports teams and entertainment at Wentworth, remember?'

Ellen relaxed visibly. Sadie watched her friend and wondered if it was the mention of Wentworth that had made her so tense. She didn't blame her; The factory had chewed them up and spat them out. Sadie still felt resentful about how they'd been treated back then, and she'd barely started at Wentworth when the strike happened. For Ellen, who had Wentworth in her bones, it must have all been so much harder to take.

'Ah, right,' Ellen said, smiling. 'Yes, I did want that. That's great it's happening now.'

'You used to talk about it all the time,' Sadie said.

'Aye, I remember.' She frowned, looking at Bridget. 'You didn't see anyone playing football?'

'Not a soul.' Bridget shrugged. 'Christina said we were too late, but she said the women play often.'

'Maybe they do, maybe they don't,' said Rachel vaguely.

Sadie gave her sister a stern look. She didn't know for sure that Rachel had been playing football but she'd always wanted to have a game when she was wee but too sickly to join in properly. Sadie suspected that now Rachel was grown and healthy, nothing would stop her kicking a ball.

'Apparently it started out just for fun,' Ida said. She was sitting on the shop counter and she leaned forward as if sharing a secret. 'But now they're a proper team. Christina said they're planning to play matches against other factories.'

'That's true.'

Everyone's heads swivelled to where Lucinda was sitting in the far corner, knitting socks. Sadie hadn't seen her come in.

'Why are you here?' she asked now, her disapproval obvious.

Ellen shot Sadie a disappointed look. 'Everyone's welcome.'

'Really?' Sadie's voice was icy.

Ellen held her gaze.

'Really.'

There was a pause and Sadie conceded, looking at her feet.

'Fine.'

She didn't have a problem with Lucinda. Not really. She was just annoyed by the whole world and she wanted someone to blame.

Ellen leaned over and touched her arm very briefly, and Sadie knew the gesture was supposed to show her there were no hard feelings. Ridiculously, it made tears spring to her eyes. She nodded to Ellen and then turned her face away before she could spot that she was crying.

'So, Christina was right?' asked Bridget, taking everyone's attention away from Sadie and Ellen – thank goodness.

'My father knows very little about football, but he's delighted,' Lucinda said. 'Apparently there is a factory down in Lancashire that's made quite a name for itself with its football team. They play matches locally and attract quite a crowd.'

'But that's not going to happen here,' Rachel said, glancing at Sadie and Ellen. 'People won't come and watch Wentworth play football?' She sounded concerned and Sadie glared at her, her suspicions that Rachel was one of the players confirmed.

'If anyone's interested in playing football, we are still recruiting at the factory,' Lucinda said, with a broad smile. 'It's hard work but there are a lot of good things about it.'

There was a murmur of interest, which annoyed Sadie.

'Are there?' Sadie said loudly, so everyone could hear. 'Are there, really?'

'Well, yes,' Lucinda said. She looked around at the women. 'I can go through them all again, if you'd like? For starters, there's the food, munitionettes get a good meal inside them every day. There's the cinema . . .'

Sadie huffed gently. On a different day, she would have admired Lucinda standing up for herself, but not today.

'I'm not talking about all the extras,' she said, interrupting Lucinda and earning a tut from Ellen in the process. 'I'm talking about the work. The conditions. These women are making explosives. Is it dangerous?'

'We have strict rules the workers follow, to make sure it's safe,' Lucinda said. 'They wear rubber boots, and of course they're not allowed matches . . .'

Sadie glanced at the corner where Bessie was sitting. Rachel said she'd been sick and now she was better, but she didn't look better. She was very frail and though she'd picked up wool to roll, she wasn't really doing anything at all. Her skin was tinged with yellow like a sickly baby, and her shoulder bones poked up through the thin fabric of her blouse.

'Does it make the munitionettes ill?' Sadie asked. She was aware that she hadn't met Bessie before she worked at Wentworth. Perhaps she'd always been weak. But perhaps not.

'Ill?' said Lucinda. 'No.'

She didn't sound as convincing about that as she had been about the meals, Sadie noticed.

'We have a doctor,' Lucinda added. 'He keeps an eye on things.'

'Right.' Sadie nodded, wondering why on earth they needed a doctor if it was as safe as Lucinda said. 'And what about the pay?'

'Well, the pay is good.' Lucinda folded her arms.

'Good?' Sadie questioned. 'Good compared to what?'

'It is good,' Ellen put in. Sadie shot her a glance and Ellen looked contrite. 'Well, I've heard it's good.'

'We pay our munitionettes twenty shillings a week,' Lucinda said. 'The standard amount.'

'The minimum amount,' Sadie pointed out.

Lucinda was unrepentant. 'It's a good wage.'

Sadie stood up.

'And what do you pay the men?'

'I beg your pardon?'

'I believe women doing men's work should be paid at an equal rate to the men,' Sadie said. 'What do you pay them?'

Lucinda frowned. 'We don't have any male munitionettes.'

'Then elsewhere in the factory. Are the women paid equal to the men?'

Out of the corner of her eye, Sadie saw Ida sit up straighter.

'I've heard some factories are changing the way jobs are described in order to avoid paying women the same amount,' Ida said. 'Is that happening in Wentworth?'

'It wouldn't surprise me,' said Bridget with a snort. There was a rumble of disapproval from the assembled women and Sadie felt a little proud.

Lucinda, though, wasn't giving up. 'I honestly don't know,' she told the women. 'But I will go straight to my father now and ask him. And if he says the men are being paid more, then I will ask him why.'

'Good,' Sadie said, the wind taken out of her sails a little. 'That's good.'

Lucinda put down her knitting, and gathered her things. 'I'll come back and let you know what he says.'

'Tell him Sadie Franklin wants to know,' Sadie said, as though she was an agitator straight from the folk organising the rent strikes sweeping Clydebank, and as though she'd not been Sadie Spark for four years.

Lucinda gave Sadie a look of sheer irritation. 'Oh, I'll tell him,' she said.

When Lucinda had gone, the women carried on chatting and knitting for a while. But Ellen looked tired and Sadie had had enough, so they packed away all their donations, agreed to sell flags to raise money for the troops and then went their separate ways.

Rachel was quiet on the way home and Sadie wondered if she was annoyed with her for speaking out about Wentworth. She felt so muddled about Rachel working there that she wasn't sure what to say.

But in the end it was Rachel who spoke, as they walked up the path.

'When you said it was dangerous working at Wentworth, what did you mean?'

Sadie paused, her key in the lock. 'Well, it's explosives, isn't it? I assume one spark could cause the whole factory to explode.'

Rachel sighed as Sadie opened the door.

'Right,' she said. 'What about what's in the explosives? What they're made of? Do you think that's dangerous?'

They went upstairs to their flat and Sadie opened that door too.

'I can't imagine it's anything nice,' she said.

Noah was sitting in the kitchen, reading. Sadie felt her bad mood lift at the sight of him.

'Hello,' she said, going to give him a kiss.

'Hello.' He put his hand on her cheek and looked at her closely. 'All right?'

'Aye,' Sadie said. 'All right.'

Noah smiled. 'What's not nice?'

'What?'

'What you were saying when you came in. What's not nice?'

'The stuff they make the explosives out of,' Rachel said. 'At Wentworth.'

Noah made a face. 'Some sort of chemical?'

'Something yellow,' said Rachel.

She put her hands out towards Sadie, palms upwards, and showed her. Sadie looked in shock at her sister's hands which had taken on a distinctive yellow tinge. Like Bessie's skin.

'It's not just my hands,' Rachel said. 'It's all over.' She tilted her face towards the window. 'Even round my lips.'

'Good lord,' Sadie said. 'You really are yellow.'

'Not as bad as Bessie,' said Rachel. 'Well, you saw her yourself this evening? She's awful yellow, and she's so weak, Sadie. Every day she seems a bit worse.'

'You said she was better.'

'Aye, well, she's not. Not really. I only said that because she was right there with me and I didn't want to upset her.'

'And this is happening to all the women?'

'It seems to affect some folk worse than others. Like Bessie. But the ones who work filling the shells are the worst. They work separately to us and I know why now. The women are all yellow, and so is everything they touch – their chairs, the locker doors, everything . . .'

'So everyone knows it's happening?' said Sadie, feeling a smouldering rage in her belly once again. 'Management know you're all turning yellow?'

'I suppose.'

'Does it wash off?' Noah asked, coming over and looking curiously at Rachel's hands. 'Can you clean it?'

Rachel shook her head. 'But it wears off, apparently, once you stop working with the shells.'

'This isn't right,' said Sadie. 'Someone needs to do something.'

Noah groaned, but Sadie thought he actually looked quite proud. 'And when you say someone needs to do something?'

'Me,' Sadie said. 'I'll do it.'

Chapter Sixteen

Rachel was a little worried she'd lit a fire under her sister. Sadie was getting herself all in a state about the conditions the munitionettes were working under and she was determined to fight to make sure they got equal pay with the male factory workers.

Noah thought it was wonderful. He'd cornered Rachel in the kitchen when Sadie had gone out to buy bread and begged her to go along with it all.

'Sadie needs a distraction,' he said.

'I thought the Clothing Exchange was the distraction,' Rachel pointed out. 'And the Belgian refugees.'

Noah had looked concerned at that. 'Aye, well, maybe this is the one thing that might help,' he said. 'A fight for what's right.'

'She does love a fight,' Rachel conceded. 'That's true enough.'

'Let her have this one,' said Noah.

And, somewhat reluctantly, Rachel had agreed.

So now she was heading to Wentworth, with Sadie's instructions to find out as much as she could ringing in her ears.

'Just wait for Lucinda's da to come home,' Rachel had said. Lucinda's father, Hamilton Blyth, had gone to Manchester for a few days.

'Convenient,' Sadie had muttered, but Rachel didn't think Lucinda was the sort to tell a lie.

She walked towards the factory, saying 'hello' as she went to the munitionettes she was getting to know through playing football. The games were becoming more organised, more regular, and more fun than Rachel had thought possible. Yesterday, Ginny, who was the star of the team, had come up to Rachel and said, 'well played, Franklin', and Rachel had thought she might die right there on the spot out of sheer pleasure and pride.

She was playing football again later, and she thought there might be some male workers watching whom she could ask about the wages. In fact, she half hoped the blond chap might be there. He'd been showing up a lot and every time he did, he caught Rachel's eye and smiled and she felt a bit hot and flustered. He was very handsome with his swept-back hair and piercing eyes. She kept catching herself thinking about him when she was waiting to finish a shell and had to force her mind back to the job. Was this how Sadie had felt about Noah before they'd got married? Rachel chuckled to herself as she walked along. It seemed unlikely. Sadie was so grumpy all the time – though, granted, she hadn't always been that way – and Noah was so, well, ungainly, with his squint glasses and his messy hair. Still, as her ma always said, it would be a boring world if we all liked the same thing.

After work, Rachel was running around the grass with the others, and Hilda – who'd somehow become their coach without anyone really discussing it – was shouting at them to keep their knees up, when she saw the young, blond man.

She smiled at him, and he smiled back at her and oof! She caught her foot in a divot and fell, ending up sprawled on the ground, dirt in her hair and her hands grazed.

Winded, she lay still for a moment, and then she pushed herself up to sitting, to see Ginny, Hilda, Ellen and the blond man all surrounding her looking worried. Ashamed that the man had witnessed her tumble, Rachel felt her face redden and she looked down at the ground.

'Anything broken?' said Hilda.

Rachel shook out her arms and straightened her legs. 'Don't think so.'

'That's a relief. Ellen's organised that match against Marlow Brothers next week and we need you.'

Pleased she was considered an asset to the team, Rachel put her hands down to help herself up to standing and winced as the grazes on her palms stung.

'Here.' The blond man bent down and took Rachel's arm, helping her to her feet. He smelled lovely, like fresh air, and as he smiled at her, she felt a little dizzy suddenly.

'Ooh, careful,' he said as she staggered. He steadied her.

'Have a sit down for a while,' said Hilda. 'Catch your breath.'

'Just for a minute.' Rachel didn't want to miss too much training.

'Come this way.' The man led her over to where a few children – including little Annie – were all snoozing on the blankets. 'Sit here.'

'Oh no, honestly, I'm fine,' Rachel said, embarrassed to be put to one side with the weans.

'I'll sit with you.'

That was all the encouragement Rachel need. 'All right, then.'

Together they sat down, watching the women kicking the ball to one another.

'I'm Lewis,' the man said.

'Rachel.' She put her hand out for him to shake then looked at her grazed muddy palms and thought better of it. 'Sorry.'

He laughed. 'Don't worry. Are you sore?'

'It's not too bad.' Rachel examined the knee of her boiler suit, which was ripped thanks to her fall. 'I can mend this.'

'Good at football and sewing?' said Lewis. 'I'm impressed.'

'And shell finishing,' Rachel joked. 'I'm excellent at that.'

'Glad to hear it.'

She looked at him. He was very handsome, with a chiselled jaw and clear blue eyes, and younger than she'd thought initially.

'You've not joined up?'

He shrugged. 'I'm too young.'

'How old are you?'

'Seventeen.'

'Me too.' Rachel was absurdly pleased about it, as if it was a good sign, though a sign of what, she wasn't sure. The thought made her feel a little giddy, so to distract herself she tore her gaze from Lewis and instead reached out and twirled one of sleeping Annie's curls round her finger.

'I've got a big brother, Daniel,' she said. 'He's in the army. He's in Belgium.'

'It's been brutal out there.'

Rachel didn't like to think about what Daniel was experiencing. It made her feel heavy inside, like her heart was too full of sadness. She knew Sadie felt the same way – it was why she was so focused on helping the Belgian refugees.

'If we help them,' she would say when they first began arriving in Scotland, 'then perhaps someone will help Daniel.'

Rachel stroked Annie's head.

'Annie's da is in the navy,' she said. 'Ellen's husband.' She nodded over to where Ellen was chatting in a very animated fashion to Ginny and a few others.

'She must miss him.'

'She's not been the same since he went.'

'I can understand that feeling. My brother's in the army,' Lewis said. 'Lachlan. He's twenty-one. My father is beside himself. And both my sisters' husbands are serving too.'

Rachel considered him for a moment. He was very well-spoken and his shirt was beautifully made. He was obviously from what her mother would call a 'good family'. But clearly they still shared the same worries as the rest of them.

'When are you eighteen?'

'End of the year.'

'Will you join up?'

Lewis nodded. 'I think so. It's better than being conscripted.'

Rachel felt a sudden, forceful desire to wrap her arms round him and make him stay. She shifted slightly on the blankets, feeling a little taken aback by her emotions.

'You've not worked here long?' Lewis said.

'Not that long, no. How about you?'

'Not long.'

There was a small pause as they both watched Ginny score an excellent goal. Even Hilda looked pleased.

'The football is wonderful,' Rachel said. 'I love it, and I know Ellen does too.'

'You're both great players.'

'You come to watch a lot.' Rachel flushed again. 'I've seen you.'

'Aye,' said Lewis. 'I like football.' He pulled one knee up and rested his arm on it. 'I've noticed you, too.'

'Have you?'

Rachel looked at him again, feeling bolder.

'I have.' Lewis swallowed. 'I was wondering if perhaps you might like . . .'

'Franklin!' bellowed Hilda. 'Are you fit?'

'Aye,' said Rachel, flustered by Hilda's whistle and Lewis's closeness. 'I'm fit.'

'Coming on? Ellen needs to go home.'

'Aye, go on, then.'

She got to her feet and ran on the spot a couple of times just to check she was all right.

'Nice to meet you, Lewis,' she said. 'Are you staying to watch the rest of the game?'

'I was planning to.'

'Then maybe I'll see you after?'

'I'd like that.'

Rachel was worried she'd be distracted with thoughts of Lewis but instead she felt his presence throughout the rest of the game like an encouraging word in her ear. She ran all over the pitch, kicked the ball with deadly accuracy and made a good couple of headers too, one that left her ears ringing with the force of the ball as she sent it into the goal, and which made her brim with pride.

At the end of the match, she stopped with her elbows on her knees, trying to catch her breath after all the exertion.

'Good work today, Franklin,' said Hilda. 'If this is what happens after you take a tumble then perhaps I need to trip you up every day.'

Rachel laughed, exhilarated by the game and the praise and Lewis.

'No need,' she said. 'This is just me.'

Hilda slapped her on the back. The other women began drifting away, chattering nineteen to the dozen, and Rachel went back to where Lewis was standing, his eyes narrowed against the weak evening sunshine. Waiting for her.

'You're really good,' he said.

Rachel grinned. 'We're all good.'

'That is true.'

'We're playing a proper match next week.'

'I heard.'

'Perhaps if we win, management will give us a proper pitch.'

'You don't like this one?'

Rachel shrugged. 'It's fine. But round the other side would be better. In between the building and the canal? Do you know where I mean? The grass is thicker, and the ground is more even.'

'The ball might end up in the canal,' Lewis said.

'Not if they put a fence up.'

'And by proper pitch, you mean?'

'Just the markings done properly, not by Hilda slopping whitewash about.' Rachel looked up into the sky, like she could see her imaginary football pitch up there. 'And real goals with nets so we don't have to scamper around collecting the ball.' She grinned.

'And there's space round there for folk to come and watch. If we play matches here, you know?'

'We could build a stand,' Lewis said. 'Charge people to get in.'

'We're not quite at that stage yet,' Rachel said with a laugh.

'No, but that's what they do in Lancashire. So I've heard.'

'Wouldn't that be wonderful?' Rachel breathed. A sudden thought occurred to her and she looked at Lewis. 'Do you work in clerical? Is that how you know all this stuff about Lancashire?'

He frowned. 'Why do you think that?'

'Well, your clothes for a start. You don't look like one of us from the factory floor.'

Lewis chuckled. 'I'm not sure whether to be flattered or offended by that,' he said. 'I suppose you could say I'm in clerical, yes.'

'Do you know about the wages?'

'Whose wages?'

'The factory workers' wages.'

'Oh,' Lewis rubbed his head. 'Not really. Why?'

'I wondered if the women get paid the same as the men?'

Lewis frowned. 'I'm not sure.'

'What do you get paid?'

He shifted slightly on his feet. 'What do I get paid? In, erm, clerical?'

'Yes.' But then Rachel thought again. 'Although that's not exactly the same, is it? As what the munitionettes are doing. We can't compare the two.'

'I suppose not.'

Rachel frowned. 'And have you ever heard anyone say anything about the work?'

'The work?'

'With the munitions. About whether it might be dangerous.'

'Well, there's always an element of danger,' Lewis said. 'It's explosives, after all.'

Rachel stuck her hands out.

'But what about what they're made of? The explosives. They're turning us yellow.'

Lewis made a face. 'Och, I don't know.' He reached out and took her hand, examining it. 'Does it wash off?'

'No,' Rachel said, giddy from the game and the feeling of his hand on hers. 'But it goes away.'

Lewis looked as though he might say something else, but Rachel, flustered by his closeness, had moved on. 'What were you going to say to me?'

'Pardon?'

'Earlier on, when Hilda called on me to come and play. You were about to ask me something.'

'Oh,' said Lewis. 'Yes I was.' He looked a little unsure of himself suddenly. 'I was going to ask if you might like to go out with me one night. Maybe to the pictures here? Or we could go to the theatre. Or just for a walk along the canal?'

Rachel felt her veins fizz with sheer happiness.

'I'd like that very much,' she said.

She'd not really noticed it happening, but somehow she was aware that she and Lewis were standing very close together. He was only a wee bit taller than she was, so she could look into his eyes perfectly. The way he was gazing at her made her feel excited and a little nervous and joyful, all at once. He seemed to like what he saw. Even though she was red in the face and hot and sweaty from running around. She hoped he didn't think she always had a face like a glowing ember from the fire.

'Are you all right?' Lewis said. 'You looked like you were somewhere else there for a minute.'

'Just thinking about football,' Rachel lied, hoping she hadn't broken the mood.

Lewis touched her arm and she felt her skin tingle under his fingers.

And then a whistle blew loudly, making both Rachel and Lewis leap apart in shock.

'Rachel Franklin,' a voice boomed at her. 'What's going on here?'

Rachel turned to see Ida's friend Christina marching towards her. She was wearing her police uniform, just like Ida's, and her face was set in a disgusted expression. She blew her whistle again and Lewis looked at Rachel.

'What is happening?' he muttered. 'Who is this?'

Before Rachel could reply, the woman reached them.

'Time to go home, Rachel,' she said. 'Off you go.'

Lewis stepped sideways, positioning himself between the two women.

'Hello,' he said amiably. 'May I ask what this is about?'

'I am Constable Christina Everidge,' the woman said. 'I'm charged with upholding behaviour here at Wentworth, and I believe a young man and a young woman here together, so long after the shift has ended, is untoward.'

Rachel swallowed her giggle. 'Untoward?'

'Indeed.'

'Well,' said Lewis, sounding very much as though he was finding it hard not to laugh. 'I certainly do not want to do anything untoward. Do you, Miss Franklin?'

'Certainly not.'

'I'm so sorry to have taken up so much of your time, Constable Everidge.'

Christina smiled at him, but Rachel thought it was a cold smile.

'Don't let it happen again.'

'It?' said Lewis innocently. 'What is "it" exactly?'

Rachel was half-thrilled, half-horrified by how casually he talked back to Christina. Rachel considered herself to be rather bold, but she'd never have the nerve to speak up to someone with authority. Even if they were as infuriating as Christina was.

'This,' said Christina.

'This talking?' Lewis looked at Rachel and then back at Christina. 'We're not to talk again? Is it just Rachel I'm not to talk to, or is it everyone at Wentworth? Because that could make things tricky. Or is it the women at Wentworth? Because my sister works here and frankly, ignoring her is not something you get away with. Or is it that Rachel shouldn't be speaking to anyone? You're going to have to make it clearer, I'm afraid.'

Rachel put her hand over her mouth, stifling her shocked laugh.

'Mr . . . Erm . . .'

'Just Lewis is fine.'

'Mr Lewis, I'll thank you not to give me cheek.'

'No cheek.' Lewis beamed at her. 'I just need to know what it is we've done wrong so we can, what was it you said? Make sure we don't let it happen again.'

Christina sighed and Lewis smiled at her. There was a pause and then Christina nodded.

'On your way,' she said.

'But . . .' Lewis began. Rachel, though, wasn't hanging around. She took Lewis by the hand and dragged him away from the grass and round the corner where they collapsed in laughter leaning against the wall, and Rachel hoped with all her heart that it absolutely did happen again. And soon.

Chapter Seventeen

Ellen held up the shirt and looked at it carefully.

'Perfect,' she said in satisfaction. 'It's perfect.'

Annie, who was playing with a little pull-along cart on wheels, looked up and nodded. 'Erfect,' she mimicked.

'It's for Mama to wear when she plays football, Annie,' said Ellen, but Annie had already lost interest.

Ellen turned her attention back to the shirt, wishing she could show James. She would draw a picture of it in her next letter, she decided, and tell him all about the goal she scored yesterday. She'd received two letters from him this week, much to her delight. That was what often happened – there would be nothing for ages and then a couple together. Each time there was a gap, she felt she was holding her breath, waiting for bad news, and then another letter would drop on the mat and she could breathe again. For a little while at least.

He'd written that he had told all his pals about his wife who was the star of the football team. And he told her how proud he was about her going to work at Wentworth, which had made her feel better about it.

'You are a strong woman,' he'd written. 'I know you will do whatever needs to be done to keep Annie and the new wee one looked after.'

Ellen had wiped away a tear when she'd read that bit. From the very first day she'd met him, James had always been her biggest supporter. It made her feel like she could do anything – lead a whole factory out on strike, start the Clothing Exchange, play football, go back to Wentworth – anything at all.

She smoothed the shirt out on her knee. It was dark blue, like the sailors wore. Ellen had thought that seemed the most appropriate colour. She'd really wanted stripes but that would be too fiddly, and her plan was to get all the women on the team to sew their own shirts. Not all of them were good enough with a needle to produce something complicated.

She had deliberately made her shirt with a bit of room in it. Her pregnancy wasn't really showing yet – it wasn't obvious in her boiler suit, or in normal clothes – but things were getting a wee bit snug. Some people knew she was expecting, but not many. The women on the football team didn't know, nor Lucinda or anyone at Wentworth really. Ellen had a horrible feeling that once they found out, they might not let her work anymore, and football wouldn't be happening either. So she was keeping things quiet for as long as she could.

In fact, she was quite weighed down by all the secrets she was keeping. Her pregnancy. Her job at Wentworth. They were heavy burdens to carry. Rachel had urged her to tell Sadie the truth about going back to Wentworth, but seeing how Sadie had reacted to Rachel taking a job there made Ellen think that was a bad idea. Rachel had only been a little girl when the strike happened – she certainly hadn't been in the thick of the action like Ellen and Sadie had – and still Sadie thought she shouldn't be working there. And there was no doubt Sadie still wasn't herself. She was grouchy and quick to anger, and Ellen knew it was taking all her friend's strength to be happy that she was expecting again. Their friendship was stretched so tight that it could snap at any moment, like a caught thread on the sewing machine. Ellen didn't want to risk losing Sadie for good.

She stood up and pulled the football shirt on over her dress.

It was plenty big enough. She was pleased. Now she just had to finish off the breeks. Some teams, she'd heard, played in skirts, but the Wentworth women were used to running in trousers because they wore their boiler suits for practice. So Ellen had come up with knee-length shorts. She was planning to knit long blue socks – there she could have her stripes – and a matching blue and white striped hat. Then they'd really look the ticket.

Not that anyone would see her of course. After they'd played an especially exhilarating match one day, Ellen had said how much she was enjoying football and mentioned that she'd heard a few of the factories roundabout had teams so perhaps they could get together. Hilda had heard her talking and before Ellen knew it, she'd arranged a proper match. They were playing Marlow Brothers, a munitions factory in Glasgow which had a proper pitch and everything. Ellen was being credited with having the idea, which ordinarily she'd have loved but it was worrying her instead. Hilda was talking about getting people to come and watch when Marlow came to play at Wentworth.

'We could put up posters,' she'd said. 'Charge folk a penny to get in. Some of the games in Glasgow get big crowds.'

Of course a big crowd was the last thing Ellen wanted. Everyone knew everyone in Clydebank. Word would soon get back to Bridget or Sadie, or both, if she was seen prancing about the football pitch at Wentworth. And then all the secrets would be revealed all at once.

In more usual times, having so much to fret about would have left Ellen tossing and turning in her bed, but she was so tired from work and football and pregnancy that she slept like the dead every night.

So the following day, she felt a bit more energetic after her shift as she and Annie headed towards the football pitch, clutching her newly made football shirt to show the other women.

As she got closer she saw that awful Christina. She was lurking a little way from where the women were gathered, watching. Ellen paused, shrinking into the shadows of one of the factory walls. She wasn't entirely sure if Christina would recognise her but she knew that if she did, she'd delight in telling Bridget she'd seen her.

'C'mon, Mama,' said Annie, tugging at Ellen's hand.

'Just wait a wee minute.' Ellen crouched down to speak to her daughter. 'Something's going on and I want to know what it is.'

Annie nodded solemnly, even though Ellen wasn't sure she understood. But nevertheless, she stood obediently by Ellen's side as they looked over at the football team. Normally the women got to playing as soon as they arrived – no one wanted to waste any time. But today they were all standing huddled in a group. It looked for all the world as though they were waiting for something. At the back of the group was Lucinda.

'Annie?' Ellen said. 'Can you run over to Lucinda, there? Get her to come to Mama?'

'Lucinda,' said Annie, smiling. She liked Lucinda, who always made an enormous fuss of her.

'That's right. Can you go to her? Go on.'

She gave Annie a gentle push in the right direction and off Annie went, scampering across to where Lucinda stood. Ellen watched as Lucinda noticed the little girl and scooped her up into her arms, making her giggle, then glanced around, looking for Ellen.

She stepped out of the shadows briefly, and beckoned to Lucinda, putting her finger to her lips to show she didn't want to be revealed.

Lucinda understood and came hurrying over, holding a giggling Annie in her arms.

'What's the matter?' she said.

Ellen pulled her round the corner, away from Christina.

'That woman – in the police uniform?'

'Aye?'

'She knows my sister.'

'She's a pain in the backside.'

Ellen grinned. 'She is that.'

'You don't want her to see you?'

'No.'

'Right.' Lucinda nodded. 'I'll get rid of her.'

She put Annie down on her little legs and made to march away, but Ellen caught her arm.

'Wait,' she said. 'What's going on? Why is no one playing?'

Lucinda smiled. 'Wait and see.'

Ellen watched from her hiding place as Lucinda walked over to Christina.

'Constable Everidge,' she said. 'How lovely to see you.'

'Hello, Miss.'

Lucinda smiled so warmly that for a moment Ellen thought she'd been teasing her when she said Christina was a pain in the backside.

'Constable, I have just heard that two women have been seen on factory grounds . . .' she paused and looked around her as if she was sharing a secret she didn't want to be overheard – 'drinking.'

Christina pursed her lips.

'Gin,' Lucinda added, with – Ellen thought – a certain amount of glee.

'Where was this?'

Lucinda pointed in the opposite direction to where they all stood.

'By the south gate. Would you mind going to check? Do whatever you need to do.'

'Certainly will, Miss.'

'And if they're not there, would you have a good old look for them? Don't let them get away.'

'Absolutely.'

'Thank you so much.'

Christina marched off and Lucinda turned to Ellen with a triumphant look.

'Coast is clear.'

'Who were the women who were drinking gin?' said Ellen, who'd been rather shocked by the thought.

'Nobody, you goose,' said Lucinda. 'I made it up.'

Ellen was impressed – and more than a little alarmed – by Lucinda's ability to lie so convincingly.

'Now will you tell me what's going on?'

'Shush,' Lucinda said, picking Annie up again so she could see. 'Here's my father.'

Ellen hadn't yet met Hamilton Blyth, the factory boss. In fact, she'd not so much as laid an eye on him since she'd started working at Wentworth, so she regarded him now with a great deal of interest.

He was younger than she'd expected, with a bushy moustache and friendly eyes. But Ellen wasn't about to trust him – she'd been caught out by good looks before and now, as Bridget would say, she only believed in deeds, not words.

'He looks tired,' Lucinda murmured. 'He's working so hard. He says it stops him worrying about my brother.'

'Poor sod,' said Ellen, slightly more sympathetic but not won over.

'Ladies,' Mr Blyth began. 'Let me say how pleased and proud I am to see you making a success of your football games.'

The women all nodded and smiled at one another. Ellen folded her arms.

'It's come to my attention that this space isn't nearly good enough for you all to play on. So if you'd like to follow me, I'll take you round to the new pitch we've had made next to the canal.'

'It's fenced off,' Lucinda added. 'No risk of lost balls.'

'Goals?' Hilda asked.

'Goals,' Mr Blyth said. 'Proper ones. With nets.'

There was a stunned silence. Ellen looked at Rachel, who seemed astonished.

'And Ellen's made a shirt,' Lucinda said. 'Haven't you, Ellen?'

'Oh aye.' Ellen held it up for everyone to see. 'Here.'

'That's smart,' someone shouted.

'We'll look like proper players,' said someone else.

'Aye,' said Hilda, with a nod. 'Not bad.'

Ellen smiled. That was high praise coming from Hilda.

'Right, come on, ladies,' said Mr Blyth. 'Let's go and see your new pitch.'

Ellen took Annie, who was beginning to look sleepy, from Lucinda. She followed at the back of the crowd as Lucinda shepherded the women round towards the new space.

But as Ellen walked along, a bit slower than the rest because Annie was heavy and she was tired, she saw – to her absolute horror and shock – Sadie crossing the courtyard, with her familiar, bustling walk. She looked like she was heading for somewhere with real purpose.

'Bugger,' she breathed.

'Bugger,' said Annie sweetly. 'Bugger, bugger, bugger.'

Ellen was so taken aback that she didn't even shush her.

With her heart pounding, she darted behind some crates. What on earth was Sadie doing here at Wentworth? Was she working here? She wasn't wearing a boiler suit, and anyway the shift finished a while ago. Sadie didn't work here, of course she didn't. So why was she here? Was she looking for her, Ellen? Was there bad news? Her heart lurched. A telegram? But no, that made no sense. Even if Sadie had intercepted a telegram, she'd not know to come looking for Ellen at Wentworth.

Was she on the hunt for Rachel, perhaps? Was it Daniel? Ellen put her hand to her mouth to stifle a gasp. She peered round the crates and looked at her friend, who had paused in the centre of the courtyard. Sadie was gazing around curiously, just as Ellen had done when she'd first returned to Wentworth. But she didn't look worried or sad, or as though she'd just had terrible news. She looked, Ellen thought, a bit like the old Sadie.

Ellen was relieved, but she realised that whatever the reason

Sadie was there, she absolutely did not want Sadie to see her. So, despite her longing to see the new football pitch, Ellen clutched Annie a little tighter, then turned on her heel and ran to the other gate, where she could head for home unseen.

Chapter Eighteen

Sadie marched across the courtyard at Wentworth, memories jostling in her head. Being there, with fire in her belly, took her right back to the strike and when she'd led thousands of workers to the factory to collect the wages they were owed.

She paused for a second, looking around her. The factory was familiar but so different in many ways. There were new buildings, and the sheds from where they'd stolen – though Sadie preferred to say liberated – sewing machine parts to use at the Clothing Exchange were gone.

It was quiet now. The shift had ended and the munitionettes were all on their way home. Taking a final glance around her, Sadie marched on, her footsteps echoing around the factory buildings as she made her way inside and up to the clerical floor where she knew Hamilton Blyth would have his office.

It was a long, wooden-panelled corridor, just as it had been back in her day. The office at the far end, where their manager Beresford had cornered many young workers – including Ellen – now opened onto the corridor through a wide archway and had four desks in it, each with a typewriter, covered over for the night.

She walked slowly along, looking at the plates on each door until she found Hamilton Blyth's name.

'This is it,' she said to herself, as she knocked sharply three times.

'Come in,' said a voice. 'But I'm going home, so be quick.'

Sadie hid a smile and went inside where a woman, perhaps a little older than she was, was putting on her hat.

'He's not here,' she said.

Sadie had a speech all prepared, about why she wanted to speak to Mr Blyth, and then she had another speech prepared to give to Mr Blyth about workers' rights and protecting the women who worked there, but the woman's blunt declaration that he wasn't there fair took the wind out of her sails.

'Oh.'

The woman rolled her eyes. 'He's gone off to see the footballers or something. He was right full of himself because he's got them a proper pitch round the other side of the factory.' She tutted. 'It's all nonsense, if you ask me. Grown women dashing about like schoolboys. But they seem to like it.'

'It's going well?' Sadie said. 'The football?'

'Mr Blyth is absolutely thrilled about it. He says it's boosting morale and keeping the girls fit and healthy.'

'He could be right there.'

'Aye,' said the woman, thoughtfully. 'I'm coming to see that he usually is.'

'I'm Sadie Spark.' Sadie put her hand out to the woman, who shook it.

'Dilys Reilly,' said the woman. 'I'm Mr Hamilton's assistant.'

'My sister works here,' Sadie said. 'I'm really worried about her.'

'Och, no.' Dilys looked concerned. 'Why's that?'

'She's gone yellow.'

Dilys chuckled, clearly relieved. 'Yes, that happens. I'm afraid. It wears off. Once they stop working with the shells.'

'That's what Rachel said.'

'Rachel's your sister?'

'Yes.'

'Well, she's right.'

'Is it not dangerous?'

'I'd not really thought about it,' Dilys said in such a light way that Sadie was immediately convinced she was lying.

'You have thought about it.'

Dilys leaned against the desk and took her hat off again. 'Some of them are so yellow, they're almost glowing. But the managers say if it was dangerous, women wouldn't be allowed to do it. They say it's as safe as travelling by train.'

Sadie raised an eyebrow and Dilys screwed her face up.

'Oh, I know it must be dangerous,' she conceded. 'How can it not be dangerous?'

'Because it's explosives,' Sadie said. 'The whole point of them is to be dangerous.'

'Yes.'

'It wouldn't be an issue if the women were being looked after. If their safety was a priority.'

Dilys rolled her eyes again. Sadie was beginning to like this woman. 'They have a doctor who checks them over every fortnight. But I've seen them go in and they're barely in there a minute.'

'The doctor's not worried about the yellow?'

'It's the same in every factory,' Dilys said. 'They call the munitionettes Canary Girls.'

'Lord.' Sadie shook her head. 'It seems much more dangerous than making sewing machines.'

'Much more.' Dilys nodded. 'But they get paid well.'

'The women get twenty shillings a week?' Sadie said casually.

'That's right.'

'And what do the men get?'

'The men don't work in munitions.'

'Aye, there aren't many of them,' Sadie said. 'But there must be a few.'

Dilys looked at her. 'Who did you say you were?'

'Sadie Spark.'

'Are you a munitionette?'

'No.'

'Then why are you here exactly?'

Sadie faltered suddenly. She wasn't here officially. She wasn't with the Industrial Workers of Scotland, as she'd been during the strike. She didn't even work at the factory.

'I used to work here, a while back,' she said. 'When there was the strike.'

Understanding dawned on Dilys's face.

'We fought really hard for better working conditions,' Sadie said. 'But now it seems all that hard work was for nothing.'

Dilys sighed. 'And you wanted to speak to Hamilton about it?'

'I did.'

'I don't think it's him you need to speak to.'

'Then who?'

'You need to speak to the women.'

Sadie felt a little ashamed of herself. She'd come marching in here, without having spoken to the people she was claiming to represent.

'You're right,' she admitted with a sigh. 'I got all fired up and didn't think it through.'

Dilys put her hat on once more and adjusted it. 'Get yourself down to the Gaiety Club,' she said. 'That's where they all go after work. They'll tell you all about it.'

'The Gaiety Club,' said Sadie in amazement. She'd pretty much always gone straight home after her factory shifts because her da had not long died when she worked at Wentworth, and her ma was sick, and Rachel was always poorly . . . 'Right.'

'I'm going there now to meet my pals,' Dilys said. 'Want to come with me?'

Sadie was relieved. 'Yes please,' she said.

The Gaiety Club had once been a music hall, but now it was sometimes a theatre, sometimes cabaret, sometimes a place for people to play cards or other games, and sometimes just a drinking den. Sadie had never been inside; it had always been a place for men as far as she was concerned. But whatever it had been before the war, now it was most definitely a place for women. In fact, the whole place was full of women. Chatting. Laughing. Dancing. There was a buzz of voices and energy. Sadie stood still in the doorway, watching. She was astonished. Why had she not been here before? It looked like . . . she thought for a moment. It looked like fun. She felt a little shiver of excitement. The war was awful, there was no doubt about that. It was awful and bloody and brutal. But with the heartbreak and the horror had come independence for a lot of women. Sadie looked around as a burst of laughter from a nearby table made her jump.

'All right?' asked Dilys.

'Aye.' Sadie smiled. 'I wasn't expecting it to be quite like this.'

'Och, it's great,' said Dilys. 'That's my lot over there.' She pointed to a group of women huddled around a table. 'But they're the ones you really want to speak to.'

At the side of the room was a large group of girls, all laughing and chattering away.

'Munitionettes?' said Sadie.

'That's right.'

'Thank you for bringing me here.'

Dilys shrugged. 'We're in strange times. The way I see it, we need to help one another.'

She blew Sadie a kiss and headed off to sit down with her friends.

Sadie went over to where the munitionettes were sitting, feeling oddly nervous. During the strike she'd never wavered in her conviction that they were doing the right thing, but back then she'd had Ellen by her side, and thousands of strikers, too. Plus, there was a different atmosphere around Wentworth now. Of course it was hard work. Backbreaking, dangerous work. But the women seemed to be relishing the challenge.

Sadie was self-aware enough to know that she'd sought out this fight. That she'd wanted a distraction. A cause to throw herself into. But that didn't mean she didn't believe in what she was doing. The safety conditions at the factory were clearly lacking, and she still hadn't had a proper answer as to whether the women were being paid as much as the men.

'Excuse me,' she said. No one paid her any attention. She cleared her throat. 'Excuse me,' she said again, louder this time.

The woman sitting closest to her turned round and Sadie gasped, because her face was yellow. Not tinged with yellow. It didn't have a yellow tint. No. Like Dilys had warned, this woman's skin was practically glowing in the dim light of the club.

'Are you all right, doll?' the woman said. 'Was it me you were after?'

Sadie tried not to look shocked. 'Aye,' she said. 'All of you actually.'

'I know you,' another woman said, older than the first but just as yellow. 'You're Sadie Franklin.'

Sadie was startled. 'I am, yes. Well, I'm Sadie Spark now.' She squinted at the woman in the dull light. 'Do you know my ma?'

'No,' the woman said. 'I know you.' She spoke to the other women around the table. 'This one here led the strike. Mind I was telling you about that, the other day?'

The women all nodded.

'It was you marched to get the wages, right?' the woman said. 'I was there that day. Not sure what we'd have done without you.'

'It was hard going,' Sadie agreed. She looked around and spotted a spare stool. 'Can I sit down?'

'Go ahead,' the woman said. 'I'm Lil.'

'Nice to meet you, Lil.'

The other women all introduced themselves and Sadie was lost in a blur of names and handshakes.

'I bet I can guess why you're here,' said Lil, when everyone had settled down and someone had put a glass of something in front of Sadie.

'Can you?' Sadie was amused. 'Go on, then.'

Lil pointed at Sadie with a yellow finger. 'Canaries.'

'Eh?'

'We're called the Canary Girls, aren't we? Because we're so yellow.' She gave a throaty chuckle. 'Though girls is a stretch for some of us, isn't that right?'

Sadie smiled. 'You're right,' she said. 'My sister's working at Wentworth now and she's turning yellow and I was worried. I'm not sure they're taking your safety seriously enough.'

'Och, it wears off,' said Lil. 'But I know it looks alarming when you see us. My husband gets a fright every morning when he opens his eyes and looks at me.'

'Dilys told me there is a doctor,' Sadie said. 'Does he check you over?'

'Not really,' one of the younger women, whose name was Joyce or Joy or something like that – Sadie couldn't remember exactly – said. 'He looked in my mouth once. And last time he asked if I was expecting. Bloody cheek. My Ronnie's been away these last ten months.'

'What did you say?' asked another woman, laughing.

'I said it was none of his business,' Joy or Joyce said.

'Typical Joy,' said the woman and Sadie made a note to remember the name.

'You know why he asked you, though?' Lil said.

'No,' Joy said. 'Why?'

'Because of Cynthia McGovern.'

Sadie sat up straighter. 'Who's Cynthia McGovern?' she said.

'She worked in shell filling until about a month ago.' Lil looked round. 'That's right, isn't it?'

The women all nodded.

'She was pregnant, but they said it was fine to carry on working. And she believed them – of course she did. But when the bairn was born, it was yellow too. Head to toe.'

'A Canary Baby,' said Joy. 'A wee canary.'

Sadie was horrified. 'The baby had turned yellow too?'

'Every inch of its skin was the colour of mustard.'

'That's dreadful.'

Lil shrugged. 'Aye. And I think it put the wind up them, because the doctor has been asking everyone now.'

'And the baby?' Sadie hardly dared ask. 'Is the baby alive?'

'Aye, all fine,' Lil said. 'But still yellow.'

'That's not right,' Sadie said. 'This is awful. How do they know what could happen to the wee tot in a year or ten or twenty? The poor thing could be damaged for life.'

Lil looked alarmed. 'I'd not thought of that.'

'Do you all feel well?' Sadie said, looking from one to another. 'Are you healthy? My sister's pal Bessie is in a state, and I think it might be because of the shell filling.'

There was a brief pause.

'I'm not right, sure enough,' said Joy. 'I've got a cough I can't shift, and I can't always get my breath.'

Sadie nodded. 'Rachel said Bessie is sick all the time. Could that be from the – what is it called, the stuff you put inside the shells? TNT?'

'That's the one.'

'Could that be making the women ill?'

Lil pursed her lips. 'Seems to me that if you're lucky, you get a cough, maybe an upset stomach, sometimes a rash . . .' She paused.

'If you're lucky?' Sadie said.

'Aye. Because the ones that get those things don't seem to get any worse. Like your cough, Joy. It's nasty right enough, and it must wear you down. But it's the same as it always was?'

'That's true,' said Joy.

Sadie hardly wanted to ask, but she did anyway.

'They're the lucky ones,' she said. 'What about the unlucky ones?'

Lil put her yellow hands on the table, gripping the edge like she was holding on for dear life.

'If you're unlucky, it gets right into you. Makes you waste away, like it's rotting you from the inside out.'

The women all fell silent. Sadie felt dizzy. Why was no one talking about this? Why wasn't the Government doing anything?

'Some folk are all right though,' said Lil, reassuringly. 'Some folk just get yellow. Maybe they're the stronger ones. The ones who don't have a weak chest, or a delicate tummy.'

Sadie thought about Rachel, who seemed hale and hearty nowadays but who'd been so poorly when she was wee. She thought about the nights she'd stayed up with her, listening to her laboured breathing, trying to ease her wheezing, and she felt a rush of fear for her sister, followed quickly by anger.

'They need to take this seriously,' she said through gritted teeth. 'They need to listen to us. To you. They need to protect you.'

'Aye,' said Lil with a shrug. 'But will they?'

Sadie bit her lip. 'I've got an idea,' she said. 'And I might need your help.'

Lil pulled her stool closer to Sadie's. 'Go on,' she said. 'Tell us.'

Chapter Nineteen

Rachel was exhausted, there was no doubt about that, but she felt strong. Physically. And that was a new feeling for Rachel. As a sickly child, she'd always been weaker than her peers. She couldn't run as fast, or pull herself up on the trees on the green. But now she felt strong as an ox. Her arms were lean and sinewy and when she ran across the football pitch she was just as quick as the other players. Quicker sometimes. And she didn't get breathless in a frightening way, like she'd done when she was wee, when her chest tightened, and she couldn't catch enough air in each gulp. No, it wasn't like that at all. Now when her heart rate quickened and her breath came faster, she felt it was a good thing. It was making her heart stronger, each pump making her more alive.

Alive. That was the word. That was how working at Wentworth made her feel.

She looked down at the paper on the kitchen table. She was writing to her brother Daniel, who was off at the Front. She was telling him everything about her job and the women she'd met. But she'd come unstuck when she had tried to find a way to describe her feelings about the factory. And now she'd found the word, but she couldn't write that to Daniel, could she? Couldn't tell him that she felt alive while he was facing death every day?

She picked up her pen and then put it down again and sighed.

'Having trouble?' Noah appeared in the kitchen doorway. His

hair was wet and his glasses were steamed up. 'It's blowing a hoolie out there.'

'It's supposed to be spring.' Rachel rolled her eyes.

'Aye, but it's spring in Clydebank,' Noah said. He nodded at the paper. 'Writing to Daniel?'

Rachel felt a little bit embarrassed. Noah was very clever and bookish – he was a schoolteacher for heaven's sake. She'd not been to school very much as she'd been so poorly, though Ma had made sure she knew how to read and write, and she was quite good with numbers, like Sadie was. Rachel's handwriting was scratchy, as though a spider had dipped its eight feet in her ink pot and gone dancing across her page. And there were quite a few splodges and splatters too. She leaned her elbow on the table so her writing was hidden from Noah, but she smiled at him too.

'Trying to write to Daniel,' she admitted. 'But I feel bad writing about being happy when he's off in Belgium, doing goodness knows what.'

Noah sat down at the table, took off his glasses and dried them on his shirt, then put them back on again, lopsided.

'Am I right in thinking that you have taken up football?'

Rachel grinned. 'How do you know that?'

'Sadie.'

'I wasn't sure she knew – she doesn't like me talking about Wentworth.'

'She doesn't like Wentworth but I think she's quite interested in the football. Though she might pretend she isn't.'

Rachel laughed.

'Strikes me,' Noah went on. 'Football could be a nice neutral topic for you to talk to Sadie about, and for you to write to Daniel about.'

Rachel looked at her brother-in-law, with a drip glistening on the end of his nose, and thought he was very possibly the kindest, cleverest man she knew.

'You're right,' she said. 'Thank you.'

*

In the end she wrote three pages, telling her brother all about Hilda's ideas for their first match.

'We've got our final practice tomorrow, then it's the game on Friday,' she wrote. 'I'm nervous but I'm so excited. We've got shirts to wear. Ellen came up with the idea. She made the first ones – she made them navy blue because so many men from Clydebank have joined the navy, and her James of course. Then she told us what to do and we made them ourselves. Some people are better at sewing than others, so they're a wee bit scrappy, but I quite like that. Because we're a bit scrappy, to be honest. Even though we've got a proper pitch now. Mr Blyth at the factory – he's the man in charge – he is a big fan of us playing football and he's being so supportive. But it's not really about the shirts or the pitch, Daniel. It's about how it makes us feel.'

She told him how she felt when she dashed across and stopped the opposing team getting the ball towards their goal. 'I like when I look round at Joan – she plays in goal – and she gives me a wee nod, like she's saying thank you for me doing my bit,' she wrote. 'Ellen says defenders are more important than goal scorers but I think we're all just as important as one another. That's the point of playing in a team, isn't it?'

She tapped her chin with the end of the pen.

'Do NOT . . .' She underlined 'not' three times. 'Do NOT tell Sadie that Ellen is working at Wentworth. She still doesn't know, and Ellen thinks she'll be furious.'

The clock on the mantelpiece chimed and she quickly signed off, then stuffed the pages into an envelope and added the address. Sadie still wasn't back. She'd gone to the Clothing Exchange, which was proving more popular than Rachel had expected. Though Sadie, Ellen and Bridget had nodded in a knowing way and said of course people needed them now more than ever, just like during the strike.

Rachel had made a little mental note to pop in after the football match and do some of the alterations that were piling up. She'd spent all her spare time recently sewing her football shirt and knitting her striped socks. She needed to do her bit to help others, too.

She glanced at the clock again and got up from the table. She didn't want to be in bed too late – she had a busy, tiring day tomorrow. There was her usual shift at Wentworth, then their last practice before their match, and – she gave a little shiver of excitement – Lewis had said he'd come to watch and perhaps they could go for a walk together afterwards.

She'd not told anyone about Lewis, or the way he'd made her feel, or how he crept into her thoughts even when she really should have been thinking about other things. She wanted to keep those feelings to herself for the time being.

Their last practice went very well. The women were playing like a proper team now. Anticipating one another's passes and runs. They'd practised some set moves and they even had little signals to tell one another what they were planning when they took a corner kick, or threw the ball in from the sideline.

About halfway through their training session, Rachel saw Lewis arrive, his blond hair shining in the sunlight. For a second she worried he'd be a distraction, until she realised she was playing better than ever, because she wanted to impress him. Her ma always said Rachel loved an audience – perhaps she was right, because Rachel felt his eyes on her as she dashed about the pitch, making her run faster, jump higher, kick harder and straighter.

At the end of the game, Hilda called Rachel over. She went to her, pushing her hair out of her face.

'Keep it up, Franklin,' she said, slapping Rachel's shoulder. 'More of the same, please.'

Beaming with pride, and lapping up the compliments from her teammates, Rachel gathered her belongings, and made her way over to where Lewis was.

'Pretty good,' he said.

'Oh, come on,' Rachel replied with a grin. 'That was better than pretty good.'

He laughed. 'Football talent and modest with it,' he said. 'What a woman.'

'You're lucky I've agreed to walk home with you.' Rachel was bubbling over with joy.

'Aye,' Lewis said. 'That I am.' He offered Rachel his arm. 'Shall we?' He gave her a cheeky glance. 'I hope that policewoman doesn't bother us again.'

'Christina,' Rachel said. 'She once got my friend Bridget thrown in jail.'

'She did?'

Rachel nodded.

'You're going to have to tell me everything about that,' Lewis said. 'Come on.'

Waving goodbye to her friends, Rachel took his arm, and they strolled off towards the factory gates.

'Where do you live?' Rachel asked him.

'Oh, out of town a bit,' Lewis said. 'I'll get myself home afterwards, don't worry. Now, where are we heading?'

'This way,' Rachel pointed down the street leading away from the factory. The thought crossed her mind that every time she asked Lewis anything about himself, he changed the subject, but she pushed it away. 'I don't live far.'

'Disappointing,' Lewis said. 'I wanted more time with you.'

Feeling warm from her head to her toes, Rachel beamed at him. 'We could sit on the green for a wee while.'

'That's a good idea.'

She led him across the road and onto the grass, where the strikers had once gathered. Last night's wind and rain had blown away and though it wasn't exactly sunny, it wasn't cold either. They found a fallen tree and sat down on the grass in front of it, leaning back against its rough trunk.

'You really love the football, eh?' Lewis said.

'So much. But it's no surprise, really. I always liked it when I was a little girl.'

'You played when you were wee?'

'Well, I was ill a lot, but when I was well enough, I liked going outside with Daniel, that's my brother.'

'The one who's in Belgium?'

'That's him.'

'And you have another brother?'

'Yes, Joseph. But he's not joined up. He's very short-sighted – can barely see his hand in front of his face without his specs.'

'What's he doing?'

'He's very clever,' Rachel said proudly. 'He's training to be a bookkeeper.'

'Impressive.'

'Yes. My sister Sadie is quick with numbers, too.'

'So there're four of you siblings?'

Rachel nodded. 'Two boys, two girls. Sadie's the oldest, and I'm the youngest.'

'There are four of us, too. My sister Leah is the oldest, then Lachlan, then . . .' He paused. 'Then my other sister and then me. Leah's having a baby.'

'Oh, how lovely,' Rachel said, feeling a wave of sadness that Sadie wasn't expecting. 'You'll be an uncle.'

He nodded. 'Tell me about your sister,' he said and once more Rachel noticed he was changing the subject. 'She was one of the strikers?'

'She's spoiling for a fight,' Rachel said. She settled back against the tree trunk and realised that Lewis had put his arm along the bark, above her shoulders. She liked it. She told him about Sadie's determination to put the world to rights, even when it wasn't wrong to begin with.

'She's worried about the explosives being dangerous,' Rachel explained. She held her hands out, palms upward. 'I told you how we're all going yellow? She thinks it could be poisonous.'

Lewis frowned. He took Rachel's hands in his and looked at them, as he'd done before. Tilting them this way and that. 'It's getting worse, I think?'

'Perhaps. Mine's not that bad. It's the girls who fill the shells who are glowing.'

'I'm not surprised she's worried.'

'She wants to speak to management.' Rachel was very aware that Lewis was still holding her hands and she was rather pleased about it. 'She says she's got a plan.'

'A plan?'

'Oh, Sadie's always got a plan. She's made friends with some woman in clerical who works with Hamilton Blyth and she says she's going to help her. And she's been speaking to all the women who are turning yellow.'

'Do you think she's right to be worried?' Lewis let go of Rachel's hand, much to her disappointment.

She shrugged. 'I feel all right.' She examined the lines on her palm which were etched in darker yellow. 'But my friend Bessie isn't doing so well.'

'She's sick?'

'She can't play football anymore.'

Lewis frowned. 'Because of the shells?'

'No idea. Sadie says it must be dangerous, because it's explosives. But all the bosses say it's no more dangerous than getting on a train. And they do look after us. We're not even allowed metal hair grips in case of sparks.'

'Right,' Lewis said. He shifted slightly on the tree trunk. 'Right. So this Betty?'

'Bessie.'

'Bessie, she's really sick?'

'Aye. I'm quite worried about her. She's so thin.' Rachel paused, thinking about her pal. 'But things are difficult for her, I think. At home. So I'm not sure she eats an awful lot.'

'It might not be the TNT, then?'

'I suppose not,' Rachel said slowly. 'Or it might be a bit of everything.' She looked at Lewis. 'Why are you so interested in Bessie?'

He looked down at his knees. 'Not Bessie,' he said. 'You.'

Rachel felt her cheeks burn. 'Me?'

'I like listening to you talk. You're so passionate.'

'Passionate?' Rachel laughed. 'You need to meet Sadie. She's the passionate one.'

'She sounds great.'

'She is.'

'Determined.'

'She really is.'

'Do you think we should warn Hamilton Blyth that she's on the warpath?'

Rachel looked at him, wondering if he was being serious, but his eyes glinted with mischief.

'Oh definitely,' she said. 'Mind you, she's not got anywhere near him yet. He's quite hard to pin down, she said.'

'What about that other woman?' Lewis asked thoughtfully.

'What other woman?'

'The one who came to your Clothing Exchange to recruit the workers?'

'Lucinda?' Rachel said. 'What about her?'

'She could help Sadie, couldn't she?'

'She's Hamilton Blyth's daughter,' Rachel said, in astonishment. 'Goodness me, yes. Lucinda! She's the person to speak to. You're right.'

Lewis grinned, looking pleased, but Rachel frowned. 'Did I tell you about Lucinda? I don't remember . . .'

'I have to go,' said Lewis, suddenly. He stood up so quickly he almost lost his footing on the uneven grass.

'Already?' Rachel said. She stood up too, realising they were standing very close together. She looked up at Lewis and he looked down at her.

He's going to kiss me, she thought. And she'd never wanted anything more. She felt like all her senses were fizzing and sparkling with life.

'I'm so sorry,' Lewis said.

He turned and walked away without even looking back at her.

Chapter Twenty

Clydebank

20 April 1916

My dear James,

I miss so much about you. I miss warming my feet on yours in bed at night, and you tutting and pretending you don't like it, but letting me do it anyway. I miss seeing you sitting with Annie on your knee by the fire. I miss you telling stories about the men at the shipyard and making me laugh. I miss the way you put your arms round me and hold me close. And James, most of all I miss you just being here to chat to. To get all my thoughts out of my head at the end of the day, and for you to say: 'Och, Ellen. Dinnae fash. It'll all come out in the wash.'

So I'm going to tell you all my worries now and pretend you're here with me, telling me not to worry. Because I am worrying, James. I'm worrying about you all the time. That's part of me now, that constant knot in my stomach, from when I wake up in the morning until I go to sleep at night. And now I'm worrying about the football match too. Because we are playing a real game in front of a crowd! A CROWD, James. And I'm so worried that I'll score a goal in the wrong net, or trip and fall on my face, or my breeks will fall down when I'm running . . .

I know you're laughing. I can picture you chuckling away to yourself.

But that's not all I'm worrying about when it comes to the football. I'm worried that Hilda thinks we're going to get lots of folk come to watch. She's put up posters all around the factory and in the streets. And apparently they're going to charge a penny to come and see us fall on our faces, and the money will go to the soldiers and sailors. And I'm really worried that Sadie will come and watch. Or Bridget, because I've still not told them I'm working at Wentworth. Even though I promised Ma I'd say something weeks ago. I've just not managed to find the words. Bridget's not keen on football. Remember how she always teases Da about being a fan? So I think I'm safe there. But Rachel's playing, of course, we'd be lost without her. And so Sadie could come to see her. And then she'll see me, and I know she'll be furious. Oh, James, it's such a mess. Perhaps I should tell Hilda I can't play? But then she'll be furious. Och, who would I rather was angry with me? Sadie or Hilda? You've not met Hilda but she's just as frightening as Sadie is. More even. See, if you were here, you'd tell me what to do . . .

And there's something else.

Something a bit more serious.

The shells at the factory are filled with explosives. Of course they are. You know that. It's something called TNT mixed with cordite, apparently. That's what they say. We have to be careful – no metal is allowed in case it sparks. That's why we wear rubber boots or wooden clogs on the factory floor. But the TNT makes our skin yellow. It happens to us all, more or less. But some are worse than others. And the yellow spreads. So we girls who fill the shells are in a separate area – we have our own dressing room and our own canteen. Because everything we touch – the chairs, our pegs . . . our children – they're all turning yellow too. They call us the Canary Girls. Imagine that! Like wee birds.

My skin's got a definite yellow tinge now and last night when I was getting Annie ready for bed, I noticed she was yellow too.

Her wee hands are changing colour. And round her hairline. And her lips.

The girls at work say it's fine. It's just the chemicals reacting with our skin. It's not dangerous, they say. And I'm sure they're right. Because it wears off, they say, as soon as you stop working with the TNT.

But I heard about this woman called Cynthia McGovern. She had a baby, and her baby was yellow too. A Canary Baby. And the wee one's fine, apparently. That's what everyone says.

But what if it's not fine? And what if our baby turns yellow too? If the wean and our Annie are being damaged by my job. What if the work I'm doing, that I thought was helping our family, is really making everything worse?

Och, now I'm getting myself all worked up about everything. And there's you out there on the ocean with real stuff to worry about. I pray you're keeping safe, my love. I was so glad to get a letter from you, finally, even if it had taken weeks to arrive. Please write back soon. We're all thinking of you and Annie has drawn you a picture. I know it looks like a big scribble but she said it's you. I show her your photo every night before bed so she won't forget you. She kisses your face and says 'Night night, Da', in the sweetest way. It fair melts me heart.

I send you all our love.

Your Ellen X

Chapter Twenty-One

Ellen was trying to follow what Sadie was talking about but she was so tired, and Sadie was really excited, and speaking very fast, and her story was jumping around all over the place, which meant it was proving a little difficult.

'So you went where?' she asked. 'Why?'

'I went to meet the workers at the Gaiety Club,' Sadie repeated, a little impatiently.

'Why?' asked Ellen again. 'Why did you go to meet the workers?'

'Because Rachel's turning yellow and I'm worried about her.'

Ellen glanced down at her own hands, safely covered in the gloves she'd taken to wearing whenever she wasn't at the factory or alone, and felt a little bit queasy.

'You think that's something to worry about?'

'I think it's something we should find out more about,' said Sadie firmly. 'Because no one seems to know for sure.'

'Right.' Ellen swallowed. 'Do you think it's dangerous?'

'I think it could be.'

'Bessie is sick.'

Sadie frowned. 'Rachel told you that, did she? Aye, Bessie is sick.'

Of course Rachel hadn't had to tell Ellen anything. She knew Bessie had been unable to play football, and was turning up to work looking frail and weak. The other women were covering for her, but Ellen wasn't sure how long that would last.

'I've heard talk that the factory has made Bessie ill,' she said now. 'Do you think it's true?'

'If Bessie was the only one, then I'd say no.' Sadie looked grave. 'But she's not the only one. Not at all.'

Ellen's stomach lurched as Sadie confirmed her fears. 'She's . . . she's not the only one?'

'I've got no proof, not yet, because folk are nervous about it, but I think she's just one of many. And then there's Cynthia McGovern.'

Ellen swallowed. 'Cynthia McGovern?' she said, feigning ignorance.

'She had a baby,' Sadie said. 'And the wee thing was yellow from head to toe.'

Ellen tasted bile in her mouth and for a second she thought she was going to vomit. 'Yellow,' she whispered.

'Aye. And they say it's nothing to worry about,' Sadie said. 'But like I say, no one really knows for sure, do they?'

'No,' Ellen managed to say.

Sadie glanced at her. 'Are you all right?'

'Fine,' Ellen lied, more than a little croakily. 'Just worried about Bessie.'

'Me too.' Sadie tucked a stray strand of hair behind her ear. 'But talking to the women at the Gaiety Club gave me an idea.'

'Oh yes?'

'In fact, I think it's the cleverest idea I've ever had.'

Ellen was almost afraid to ask. Her head was spinning.

'Cleverer than marching to get our wages during the strike?'

'Well, no, probably not,' Sadie said. She stopped pacing the shop floor and pulled herself up to sit on the counter, where Ellen was leaning. 'But it's still clever.'

Despite herself, Ellen smiled. This was all worrying, but it was nice to see her friend happy and interested in something after seeing her sad for so long. 'Tell me.'

Sadie made a face. 'I will, but first I just want to get everything straight in my head. Work out how to make it happen.'

'What do you want to happen?'

'I want to know it's safe for women to work with the munitions.'

'I want to know that too,' Ellen said, nodding vigorously. Surely, she thought, it is safe? Safer than railway travel, remember? But it would do no harm to have someone with the right knowledge to confirm that. It would stop Sadie fretting, and reassure them both.

'I suppose you need to speak to management,' she said. 'They're the ones who'll know one way or the other. But we know that's the tricky bit.'

'Aye.' Sadie nodded. 'I've met Hamilton Blyth's assistant now, Dilys, but she says he's all over the place, all the time. Hard to pin down, she says.'

'He sounds quite different from management back when we were striking,' Ellen said, making a face at the memory. 'Mr Beresford and the others.'

Sadie frowned. 'I suppose he does.'

Ellen thought about pointing out that Sadie didn't work at Wentworth now. That this fight – if that's what it was – wasn't hers to have. But then she thought about how sad Sadie had been and how she was looking more like herself for the first time in ages, and how she really wanted to know it was safe too, and so she kept her mouth shut.

'That's why I'm here,' Sadie was saying.

'Here at the Clothing Exchange?' Ellen raised an eyebrow at her friend. 'And here's me thinking you're here because you work here.'

Sadie waved her hand. 'Yes, I'm here to work, but also I wanted to see Lucinda.'

Ellen stood up a bit straighter. 'Lucinda?'

'Yes.'

'Why?'

'Because she's Hamilton Blyth's daughter,' Sadie said, like it was the most obvious thing in the world. 'And she can tell me where he's going to be.'

'Well, that's a bit of an unfair position to put Lucinda in,' Ellen said, rubbing her forehead. 'Do you really need to speak to her?'

Inwardly she was groaning. Goodness, this was becoming the most awful mess. She should have told Sadie the truth from the start – admitted she was working at Wentworth and explained why. She'd have understood, surely? Though she was still being a little frosty with Rachel, and she hadn't even been part of the strike at the time. And then there was Bridget – the strike had changed every part of her life. If Ellen's secret was revealed now, then her sister was bound to be furious too. Ellen might even have to leave Wentworth, and stop playing football and she'd have no money and . . . she took a deep breath, trying to calm herself.

'Sadie,' she began.

She was interrupted by the ding of the bell on the shop door, and in walked Lucinda. Ellen's stomach lurched.

'Lucinda,' Sadie said, sounding delighted. 'Hello!'

Lucinda looked at Sadie, who'd never been anything other than rather rude to her, with a suspicious expression that would have made Ellen laugh if she'd been less worried.

'Hello?'

'Nice to see you,' Sadie said.

'Is it?' Lucinda was still cautious. 'Why?'

Sadie floundered. 'Well,' she said. 'It's just nice.'

Ellen rolled her eyes. 'How can I help?' she said to Lucinda.

Lucinda held up a bag.

'I brought some donations,' she said. 'My sister lives in Edinburgh, but I told her about the Clothing Exchange and she has been collecting at church. It's mostly children's clothes.'

'That's so kind,' said Ellen, taking the bag and realising it was gratifyingly heavy. 'Please thank your sister for us.'

'I will.' Lucinda nodded. 'She likes to be helpful.'

Sadie slid off the counter.

'Lucinda,' she said. 'I wanted to ask you a favour . . .'

'Rachel told me about the factory football match,' Ellen said, interrupting her. She didn't want Sadie sniffing around Wentworth. 'Is it this afternoon? Did you know about that, Sadie? Rachel's quite the star, so she tells me.'

Sadie gave a small smile. 'She's always enjoyed football.'

'Who is it they're playing, Lucinda? Do you know?'

'Another factory, I believe. I don't know much about it.' Lucinda gave Ellen a wide-eyed, innocent look and Ellen felt a rush of affection for her new friend, followed immediately by a flicker of guilt that she was being disloyal to Sadie.

'Will there be a crowd?' Sadie asked. 'Rachel loves an audience.'

Ellen chuckled. That was true enough.

'I believe they are expecting a few people,' said Lucinda. 'Now I really must get off . . .'

Sadie clapped her hands together, making Ellen and Lucinda both jump. 'I've just had the most marvellous idea,' she said. 'Lucinda, I don't want to make life difficult for you, in any way, of course . . .'

'Of course,' said Lucinda wryly.

'But I need to speak with your father. I'm worried it's not safe for the women to be working in the factory.'

'You don't think it's safe?' Lucinda said. 'But you don't work at the factory.'

'Well, no,' Sadie said. 'But I've been speaking to a lot of the workers and I've seen how yellow they are. And then there's Cynthia McGovern, and Bessie, and really we just need him to confirm that it's not dangerous.'

'They say it's no more dangerous than—'

'Railway travel, yes I know.' Sadie waved her hands like she was brushing away an annoying fly. 'But I want to know how they know.'

'Right.' Lucinda nodded.

'I've been trying to track down your father but Dilys, his assistant, says he's terribly busy.'

'You know Dilys?' Lucinda sounded impressed. 'How do you know Dilys?'

'Och, we just got chatting,' said Sadie. Ellen hid a smile. She liked Lucinda, but she had no idea how tenacious Sadie could be when she got going. 'Anyway, he's proving quite tricky to get hold of, but I've heard he's a big supporter of the Wentworth football team. And now I'm just thinking perhaps I should go along to the match, and speak to him there. What do you think? And it would be nice to see Rachel play, too. Give her some support.'

Ellen stifled a gasp. If Sadie came to watch the football match, then the game would be up. Her secret would be out. She knew she was going to have to tell Sadie soon but she needed time to think about it properly. To work out how to say it, so she didn't lose her rag. Or worse, be upset. Ellen was already horribly aware that Sadie had used every ounce of her kind-hearted nature to be pleased for her that she was having another baby. She didn't want to push her luck.

Now she looked at Lucinda in horror, unable to come up with a reason why Sadie shouldn't go to the match,

'Oh no,' said Sadie. 'I said I'd watch Annie for you, didn't I?'

'Yes!' Ellen was almost dizzy with relief. 'You did! And I really need you to look after her for me, because I've got that thing.'

What was the thing? She had no idea at this moment what she'd said when she'd asked Sadie to care for Annie for the afternoon.

'Where is it you're going?' Sadie asked, her brow furrowed.

Lucinda, bless her, leapt in. 'She's going to speak to some of my friends. They're setting up their own Clothing Exchange. I really think this could be the first of many.'

Sadie looked impressed. 'Good idea,' she said. Ellen made a mental note to spread the word about the Clothing Exchange to everyone Lucinda had ever met as soon as this damn football match was done and dusted.

'I've got an idea,' Lucinda carried on. 'Sadie, let me speak to my father, and I'll arrange a meeting for us. I'm sure he'll be thrilled to meet you.'

'Do you think so?' Sadie looked doubtful.

'I know so.' Lucinda smiled. 'My father has his faults, but he has learned never to ignore a clever woman.'

Sadie preened just a little and Ellen leaned against the counter feeling like she'd had a lucky escape. Which she had done, really, all things considered.

Lucinda looked at the clock on the wall. 'We should get going,' she said to Ellen. 'If you're ready?'

Ellen thought she'd never felt less like playing football, but she nodded. 'Annie's having a nap in the back,' she told Sadie.

'I'll give her some food when she wakes up,' Sadie said. 'Take her for a runabout on the green, maybe. We'll have fun.'

Impulsively, Ellen threw her arms round her friend and squeezed her tight. 'Thank you for being so kind,' she said. 'You're a good person.'

Sadie laughed, but she hugged Ellen back. 'Go on, off you go,' she said. 'Good luck with Lucinda's friends.'

In the end, even though her head was full of worries before the game, and she felt sick with nerves about playing in front of a crowd, and about her secret being revealed, Ellen thought the match was a triumph.

It was a draw. Both teams scored one goal – Ginny scored for Wentworth, with Rachel making a rather impressive run down the length of the pitch, darting past the opposition players, before she passed and Ginny kicked the ball into the net.

And the roar of the crowd was thrilling. Some folk had come with dark blue scarves, the same colour as the Wentworth jerseys. Ellen had been astonished by that. She'd been astonished by the whole thing, really. She'd expected to see maybe ten or twenty people gathered to watch the game. But actually it had been more like a hundred. Maybe more. Hilda had been delighted. And Lucinda was pleased, too.

'My father is thrilled to bits,' she said. 'He thinks this is going to put Wentworth on the map.'

'In a more suitable fashion than the strike, eh?' said Ellen, rubbing her face, which was sticky with sweat and dust.

Lucinda raised an eyebrow. 'He knows that the football team will help morale,' she said. 'Heavens, aren't our boys playing in the trenches? Wasn't there a truce at Christmas for them to play?'

Ellen thought that story had to have been exaggerated, but there was no denying the women all felt a proper bond now they were playing football. More and more workers were coming along to practice and Hilda was talking about forming another team.

'Father is busy making lists of all the other factories we can play against,' said Lucinda. 'He thinks we can charge people to come and watch.'

Ellen pulled off her boot and wiggled her toes. 'He does realise we are supposed to be making munitions too.'

'He says happy workers are faster workers.'

'Gosh, he sounds like Sadie.' Ellen giggled, taking off her other boot and standing on the grass in her socks. She felt full of life after dashing about all afternoon. 'Look, there's Rachel. Who's that she's with?'

Lucinda looked where Ellen was pointing and made a face. 'No idea.'

'He's rather handsome,' Ellen said. Rachel was standing very close to a tall blond man whom Ellen had seen around. 'Who is he? Do you know?'

Lucinda shrugged, looking vague.

'I'm going to go over,' Ellen said. 'I want to know what's going on.'

'Leave this to me,' said a shrill voice. Feeling suddenly sick, Ellen turned to see Christina bearing down on them. 'I've had to speak to Franklin about her conduct before.'

Ellen looked round wildly, wondering if she could make a run for it, but it was madness, because Christina was there, standing next to her. 'Hello, Ellen,' she said, her voice dripping with triumph. 'Fancy seeing you here.'

Ellen thought about saying she'd come to watch the match, but there she was in her blue jersey and striped socks. There was no chance of lying her way out of this one. She swallowed.

'Hello, Christina.'

'Good game?'

'Yes, thank you.'

'Glad to hear it,' Christina said. She looked Ellen up and down with absolute disdain. 'I'm sure your sister will be glad to hear all about it, too.'

'No, Christina,' Ellen started, then she stopped talking because what was the point?

'I remember folk used to say you Kelly girls ran towards a fight, instead of away from one,' Christina said. 'Like you were brave and bold,' she scoffed. 'But you're just as cowardly as the rest of us. Now if you'll excuse me, I must get on.'

She nodded at Ellen and marched on by, heading for Rachel, who was still standing close to the blond man.

Ellen watched her go, feeling utterly wretched. 'That's that, then,' she muttered to Lucinda. 'The final whistle has blown.'

Chapter Twenty-Two

Cynthia McGovern's baby was a sweet wee thing. Bonny and bouncing, with long eyelashes that brushed his round cheeks.

And he was as yellow as a canary – just like his ma.

Sadie looked down at him in his crib and then at Cynthia.

'Is it fading?' she asked.

Cynthia, who looked tired and sallow, but content, held out her hands.

'I don't think so.' She examined her palms. 'Maybe a wee bit? But it's not been that long.'

'And you feel well, apart from the yellow?'

'Aye.'

'And the wean?'

'He's grand,' Cynthia said with a smile. 'Grand.' Her smile faltered a little bit. 'I think.'

'He looks grand.'

'Aye.' Cynthia took a breath. 'But what happens if he isn't?'

'What do you mean?'

'There's lassies from Wentworth who are sick,' Cynthia said. 'That Bessie, for one. She's struggling.'

'I heard.'

'She's not the only one. There are others. Rita Milligan. Irene Stewart. Moira Vairey.'

Sadie wanted to write the names down, but she didn't feel she could start scribbling when Cynthia was sharing her worries. She repeated the names in her head. Rita. Irene. Moira.

'And when I look at my wee Walter there, I wonder,' Cynthia went on. She breathed in deeply. 'Because no one has done this before, have they? Worked in munitions factories like this, the way we're doing it.'

'No,' Sadie said, shaking her head. 'No one has.'

'And it might be fine now. But we're breathing in this stuff from morning until night. And touching it. And smelling it. And it's doing something to us, right enough. Because look at the colour of us.'

'Yes.'

'So who knows what could happen in a year. Or two years. Or five, or ten?'

'How do we know it's safe?' Sadie said.

'Exactly,' said Cynthia. She leaned over the crib and very gently stroked Walter's yellow cheek. 'How do we know?'

Sadie felt a rush of determination and purpose. She liked it.

'I promise you, I'm going to do my very best to find out,' she said. 'I promise you and Rita and Irene and Moira. I will find out.'

Cynthia nodded.

'You do that, doll.'

Later that same day, Sadie looked around at the faces gazing up at her and thought she was absolutely where she belonged. Perhaps she'd not have predicted that balancing on a table at the Gaiety Club would be where she felt most at home, but life was nothing if not surprising.

She took a deep breath.

'Sisters,' she said. Everyone cheered and she grinned. How lovely to be listened to. To feel like what she was saying really mattered. 'Sisters, things must change.'

'What's your plan?' shouted Dilys from near the back. Sadie chuckled.

'I'm getting to that,' she said. The buzz of voices in the room quietened down and Sadie spoke again – more calmly this time.

'Today I met some of the workers from the factory who have been affected. I met Cynthia's wee Canary Baby Walter.' She smiled. 'He's a smasher, but Cynthia's terrified he's been affected forever.'

'No one knows,' Lil shouted.

'Exactly,' Sadie said. She breathed in deeply. 'And then I went to see Rita, Irene and Moira, and they're all suffering. Irene's got trouble with her stomach. She's fading away because she keeps being sick. And Moira, she can't always catch her breath. She says she could run up the stairs to her flat without stopping and now she can't go out because she worries she won't get back again.'

There was silence. 'And then there's Bessie.' Her voice cracked a little and she took a second just to gather herself. 'She didn't want to see me at first, but her ma is so worried and wanted me to see just how bad she is.'

Sadie felt tears fill her eyes as she remembered the shock she'd had when she'd seen Bessie. 'You all know Bessie? She's twenty-one years old. She's got that curly hair that always looks wild no matter how much she tries to tame it? She works hard to keep her brothers and sisters fed. She loves playing football.'

Voices murmured and Sadie was glad folks knew who she was talking about.

'But not anymore,' she said. 'She was sitting beside the fire, covered in a blanket, like an old wifey. She could be sixty years old. There's nothing of her. She's skin and bone. Her eyes are huge in her head. And they're yellow. The whites of her eyes are pure yellow. Her hair's falling out.' She swallowed. 'Her ma said every day she wakes up and Bessie's still with her is a blessing. She says . . . She says the priest's going later . . .'

Sadie couldn't finish the sentence. But she knew the women would know what it meant.

She wiped her eyes with her thumb and tried to focus.

'Bessie's never been sick before,' she said. 'Her ma said she was always healthy until she started working at Wentworth. And she was one of the first lot. The first bunch of women to start work more than a year ago.'

'What are we going to do?' Dilys asked, sounding shaken. 'What can we do?'

Sadie pulled herself up to her full height. Because she knew what she wanted to do, but she needed everyone to understand what she was saying.

'When I worked at Wentworth back in 1911, and we went out on strike, that was a big thing,' she began. 'Not just big, huge. We needed something enormous to make everyone listen.'

'What's the big thing this time?' a woman called across to her.

Sadie looked straight at her, then around the room, taking in the expectant faces.

'It's not a big thing this time,' she said. 'It's a tiny wee thing.'

There was silence, then a murmur of disappointment. Sadie held her hands out, showing she wasn't finished.

'It's just three little words,' she said.

'Get tae—' someone said loudly before being quickly shushed.

'What are the words?' Dilys asked.

Sadie planted her feet more securely on the tabletop. 'Everyone says that working in munitions must be safe, because they'd not ask you to do it if it wasn't. Right?'

'Right,' everyone agreed.

'They say, "Och it must be fine, or they'd not let women work there if it wasn't safe", right?'

'Right.'

'As safe as a railway journey, eh?'

'Right.'

'So the three words I think we should take to management?' Sadie looked around again. '*You do it.*'

Everyone stayed silent. Sadie pushed away her nerves and tried to explain.

'When we see management, and tell them about your yellow skin, and the weans turning yellow, and the babies being born yellow, they'll say they know that's happening. They'll say they're sure it's safe,' she said. 'Of course they will. They'll claim the explosives you shove into shells all day every day aren't poisonous, or dangerous in any way.' She took a breath. 'And then we'll tell them that if it's so safe, then they can do it. Or their pregnant wives can do it. Or their daughters.' She shrugged. 'If they won't do it, then we'll know.'

There was a moment of hush and then the room erupted in chatter. Sadie put her hands to her chest in relief and thanks. They understood, she thought. They understood what she was trying to tell them.

'So what do you think?' she asked. 'Shall we ask them to do it?'

There was a chorus of 'aye' and 'absolutely' and 'why not'. Sadie nodded. 'And are you all happy for me to represent you with management?'

Again the room filled with confirmation.

'I'll sort you a meeting,' Dilys called. 'I'll put something in Mr Blyth's diary for you. Just say the word.'

Sadie smiled her thanks. 'My sister is a munitionette,' she told everyone, crossing her fingers behind her back and hoping that Rachel would agree when she asked her to get involved. 'I'll bring her to the meeting too.'

The women all began talking among themselves and across the room, Sadie spotted Lucinda. She was so surprised to see her, she almost tumbled off the table and for a moment she thought the other woman would be angry. But their eyes met and Sadie realised Lucinda looked half amused and half – Sadie was fairly sure – impressed.

Lucinda smiled and Sadie clambered down from the tabletop and weaved her way through the women to get to the back of the room where Lucinda was waiting.

'The women are really sick?' Lucinda asked as she approached. 'Bessie and the others? It's all true?'

'I didn't want to believe it, but they are.' An image of Bessie, curled up by the fire popped into Sadie's head. 'Bessie's really suffering.'

'*You do it*?' Lucinda said, echoing Sadie's words.

'It's just an idea.'

'It's a good idea.'

Sadie preened. 'I'm glad you think so.'

'There's just one problem.'

'What's that?'

'My father prides himself on never asking anyone to do a job he'd not do himself. He's been that way his whole career. At his last factory, he often worked shifts in various departments.'

'Right,' said Sadie. 'Did he?' She smiled. 'Sewing machines are different though. Not much danger in polishing a cabinet.'

Lucinda shrugged. 'When Wentworth got the government contract for the munitions, he spent a few days down in Barrow-in-Furness alongside the workers. He filled shells with his own hands.'

Her expression was less amusement now and more relief. The realisation made Sadie feel prickles of annoyance down the back of her neck.

'So, I'm afraid that while your "you do it" plan is undoubtedly a good one,' Lucinda said, 'my father is one step ahead.' She made a face. 'He usually is, to be honest. Drives me mad.'

Sadie didn't want to start acting pally with her now.

'You think your father would work filling shells?' she said.

'I know he would work filling shells.'

'And what about you?'

'What about me?'

'Would you do it?'

Lucinda looked startled. 'Yes,' she said. She frowned. 'Yes, I think so.'

'You think it's safe?'

'Yes.' Lucinda sounded less certain.

'Once wouldn't be enough,' Sadie said. 'You'd have to do it every day for weeks. A year, like Bessie. Longer. You'd have to watch your hands turn yellow and your hair and your face. Would you do it?'

'Yes.' Lucinda's voice was quiet and unconvincing.

'And you've a sister in Edinburgh?' Sadie went on.

'I do.'

'Ellen said she's expecting?'

'Aye.' Lucinda's expression softened. 'It's her first baby.'

'Would you let her do it?'

'Work in munitions?'

'Yes. Knowing the wean would be born yellow. Knowing there's no telling what could happen to that babby.'

Lucinda sighed. 'We have a doctor who checks the women are healthy.'

'Does he ask if they're expecting?'

'I don't know.'

'They could lie,' Sadie pointed out. 'Even if he asked, they could lie.'

'Why would they lie?'

'Because,' Sadie said through gritted teeth, 'not everyone has the choices you have, Lucinda. Not everyone can turn down the chance of a weekly wage, even when the work could be dangerous.'

Sadie felt her insides twist at the thought of innocent wee babies like Walter being exposed to goodness only knew what through their mothers' skin. She couldn't imagine the awful situation the women were being put in – forced to work for money knowing they could be harming their unborn children.

'So, I ask you again, would you let your sister work in munitions?'

Lucinda hung her head. 'I can't tell her what to do,' she said. 'She never listens to me anyway.'

'Aye,' Sadie allowed herself a small smile. 'I know how that feels.'

There was a pause.

'No,' Lucinda said. 'I wouldn't want her filling shells.'

Sadie lifted her chin. 'Right,' she said. 'What about your da? Would he let her do it?'

'Not a chance.'

'That's our answer, then. If it's not safe for a Blyth woman, it's not safe for any woman.'

Lucinda didn't speak. Instead she chewed her lip, looking worried.

'My father asked me to recruit more women,' she said. 'We need workers. What will happen if we can't fulfil our government contracts?'

Sadie made a face. 'When we were striking, I realised that small wins were worth a lot,' she said. 'Tiny victories that made a difference.'

'Right,' said Lucinda, looking baffled.

'How about we start with your doctor?' Sadie suggested. 'Make sure he gives any pregnant women extra checks? Moves them off shell filling if there's any suggestion of their babies being at risk.'

'Shell fillers get paid more,' Lucinda pointed out. 'They'd not want to move.'

Sadie waved her hand. 'We'll worry about that later,' she said. 'What do you think?'

'Yes,' Lucinda said doubtfully. 'It could work.'

'Good.' Sadie folded her arms. 'Then that's what we'll ask for.'

'We?'

'Surely you're coming to the meeting?'

'I suppose.' Lucinda didn't look very happy about it. 'So we'll ask for the extra medical checks and that's all.'

'That's all,' Sadie said. *For now*, she added silently in her own head. That's all for now.

Chapter Twenty-Three

Clydebank

27 April 1916

My dear James,

I feel like a condemned woman waiting for the executioner's axe to fall. I can picture you reading this, and tutting, and saying I am being dramatic – just as you always do – but that is how I feel.

Because awful, interfering Christina saw me after the football match yesterday. She saw me in my football jersey and there was no way I could have denied being part of the team. And of course the team is all Wentworth workers. So now she knows that I am working at Wentworth, and I'm absolutely sure she won't keep it to herself for long – she'll be rushing off to tell Bridget as soon as she can.

I've not seen my sister yet today. But goodness me, you can't avoid folk in Clydebank for long, can you? So it's only a matter of time before she finds out the truth. Then Sadie will know. And I have no idea what they will think. Perhaps they'll be fine with me going back to Wentworth, despite our history with the place. Perhaps they'll understand? But I have an awful feeling that even if they do, they'll be upset that I've not told them before now.

I feel I've made a terrible mistake.

So here I am getting myself all worked up again. As a distraction, let me tell you about the football match, because it was wonderful.

A lot of people came to watch and cheer us on. Some of them even had scarves in our dark blue colour – can you imagine? Men and women. Hilda says that those men who love the game are missing going to matches now it's all stopped. So they'll come to watch us play instead. I can't imagine Da's pals all trooping to a patch of grass round the back of the factory instead of going to watch Celtic, but perhaps Hilda is right. Perhaps we're better than nothing!

A lot better, in fact. Because I feel we played really well. I mean, I'm no expert, but it just felt right, you know? Like it all came together. Everything we'd practised. We drew 1–1. Ginny scored our goal. She's very good.

Hilda's not one for doling out a lot of praise – if she says something's good then you know she really means it. And James, she was delighted. She could hardly speak. She got us all in a wee huddle and then she just patted us on our backs and said, 'Good work, lassies'. I thought she was going to cry.

She says there's a competition. The Munitionettes' Cup. It's all the factories who have teams, playing against one another to see who's best. She says she's going to speak to Hamilton Blyth and if he says it's all right, then she's going to enter us. Fancy that! We'd have to travel. I think there are factories from England and all over Scotland entering. We might even get to see Malcolm!

I'm not sure how much longer I can keep playing, mind you. I'm starting to show, though no one has said anything because I've been letting out my skirts and my boiler suit at work. But this wean is definitely making himself known. My belly is round and hard and I think it'll only be a few more weeks before I can't hide it anymore. And James, I can feel him kicking now, and wriggling about inside. I think he's a footballer, too. Like his ma!

He's very active early in the morning. I lie in bed, before Annie wakes up, and feel him jiggling about. And I put my hand on my belly and I think 'Hello, wee man' and I tell him we love him and you'll be home soon.

I definitely think he's a boy. I've got a lot more energy than I had with Annie and my hair's not so lank. Or perhaps I'm remembering it wrong and this is another wee girl. I wouldn't mind either way, would you?

Look at me, rambling on about rubbish. How are you? Are you keeping warm? Getting sleep? I can't imagine what it's like out there in the middle of the ocean, with no land in sight. Worrying about mines or U-boats. I bet you'd love to have the chance to play a game of football, eh? I'm sending you more socks to keep your feet warm, and I've drawn another wee picture of the football game.

Now I really must go because Annie is running around like a mad thing and she needs some fresh air. And if I bump into Bridget on the way, well. I'll let you know what she says.

We all love you and miss you dreadfully. Come home safe and sound.

Your Ellen X

Chapter Twenty-Four

'I don't understand why you need me to come,' Rachel said. 'This has nothing to do with me.'

'It has everything to do with you.' Sadie reached across the table and tugged at Rachel's hands. Rachel tried to pull them away from her sister but Sadie was too quick. 'Look,' she said, jabbing her finger at Rachel's palms. 'Yellow.'

'It goes away when you stop working with the shells,' Rachel said, yanking her hands out of Sadie's grip. 'I don't know why you're making such a fuss.'

'How do you know it's safe?' Sadie said.

Rachel frowned. 'Well, it must be. They'd not let us do it if it wasn't.' She winced at her sister's furious expression. 'Would they?'

'Bessie's ma would say different. And Rita and Irene and Moira, and the others.'

'Is Bessie really bad?' Rachel closed her eyes briefly, thinking of her friend.

'She's being well looked after,' Sadie said, with a tone that suggested to Rachel that she'd chosen her words very carefully.

Rachel felt uncomfortable. She tucked her yellow fingers underneath her thighs and said: 'Management says it's safe.'

'In my experience, managers do whatever they need to do, and say whatever they need to say, in order to make money,' Sadie said.

'These are government contracts,' Rachel pointed out. 'It's not like when you went on strike.'

'Isn't it?' Sadie said darkly.

Rachel felt arguing was hopeless. 'I don't want to annoy anyone, Sadie,' she said. 'I like working at Wentworth.'

Sadie glared at her, but Rachel carried on regardless. 'I'm paying you proper rent now,' she said. 'I know that's helping a lot.'

Sadie nodded, but she looked a little grumpy about it.

'I like being independent,' Rachel said. 'I've got friends, Sadie. Proper friends, Bessie and . . .' she wanted to say Lewis, but she hugged her feelings for him close and instead she said: 'And everyone on the football team. I love playing football. It makes me feel alive.' She sighed. 'I don't want to do anything to spoil it.'

'This won't spoil it.'

'You went on strike, and then you didn't work for Wentworth anymore.'

'This is different,' Sadie said. 'I don't want anyone to strike. I just want to make sure everyone's being looked after. That the work is safe.'

'How are you going to do that?'

'Well,' said Sadie, 'that's what I've been trying to explain. If you'd let me get a word in.'

Rachel rolled her eyes. 'Go on,' she said.

'We're going to focus—'

'Who's we?'

Sadie sighed. 'Lucinda and me.'

'You're working with Lucinda?'

'Yes.' Sadie tutted. 'We're focusing on pregnant women for now. We don't want to risk any babies being harmed and we've got Cynthia McGovern's wean as proof that the babies are being affected. We just don't know what will happen to them. So we're going to ask for the doctor to check over the women working on filling the shells.'

Suddenly it all made sense to Rachel. Sadie had latched on to this as a way of distracting herself from her own longing to have a baby. And now she felt she was protecting other women's children. The realisation made Rachel feel very sad for her sister, and a little uncomfortable.

'Does Noah know what you're up to?' she asked.

'He does,' Sadie said. Then she shrugged. 'Well, more or less,' she admitted. 'He's that busy with school and the Belgians that we've barely seen one another.'

Rachel paused.

'All right,' she said. 'I'll come with you.'

Sadie gave her a hug. 'Thank you.'

'How are you going to approach this?'

'Lucinda's sister is expecting,' Sadie said. 'I'm simply going to ask Mr Blyth if he'd be happy with his pregnant daughter working filling shells, and giving birth to a Canary Baby.'

Rachel felt a little glow of admiration. 'That's clever,' she said. 'You're clever.'

Sadie nodded modestly. 'We're calling it the "you do it" campaign,' she said. 'If the managers say the jobs are safe, we'll say, "You do it, then."'

'And what if the doctor says it isn't safe?' Rachel said, thinking suddenly of Ellen, whose job was a secret at home and whose pregnancy was a secret at work. Rachel wasn't entirely sure who knew what about Ellen. The thought made her feel nervous. 'The women won't lose their jobs?'

'No. If it's causing an issue, we'll get them moved to a different part of the factory.'

'Shell filling gets paid more,' Rachel said. 'Women might not want to move.'

'We'll work something out.'

'Will they listen to you? You don't work at Wentworth.'

'No,' Sadie said with a grin. 'But you do.'

Rachel looked down at her yellow palms. 'Aye,' she said doubtfully. 'I do.'

'Right.'

'When are we going?'

'Tomorrow.'

'Tomorrow? But Hilda wants us to have football practice. We've got another game next week and she's desperate for us to enter the Munitionettes' Cup.'

'You can do both,' said Sadie airily. 'You've got nothing else on, have you?'

Rachel had been hoping to see Lewis because she hadn't stopped thinking about him since he'd walked away from her. She'd seen him at the football match and he'd been just as lovely and friendly and kind as ever, but she was desperate to get him alone. She wanted to know why he'd almost kissed her and then stopped himself. She felt that if she didn't find out, she would go quite mad with the wondering. But now she looked at her sister, who was suddenly looking more like her old self, and she shook her head. 'I don't have anything on, really.'

'Then it's settled.'

Rachel had never been in the main factory building before. It was impressive and imposing, with wood panelling on the walls and long corridors that echoed with their footsteps. She adjusted the waistband of her boiler suit and Sadie tutted. 'Stop fidgeting,' she whispered. 'Here we are.'

She showed Rachel into a side office. Inside, an older woman was sitting at a desk. 'Hiya, Sadie,' she said. 'And you must be Rachel? I'm Dilys.'

'Nice to meet you,' Rachel said politely.

'He's just in with Lucinda. Won't be long,' Dilys said. She leaned over the desk and looked at Rachel. 'Saw you in the football,' she said. 'You're really something.'

Rachel was startled and delighted. 'You did?'

'Och, yes. We all thought you were great. We're coming along to the next game and bringing more of us next time. Everyone's really fired up about it.'

'I'm really pleased,' said Rachel. 'Hilda, that's our manager, she says everyone will know our names soon.'

'I think she's right,' Dilys said. 'Enjoy it.'

'I will,' said Rachel. Then she frowned, thinking of Ellen. 'Not sure all the girls feel the same, mind you. I think some of them would rather stay unknown.'

'I heard some of the football matches down south are getting thousands of spectators,' Dilys said. 'They made hundreds of pounds for wounded soldiers.'

'Really?' said Rachel, impressed. 'That would be good. Wouldn't that be good, Sadie?'

Sadie was pacing up and down, looking nervous.

'What would be good?' she asked.

'Just talking about football,' Rachel said.

Sadie sighed. 'Do you ever talk about anything else?'

The door to Hamilton Blyth's office opened and there stood the man himself. He was younger than Rachel had expected, with a blond moustache and an upright stance. He smiled.

'I talk about football too much also,' he said to Rachel with a broad smile. 'I understand.'

Rachel warmed to him immediately, grinning back at him, and then tried to look serious in case Sadie thought she was siding with the enemy. Not that Mr Blyth was the enemy. But still.

'You're Rachel Franklin,' he said. 'I saw you in the match. Impressive stuff. And that red-haired girl?'

'Ginny, sir,' said Rachel.

'Ginny.' He nodded. 'Very fast.'

'Och, she's terrific,' Rachel said. 'We need a couple more like her, then we'd be unstoppable.'

Behind her, Sadie gave a tiny cough.

'This is my sister, Sadie Spark,' said Rachel.

'Your sister?' Hamilton Blyth was obviously putting two and two together.

'That's right.' Sadie stepped forward and shook his outstretched hand. 'Spark is my married name. I was Sadie Franklin.'

'Sadie Franklin from the strike in 1911?'

'The very same.'

Rachel watched as Mr Blyth regarded Sadie with what Rachel thought was something akin to admiration. 'Sadie Franklin,' he said. 'And what of your friend? Kelly?'

'Ellen Kelly, sir,' said Sadie. 'Now Ellen McCallum. She runs the Clydebank Clothing Exchange with me. And Ellen's sister Bridget.'

Mr Blyth looked a little dumbstruck. 'All these sisters,' he muttered.

Lucinda appeared behind him. 'Come in,' she said. 'Come and have a seat.'

Mr Blyth's office was the nicest room Rachel had ever seen, including the rabbi's office at their shul. It was enormous, with a huge window overlooking the courtyard and – in the distance – the new football pitch.

'Sit, please,' he said.

The women sat in front of the desk, and he sat behind it. 'Lucinda said there was something you wanted to discuss?'

Sadie took Rachel's wrist and thrust her hand towards him. 'Your munitionettes are turning yellow. They're being called Canary Girls.'

'Aye,' Mr Blyth said, looking unconcerned. 'It's happening everywhere. It goes away when they stop working with the shells.'

Rachel shot Sadie a glance that was meant to say 'See!' but Sadie didn't look at her.

'But why is it happening?'

He frowned. 'What?'

'What's making them yellow?'

'The TNT, I believe. It reacts with something in the skin?'

Sadie nodded. 'Right. And the TNT only affects the skin? It's absorbed enough to make the girls bright yellow, but it stops there?'

Mr Blyth was looking less admiring now. 'Well, yes . . .'

'Some of the girls have reported stomach pains,' Sadie said. 'Did you know that?'

'No, I didn't . . .'

'Coughs,' Sadie said. 'Sickness. Dizziness. Some of them are really sick.'

'But they're a different colour yellow,' Rachel put in helpfully, still not wanting to believe that Bessie was suffering so badly. 'The girls who are sick aren't bright yellow. More sallow. It doesn't spread either – not like the canary yellow. That turns everything we touch yellow.'

Mr Blyth looked alarmed. Sadie looked triumphant.

'They're given check-ups by a doctor?' she asked.

This time Mr Blyth seemed surer. 'Yes, regular checks.'

'He looks in their mouths?'

'He does?'

Rachel nodded. 'He does.'

'Is that enough, do you think?' Sadie sounded interested but Rachel knew she knew the answer.

'Well,' Mr Blyth said, 'we give them milk to drink.'

Sadie simply raised an eyebrow. Rachel hid a smile.

Mr Blyth put his elbows on his desk, put his hands together like he was praying and tapped his forefingers against his moustache.

'Mrs Spark,' he said. 'I think it's fair to say the workers of Wentworth owe you and your friend Ellen a great deal. Your strike didn't succeed in its main aims, but there's no doubt you changed the way this factory thinks of its workers.' He smiled. 'We value them. And with the men away, the workers we value are the women. We need them and they need the jobs we're providing. They scratch our backs . . .'

Sadie nodded. 'Right,' she said.

'So you see, it's important to us that our workforce is looked after.' He glanced round at Lucinda, who was standing silently beside the window. 'That's what I told Lucinda. It's why I agreed to speak to you. I wanted to show you that it's all completely safe.'

'Right,' said Sadie again. 'Safe?'

'Yes.'

'Would you do it? Work assembling shells?'

Mr Blyth didn't hesitate. 'I would indeed. In fact, I have done.'

'And Lucinda?' Sadie asked. 'Would you want her assembling shells?'

This time Mr Blyth did hesitate, for a fraction of a second. 'If she wanted to, I would support her.'

Sadie nodded. 'You know there are babies being born who are yellow.'

'Canary Babies,' said Rachel, mostly because she quite liked the phrase.

'Somehow the part of the TNT that is turning women's skin yellow but, as you said, going no further, is also affecting their unborn children.'

Mr Blyth had gone rather pale. Rachel thought Sadie was like a cat playing with a mouse, waiting for the moment to pounce.

There was a brief silence and then Sadie said: 'What about your other daughter? I hear she's expecting a baby?'

Mr Blyth sighed, obviously understanding exactly what Sadie was doing. 'She is.'

'And would you want her to fill the shells?'

He shook his head. 'I would not.'

'And I don't blame you for that.' Sadie smiled. 'So, what are we going to do to make things safer for the munitionettes?'

Chapter Twenty-Five

Ellen couldn't quite believe what she was hearing.

'We need to know if any of you are expecting a baby,' the doctor said again, raising his voice a little to speak over the confused chatter.

'Why?' asked Ellen, rankled by the question. 'Why is that any of your business?'

The doctor held his hand up for hush, and – eventually – the voices quietened down. 'Because,' he said, 'Mr Blyth is concerned.'

'Concerned he might be employing pregnant women?' Ellen scoffed.

'No.' The doctor looked straight at her. 'Concerned this work is dangerous.'

'We're working with explosives,' another woman, standing next to Ellen, said. 'Course it's dangerous. But we know what to do to keep everyone safe.'

'That's not the issue,' the doctor said. 'The issue is your babies could be at risk.'

Ellen felt a lurch of fear. 'What kind of risk?'

'It's the erm . . .' the doctor looked down at the notes he was holding. 'The erm, chemicals in the explosives – the ones that make your skin yellow. Mr Blyth is concerned they are being absorbed into your bodies and therefore into your unborn babies.'

'The babies are born yellow,' someone said from behind Ellen.

'And my weans at home have a tinge now, just from me touching them.'

Ellen thought about Annie, whose hands were distinctly yellow and whose hairline had a definite hint of mustard, and felt a little sick.

'I thought the yellow was just the chemicals reacting to something in our skin,' she said. 'I didn't think they soaked into us.'

The woman standing next to her gave her a disparaging look. 'Did you not hear about Cythnia McGovern's wean?'

'Well yes,' Ellen said. 'But I didn't think . . .'

The woman shrugged.

Ellen put her hands to where her boiler suit was beginning to pull tight across her swelling belly. She'd already let it out as much as she could, and she was planning to unpick the seams and put in an extra panel when she had time. Then she looked at the yellow hue of her fingers against her own abdomen and took them away again.

'It's dangerous?' she said to the doctor. 'The chemicals are dangerous for our babies?'

The doctor's expression softened as he looked at her. 'That's the thing,' he said. 'No one knows for sure.'

'What about our children at home?' Ellen asked, her voice sounded shaky and uncertain to her own ears. 'My daughter's hands are yellow.'

'She'll be grand,' said the woman next to Ellen. 'I'm sure of it.'

But Ellen wasn't convinced.

'Bessie is sick,' she said. 'And others.'

'Aye,' said another woman. Ellen thought her name was Lil. 'That's what started all this.'

'All this?' Ellen said but the woman was deep in conversation with a worker next to her.

'What's to be done?' she asked. 'What will make this safe?'

This time it was Lucinda who answered. Ellen hadn't even seen her standing at the side of the room. She looked worried.

'Hello, everyone,' she said, loudly, waiting for the buzz of voices to calm down before she spoke again. 'At first we thought we could move the women who are expecting from shell filling to elsewhere in the factory.'

Ellen nodded. That was fine. It was slightly less money but she could make it work. And if it kept her baby safe, then so be it.

'But my father is still worried,' Lucinda went on. 'After all, even the women who are working making horseshoes, on the other side of the factory, are beginning to show a tinge of yellow. It's everywhere.'

'Aye,' said a few voices around Ellen. 'It's in the air,' someone added. 'We're all breathing it in.'

Ellen pinched her lips together, as though she could stop breathing.

'My sister is expecting a baby,' Lucinda went on. 'And the more my father thought about Leah working in the factory, the more he thought that couldn't be allowed to happen. He said he couldn't in all honesty ask you to do work he wouldn't want his daughter to do.'

Suddenly, Ellen realised where this was going.

'Oh no,' she breathed.

'So, I'm sorry,' Lucinda said. 'But if you're expecting a baby, you can't work here anymore.'

Ellen walked home in a daze. She couldn't quite believe what had happened. Of course she didn't want to work at Wentworth if there was a chance it would harm her unborn baby, or – she shuddered – had already harmed her Annie. But, but, but . . . What was she to do without the extra money her job had been bringing in? She felt a cold trickle of fear down the back of her neck. She would have two children to look after and barely the means to put food on the table.

Still, she had James's wage. And there was the Clothing Exchange, which didn't bring in much money but meant she wouldn't go short of clothes for the weans or food. She sighed as she crossed the road. This was a problem, that was for certain. But it wasn't a disaster. Sure, wasn't the strike back in 1911 much harder than this? When there'd been no end in sight and no other options available to her?

She took a deep breath. And of course, things were always made easier by the women she had around her. She would support Sadie through her sadness at not having a baby, she'd stand by Bridget as she worried about Ida in the police service, and in turn they would help her. They'd always been better as a team. Like single threads in a rope, made strong by pulling together. And this way, no one would ever need to know that she'd been working at Wentworth. Her secret would remain hidden.

Feeling a little cheerier – though still worried, of course – she pushed open the door to the Clothing Exchange and went inside.

Standing by the counter were Bridget, Sadie and Ida. Annie – who had been with Bridget today – was playing on the floor. No one looked at her as she came in – they were all looking at Christina, who was standing on the opposite side of the room, with her arms folded, imposing in her police uniform and unsmiling.

'What's the matter?' Ellen asked, suddenly remembering Christina had seen her at the football match – how long ago that felt. 'What's happened?'

She scooped up Annie and kissed her and made her giggle, then she turned to Bridget and asked again: 'What's happened?'

'Nothing.' Bridget leaned against the counter. 'Christina was just leaving.'

'Why are you here?' Ellen asked Christina, rather rudely. 'No one wants you here.'

'I just popped in to check the rota with Ida.'

Ellen looked at Christina. 'Is that all?'

'Yes,' Christina said sweetly. 'That's all.'

With Annie in her arms, Ellen stood by Bridget's side. She and her sister, Ida and Sadie all stood facing Christina. It was a little like she was taking a free kick and they were the defenders, Ellen thought.

The bell on the door tinkled and Rachel came in. She looked worried, and her expression grew confused as she looked from Christina to the other women.

'What's going on?' she asked.

No one said anything. Ellen rolled her eyes.

'Och, Christina, off you go or I'll give you some socks to knit.'

'I'm going,' Christina said.

She turned to leave, and Rachel went to Ellen. 'Are you all right?' she asked. 'Did you . . .?'

Ellen shook her head, very slightly, and Rachel stopped talking.

But Christina, damn her, had spotted their exchange.

'What's the matter, Ellen?' she said sharply. 'Still keeping secrets?'

'Shut up, Christina,' Ellen said.

Christina's expression darkened. 'Don't speak to me like that.'

'Oh get over yourself,' Ellen growled, her patience running out. 'You're a sour-faced crone and you make yourself feel more important by telling tales about folk.'

There was a pause and Ellen screwed her face up, thinking she'd gone too far.

'I don't tell tales,' said Christina, looking martyred. 'I just think it's not on for people like you to lie to people who trust them.'

She took a breath and Ellen glared at her.

'What you don't all know about precious Ellen,' Christina began, looking at the other women. 'Is that she's lying to all of you . . .'

'Put a sock in it,' Bridget said mildly, standing up straighter and taking a step towards Christina. 'No one is interested in what you have to say. You're not judge, jury and executioner around here, no matter what you might think.'

Christina's expression went from irritated to angry. 'No one is interested?' said Christina. 'On the contrary, I think they'd be very interested in the truth about you and your friend Ida.' She emphasised the word 'friend' and Ellen watched as her sister's face grew red and her eyes widened. She looked, Ellen thought, horrified.

'Christina,' Bridget said, her voice thin and reedy. 'Christina, please . . .'

'And you a married woman,' said Christina gleefully. 'Dreadful business.'

Ellen was bewildered. What on earth was Christina implying? Surely she didn't mean . . . She looked from Ida to Bridget, noticing how close they were standing to one another and felt dizzy all of a sudden.

'This is none of your business,' Rachel said, putting herself firmly in between Bridget and Christina. 'You need to leave.'

'Och, don't worry, I'm going,' said Christina. 'But you're not so smart yourself, Rachel Franklin. Perhaps you need to ask your young man what he's not telling you. Or perhaps ask that Lucinda . . .'

'What's Lucinda got to do with anything?' asked Sadie.

Ellen's head was spinning with the accusations flying about, and Christina's smug expression was making her furious.

'You need to leave,' she said. She put Annie down on the floor and gave Christina a little prod to encourage her to move. 'Go.'

Christina marched to the door of the Clothing Exchange and Ellen breathed out in relief. But then Christina turned back.

'You should all know that Ellen's working at Wentworth,' she said with satisfaction. 'Quite the star of the football team.'

Then she pushed open the door and walked out with the bell tinkling as she went.

Ellen turned to face her friends.

Sadie was the first to speak. 'You're working at Wentworth?' she said, shaking her head.

'No,' said Ellen. 'Well, yes, I was working there, but I'm not now.'

'You didn't tell us?' Sadie said. 'Why didn't you tell us?'

'I thought you'd be angry.' Ellen looked at her boots. 'Because you were angry with Rachel.'

'Oh, I'm not angry,' said Sadie, lightly. Ellen's heart lifted. But Sadie was glowering at her. 'I'm absolutely flaming furious. How could you, Ellen? After everything they did to us?'

'I needed the money,' Ellen said, annoyed at Sadie's reaction. 'Because my husband has gone and I have a baby on the way. So don't stand there all holier than thou, Sadie Spark, because you don't know what it's like to be a mother.'

There was a stunned silence. Sadie's face crumpled for a second and then she gathered herself. Ellen felt sick.

'Sadie,' she said. 'I didn't mean that . . .'

But Rachel jumped in.

'What did you mean, you're not working at Wentworth anymore?' she said. She looked at Sadie. 'Why not?'

'They sacked all the pregnant workers,' Ellen said, suddenly weary. She sank into a chair and put her head in her hands. 'They let us all go.'

'Go from shell filling?' Sadie said. 'But not from the factory as a whole? That wasn't the plan.'

Ellen shook her head. 'Even women working on horseshoes are going yellow,' she said wearily. 'The poison is in the air. It's everywhere. We've all been told not to come back. Just in case.'

She looked at Sadie, who was biting her lip. 'What do you mean that wasn't the plan?'

Sadie paled. 'Well, I . . .'

Ellen eyed Sadie.

'Sadie Spark,' she growled. 'Was this you? Was this your fault? You and your blooming campaigning?'

'No,' Sadie said immediately. Then she dropped her head. 'But yes, in a way it was.'

'What did you do?'

'Rachel and I just went to see Hamilton Blyth . . .'

'WHAT?' Ellen couldn't believe her ears. 'Sadie, what?'

'I went to see him and asked if he'd let his pregnant daughter work on the shells.'

'And he said no?' Ellen said. 'And then he sacked us all.'

'I thought he'd just move you round,' Sadie said miserably. 'I didn't know he'd sack anyone.'

Ellen rubbed her forehead. 'You can never leave well enough alone, can you?'

'I thought I was doing the right thing,' Sadie said.

'It's not Sadie's fault,' Bridget said. 'If you'd not lied about working at Wentworth, she'd have known this affected you.'

Ellen turned on her sister. 'Oh shut up, Bridget,' she said. 'How dare you criticise me. Like you didn't spend months lying to your own husband?' She glared at Bridget, who shifted closer to Ida. 'Like you don't lie to everyone every single day,' Ellen added pointedly. 'Every day.'

She whirled round and faced Sadie. 'And you, Sadie Spark. So caught up in your campaigning, so desperate for a distraction from your own trouble getting pregnant, that you ruin everything for everyone else. Just because you want to be hailed a heroine.'

'Ellen, that's not fair,' said Rachel.

'Shut up,' Ellen said furiously. 'You knew what Sadie was up to and you never said a word.'

Ellen looked at the women and then down at little Annie who was hugging her knees. She bent down and picked up her daughter, holding her tight.

'Do you know, on the way here I was thinking how pleased I was to have you all. I was thinking how strong we were together.' She snorted. 'How could I have been so wrong?'

She marched across the room to the door and yanked it open.

'Get out,' she said. 'All of you, get out. I got sacked, and now I'm sacking you. I run the Clydebank Clothing Exchange now. And I don't need any help from any of you.' She marched over to the door. 'You're not welcome.'

Silently, the other women filed out of the door. 'Go on, go!' Ellen screeched after them, knowing full well her ma would have kittens if she saw her girls brawling in the street. 'You bloody traitors!'

Above her, the sign she'd stitched to recruit new volunteers at the Clothing Exchange flapped in the breeze. 'Join us,' it read.

'It's finished,' Ellen said to Annie.

'Finished,' Annie agreed happily. Ellen put her down and then reached up and tugged at the sign hard. It came loose easily and Ellen pulled it from the fixings and crumpled it up. Then, to Annie's delight, she dropped it into the puddles in the gutter and stamped on it.

'It's over,' she said. Then she burst into tears.

Chapter Twenty-Six

Clydebank

2 May 1916

My dear James,

There was a raid in Edinburgh. Two airships started by dropping bombs on the docks. They said they were aiming for the castle, and one bomb even hit the castle rock. It seems some folk had a lucky escape, but others weren't so fortunate – thirteen people were killed. Suddenly the war seems very close by.

Is this what you face every day, James? Bombs falling and the sudden cold fear that this is real? You're so brave, my darling. So very brave.

And as for me. Well, I'm falling apart. I hate to pour my heart out to you, when you're facing real danger, but I have no one else to talk to.

All my lies and tall tales have been uncovered, as they always are, of course. My ma told me that weeks ago when she was cross with me for fibbing to Bridget. Ma's gone to stay with Auntie Peggy in Fort William, with my da, so she's not here to say 'I told you so'. I'm glad about that but I miss her too.

I've made such a mess of everything, James.

I've lost my job, that's the first thing. They say it's not safe for pregnant women to work in munitions, and maybe that's true. But I will miss the money, there's no doubt. And the football. How I'll miss the football.

And that's not the half of it. Sadie's not speaking to me, because she's so cross that I was working at Wentworth, and I'm furious with her because it's her meddling that's cost me my job. You'd think that would make us even but it doesn't, because I said some cruel things, James. Awful things.

And then there's Bridget. Where to begin? I know I don't know much about the world. I'm not clever like Noah, or street smart like my da. But I thought I knew my own sister. And I knew she never really wanted to marry Malcolm all those years ago, and I was quite impressed with the way they'd handled things. How they stayed pals – stayed married – but did their own thing. I know Ma was upset at first, but Bridget was never this happy when she and Malcolm were together.

And – oh gosh, how silly and naive this seems now – but I thought Bridget and Ida were just good friends. Like Sadie and me. And I was glad, James, that Bridget had someone like Ida to rely on.

But it seems I was wrong. I can't even write the words, but Bridget and Ida are more than pals. They are living together like a married couple. And I can't make it make sense, James. Not one tiny bit.

There was a big row in the Clothing Exchange. That insufferable Christina was to blame but I suppose we were all to blame in a way. Anyway, I was screeching like a fishwife and I threw everyone out. And I've not seen anyone since.

Except Bridget. She came by this morning. Standing in the doorway, her hat in her hands like she was a witness in court. And she begged me to listen to her, but I couldn't, James. I couldn't bring myself to listen to what she had to say.

To think, she's always been someone I looked up to. Someone I wanted to be more like. But not now.

All I said was 'Does Malcolm know?' and she sort of gasped and said of course he didn't. And I said she wasn't the person I thought she was. And she cried and said she couldn't lie anymore. But her tears just made me cross, and I said she blooming well should keep lying because if what Christina said about her and Ida was the truth, then absolutely no one would want to hear it. I said she was disgusting and I was ashamed of her. And then I shut the door in her face. She stood there for ages. It was a good ten minutes before I heard her footsteps going down the stairs.

I know what you're thinking. I've hardly covered myself in glory, have I? But I was so cross, James. Cross and scared and fed up and confused. All those things, all at once. And I really don't think I was the only one in the wrong. I'm certainly not the only one who's been lying.

But I don't know what to do to put it right.

Please tell me what to do, James. Please tell me.

Your hot-tempered but apologetic wife,

Ellen

Chapter Twenty-Seven

'I'm full of beans,' Sadie told Noah. 'I've been revitalised. Like the wind has caught my sails.'

Noah looked more than a little alarmed. 'Don't do too much, Sadie,' he warned.

Sadie scoffed. 'I'm not doing too much,' she said. 'I've got lots of time on my hands now Ellen's thrown us out of the Clothing Exchange.'

Noah frowned. 'Aye, but I'm not sure that's a good thing.'

'Course it is.' Sadie stood up. 'It gives me more time to focus on the important things, like keeping an eye on Bessie, and helping your refugees.'

'They're not my refugees,' Noah said. 'And they're fine. All settled. No more expected for now. I'm glad to have the chance to get back to normal school business.'

Sadie made a face. She didn't want anything to get back to normal. Well, to be honest, she wasn't really sure what normal was anymore. But her head and her days were full and she didn't have time to think about that now.

'Of course, the biggest thing is the campaign,' she told Noah.

He nodded. 'Aye,' he said. Sadie thought he sounded a bit tired. 'Still going, is it?'

'Oh yes. I've heard there are more women who are sick.'

'Good,' said Noah half-heartedly. 'Well, not good, of course. That's not what I meant.'

Sadie rolled her eyes. 'I'm off out actually,' she said. 'Just off to see Bessie.'

'Good,' he said again.

'Are you all right?'

'Yes. Why wouldn't I be?'

'You just sound a bit tired,' Sadie said. 'Weary.'

Noah smiled at her, but she thought it was a bit forced. 'I might go to bed early,' he said.

'You should.' She went over to where he sat, a book in his hand and his glasses skewwhiff, and gave him a kiss. 'I'll see you later.'

Noah caught her hand. 'Sadie,' he said. 'Are *you* all right?'

Sadie paused. 'Yes.'

'Are you sure?' Noah sighed. 'Because I'm not sure you are.'

Sadie wasn't sure, actually. She wasn't sure at all.

Because she'd not spoken to Ellen for almost a month and that was the longest they'd ever gone without speaking. And she missed her. And she missed Annie.

And Bridget – whom Sadie was half desperate to speak to and half excruciatingly embarrassed about – had gone quiet and retreated away to McKinley's, and Sadie had barely seen her. And Rachel was either working, or playing football, or doing goodness knows what, and she was never home. Sadie only knew she still lived with them because she saw her washing hanging on the line out the window.

Then there was the campaign. Which, if she was going to be honest, had lost some of its shine now Ellen and the other pregnant women had all been ousted from Wentworth. That hadn't been Sadie's intention at all. And Dilys was keen as mustard, but Sadie had a horrible feeling that Dilys – as fun and likeable and clever as she was – just liked stirring up trouble. She longed to talk to Ellen about it. But she couldn't, because Ellen wasn't speaking to her. Which was fair enough really.

Then there was the nagging feeling that what Ellen had said – about Sadie throwing herself into the campaign as a distraction because she wasn't pregnant – was true. And, as it happened, she wasn't feeling revitalised at all. She was absolutely exhausted, she was terrified that Bessie wasn't improving, she missed her friends desperately, and she felt as guilty as could be about Ellen being sacked.

But she didn't say any of that to Noah. Instead, she squeezed his fingers.

'I'm sure,' she lied.

It didn't take long to get to Bessie's, but Sadie's steps were slow and heavy. When she saw Ida approaching, she almost hurried away but decided she didn't have the energy, and anyway, she thought it might be good to speak to her.

They stepped towards one another almost gingerly.

'Hello,' said Sadie, cautiously.

'Hello,' said Ida with even greater caution.

Sadie wondered if Ida was expecting to be treated differently after what Christina had revealed, and then she wondered if she should treat Ida differently. She'd heard about women being romantically involved before, but she'd never known anyone . . . well, as far as she knew, of course. She looked at Ida, who looked just the same as always, with her funny crooked smile and sharp eyes, and felt an unexpected rush of affection.

'It's nice to see you,' she said.

Ida's shoulders dropped in relief. 'And you,' she said. She reached out and took Sadie's hand. 'It's very nice.'

'It's been awful,' Sadie admitted. 'Have you seen Ellen at all? Has Bridget spoken to her?'

Ida looked stricken. 'No,' she said. 'Not a word. Bridget went round and Ellen wouldn't speak to her. Bridget was dreadfully upset.'

'Oh lord.' Sadie scratched her head. 'What about Mrs Kelly? Has she seen Ellen?'

'She's gone to stay with her sister in Fort William,' Ida said. 'She doesn't know the girls have fallen out.'

'Goodness what a mess.'

'Aye,' said Ida darkly.

'It's my fault.'

'No,' Ida said. 'No. Everyone's been keeping secrets. Ellen's upset with everyone. And Bridget's upset that Ellen didn't tell her about working at Wentworth.'

Sadie nodded. 'I would be too, except I'm too busy feeling guilty that I lost her the job to feel betrayed that she had the job in the first place.'

Ida put her hand on Sadie's shoulder and smiled her crooked smile. 'Sadie,' she began. 'About what Christina said . . .'

Sadie felt a little embarrassed. She put her hand on top of Ida's and tried to smile reassuringly. 'It's fine,' she said. 'Honestly. I've barely had time to give it any thought. It doesn't change anything.'

'Well, if it does . . .' Ida began.

'It won't,' said Sadie firmly, though truthfully, it wasn't that she'd not had time to think about it, it was more that she didn't even know how to think about it. 'Honestly, it's the very least of my worries.'

She gestured towards the direction she'd been walking in. 'I have to go, Ida. I'm visiting Bessie.'

'How is she?'

'Not so good.'

There was a small, awkward pause.

'It will all be fine in the end,' said Ida.

'Will it?' Sadie felt bleak. 'But what if it isn't?'

'Then it isn't the end,' said Ida.

She gave Sadie a quick pat on her upper arm, then headed off.

Sadie, more slowly, carried on walking towards Bessie's flat.

Bessie's ma was pleased to see her. Sadie gave her the little parcel she'd put together – some bread and milk and a few bits of clothes from a Clothing Exchange donation she'd had in the flat and not got round to delivering.

'You should go and see Ellen,' she told her. 'At the Clothing Exchange. Don't worry about not having anything to swap – she'll let you take what you need.'

'I've been these last three days,' Bessie's ma said. 'But it's closed every time.'

'Really?' Sadie was alarmed. 'Did you chap on the door?'

'Aye.'

'And there was no sign of Ellen, or anyone?'

'No, it was all dark and closed up.'

'I'll find out what's going on,' Sadie said, trying to dampen down her worries. 'How's Bessie today?'

'She's just sleeping all the time,' her ma said.

'Well, sleep is a good healer.'

'I hope so.' Her ma bit her lip. 'I'm not so sure.'

'Can I see her?'

Bessie's ma tilted her head wearily. 'Go on through.'

Bessie was so still in her bed that for a moment Sadie thought the worst. Then she sighed and shifted slightly, much to Sadie's relief. But she didn't stir the whole time she sat with her, and her hand on the bedclothes was skeletal. Sadie tucked it under the sheet, noticing how cold she was.

She thought that if Bessie died, Hamilton Blyth would have her blood on his hands.

It was with a heavy heart that she headed home again, even more slowly than she'd walked to Bessie's earlier.

She turned the corner into her street and there, sitting on the wall outside their flat, was Bridget. Sadie's tiredness lifted, just a little, and her steps quickened.

'Bridget,' she said, trying to sound warm and reassuring. It obviously worked, because Bridget's expression changed from one of concern to one of relief.

'Ida said that you don't hate me?' she said as Sadie approached. 'Hate us.'

'Of course I don't.'

'You're not . . .' She made a face. 'Disgusted?'

'Lord, no,' Sadie said, realising almost to her own surprise that she was telling the truth. 'No.'

Bridget closed her eyes.

'That's what Ellen said.'

Sadie sat down on the wall next to her friend.

'Ellen said a lot of very hurtful things.'

'She did.'

'But we have to remember that she is my friend, and your sister, and we know her as well as we know ourselves. And we know that she is a good, kind woman, who loves us. And at the moment, I believe she is like a wounded animal, lashing out and biting whoever comes close.' She took Bridget's hand. 'But she won't be like this forever.'

Bridget squeezed Sadie's fingers. 'Goodness me, you're very wise, Sadie.'

Sadie smiled. 'I'm really not. I just learn lessons from all the mistakes I've made.'

'We should all do that. The world might be a better place.'

'It would.' Sadie gave her a little nudge. 'Do you want to come inside?'

'Yes please.'

Upstairs in the empty flat – Noah had gone out and there was no sign of Rachel, of course – Sadie made tea, then they sat beside the fire.

'I've been feeling awful,' Bridget said.

'Me too,' Sadie admitted. 'Rotten.'

Bridget wrapped her fingers round her mug. 'Do you remember how me and Ellen fell out when I wasn't striking and you were?'

'I do remember.'

'That was rotten, too. I was so cross with her for not seeing things my way.'

'Aye.'

'And now I feel exactly the same.'

'I understand that,' Sadie said. 'She didn't think about how we would feel if she went to work at Wentworth again.'

'No, she didn't.' Bridget took a deep breath. 'But we didn't think about how hard things are for her.'

Sadie felt her words like prickles on her skin. 'We didn't.'

'James is away,' Bridget said. 'And she's got Annie, and another wean on the way. And money is tight. We should have thought about that.'

'And now I've made everything so much worse,' said Sadie, feeling awful.

'You weren't to know,' Bridget said. Then her expression hardened, briefly. 'Because blasted Ellen didn't tell us.'

'God, we're all as bad as each other,' Sadie said with a groan. 'I hate not speaking to Ellen.'

'Ida says everyone has been lying to everyone else.'

'Ida's right,' said Sadie. 'What a mess. I just wish I knew how to put it right.'

'I don't know,' Bridget said. 'But I think we should do something. Try to do something at least.' She looked at Sadie with a hint of devilment in her eyes. 'There is one good thing about all this,' she said.

'Is there?'

'Ellen won't be yellow anymore.'

Sadie laughed and then suddenly found she was crying. Bridget went from chuckling to concern and gathered her into her arms.

'This is all my fault,' Sadie sobbed into Bridget's shoulder, letting out all the emotions she'd been feeling for days, and weeks.

'No,' Bridget soothed. 'That's not true.'

'I've made such a mess of everything. And I'm only doing it because I'm not having a baby.'

'Oh shhh,' Bridget said, offering Sadie a handkerchief. 'Ellen shouldn't have said such a thing. It was cruel.'

'She was right,' Sadie said. 'I'm sticking my nose in where it doesn't belong just to keep busy. I'm campaigning for better conditions at Wentworth, and I don't even work there.' She tried to smile but it wasn't working.

'Och, Sadie, don't apologise for trying to help folk,' said Bridget.

Sadie nodded, managing a smile this time. 'I suppose. After all, the Clothing Exchange is where all this began.' Then she clutched Bridget's arm as a thought struck her. 'The Clothing Exchange.'

'Yes,' Bridget said doubtfully. 'What about it?'

'Ellen needs it.'

'Ellen threw us out.'

'I don't mean she needs us to work there – though she does,' said Sadie. 'She needs to make use of it.'

Bridget frowned. 'Go on.'

'Things must be hard,' said Sadie. 'No money coming in, and Annie's a handful, and she must be fair worried about James.'

'Yes.'

'So, let's help her, the way we've helped scores of other women these past five years.'

'She won't want our help.'

Sadie scoffed. 'Of course she won't. And that's why we won't tell her it's from us.'

Understanding dawned on Bridget's face. 'Right,' she said. 'This could work, Sadie.'

'It'll work,' Sadie said. She smiled – properly this time. 'My ideas always work.'

Chapter Twenty-Eight

Rachel was carrying a parcel tied up with string, but it was heavy and bigger than she'd expected, so she was struggling a little bit.

'Blasted Sadie,' she muttered under her breath as she crossed the road. It was raining and it was so early that it wasn't light yet, and the parcel kept threatening to slide out of her arms.

She didn't even know what was inside it, not really. Sadie had spent most of yesterday putting it together. She said even though Ellen had shut the doors of the Clothing Exchange, they weren't going to ignore her.

Rachel knew Agnes, one of the newcomers to the Clothing Exchange, had made a loaf of bread, and Isobel, another recent arrival, who seemed to know everyone in Clydebank, had added some eggs and a pint of milk. There was potted meat, a jar of jam, and a copy of the newspaper that had a write-up about the last football game in it, where Ellen was called 'talented'. And Noah, who was just a big softie when you really thought about it, had put in some wee bits for Annie – a fruit bun, and a little knitted bear someone had donated for his refugees who were all too old for soft toys.

Rachel thought there were some clothes for Annie too, and maybe even a baby blanket, though Ellen's wean wasn't due for ages yet.

The whole thing was lovely, but it was heavy, and Sadie had

told Rachel she wasn't to let Ellen see who delivered it, and she wasn't sure how she would do that, being as she couldn't get into Ellen's stairway without pulling the bell, and it was so early, she didn't really want to wake Ellen up, though she might be awake already because Annie was an early riser. But then what if she came down to open the main door too quickly and caught sight of Rachel lurking there?

The milk cart rattled past and sent splashes up the back of Rachel's skirt.

'Stupid, bloody Sadie,' she swore again, adjusting her grip as the parcel took a dive out of her arms and into the wet gutter.

'Easy, there,' a voice said, as someone caught the parcel before it landed. It was Lewis. Rachel was absolutely delighted to see him and not just because he'd averted disaster.

'Hello,' she said.

'Hello.'

For a second, they both stood there, smiling at one another, then a raindrop rolled its way down Rachel's neck and she shivered.

'Why are you here?'

'To see you.'

'Really?' Rachel was absurdly pleased. 'Truly?'

'I woke up early and I missed you, so I thought I'd come over and catch you on your way to work, and we could walk to the factory together.'

'That's so nice.' Rachel smiled. 'Was it far?'

'Pardon?'

'Did you have to walk far, from where you woke up?' Rachel knew that was an odd question to ask but she kept hearing Christina saying she didn't know the truth about Lewis, and she couldn't for the life of her stop wondering what he was hiding.

'Not far,' Lewis said, gazing at her quizzically. 'Though I'm surprised you're here . . .' He checked his pocket watch and again Rachel's mind went to Christina's accusations. She wondered exactly what Lewis did at Wentworth to dress so smartly every day. But then he smiled at her again, and put his hand on her arm, and she melted.

'You're here and it's still early,' he said. 'What are you up to?'

'I need to take this parcel to Ellen's,' she said. 'Secretly.'

'Ooh,' said Lewis in delight. 'We're going behind enemy lines.'

Rachel gave him a good-natured shove. 'No, we're going to deliver some potted meat that my pig-headed sister doesn't want Ellen to know came from her.'

'That doesn't sound nearly as exciting,' Lewis said. He offered her his arm and Rachel took it.

'No, but it is our good deed for the day.'

'Fine.' He put the parcel up onto his shoulder and together they walked towards Ellen's tenement building.

'I don't want to wake her up,' Rachel said as they drew closer. 'But how will I get through the main door without ringing the bell?'

'I have an idea,' said Lewis. 'Let's just wait a wee minute. There are bound to be folk leaving for work.'

They perched on a wall nearby, and sure enough, after a little while, a man came out of the main door dressed in work boots.

'Hold the door, pal,' Lewis called, darting over. He nodded to the man, holding the door for Rachel. 'Go on, then,' he said, giving her the parcel. 'Do your good deed.'

'Righto.'

Rachel dashed up the stairs, in rather a clumsy fashion because her burden was quite heavy and cumbersome, and left the parcel on the doormat, crossing her fingers that one of the toerags who lived on the top floor wouldn't pinch it and take it home for their ma. Mind you, their mother would give them a clip round the ear if she thought they'd stolen it, so best to be sure it was obvious who it was for. She dug into her pocket and found a stub of pencil, then wrote 'ELLEN McCALLUM' in large letters on the top of the parcel.

Then she shoved the pencil back into her pocket and ran back downstairs to where Lewis was waiting.

'All done?'

'All done,' she said.

She tucked her hand into his arm once more and they continued through the early morning gloom towards the factory. And even though the rain was heavier now, and Rachel's ankles were damp and her face was running with drips, she honestly thought she'd never felt quite so content as she did right at that moment.

But was it wrong to feel that way? She sighed and Lewis glanced at her.

'Not looking forward to work?'

Rachel shrugged. 'No, it's not that,' she said.

Lewis stopped walking and turned to face her. 'Then what?'

'My sister is in a state,' Rachel said. 'She's not herself even though she's pretending everything is fine. And Ellen, well, she's not happy, is she? Even Bridget who's always so calm, is . . .' She spread her fingers out, trying to show how everything had exploded between the women who'd been such an important part of her life for so long.

'But . . .'

'But,' Rachel said, frowning. She felt a flutter inside, like she couldn't believe what she was about to say. 'But I'm completely happy.'

Lewis looked into her eyes and Rachel wondered if there was a name for this perfect, joyous, agonising pleasure she was feeling.

'I'm completely happy too,' he said.

Surely now he would kiss her? Surely.

But overhead, the factory clock chimed the hour and he looked alarmed. 'I have to dash. Can I walk you home after your shift? Are you playing football?'

'Of course,' Rachel said, disappointed but trying not to show it. So she shook her head comically at the ridiculous notion that she wouldn't be playing football. 'But I could meet you after that?'

'Done,' Lewis said.

'Do you want to meet Sadie?' she said suddenly, once more thinking of Christina's strange words. 'I want you to meet her and Noah.'

Lewis looked startled. 'Yes,' he said. 'Definitely.'

'When?'

'Oh, soon.' He sounded vague. 'One day very soon.' He gazed up at the clock. 'I have to go,' he said. 'See you later.'

He melted away into the crowd and Rachel was left behind, still wondering what he was hiding and if she'd ever know for sure. Was he married? Surely not – he was too young, wasn't he? Or was he one of those awful people who didn't like Jewish folk and made it horribly obvious? Rachel had crossed paths with them before. Though, she thought with a sigh, if he didn't like Jews then he would hardly be getting out of bed early to come and meet her in the rain.

And so, she came up with a plan; She would meet Lewis after football and she would go via McKinley's, because she knew Sadie was planning to pop into the shop later and hopefully they'd walk past, just as Sadie was arriving.

'Sadie,' Rachel bellowed, spotting her sister right at the end of the street. 'SADIE!' She waved madly.

Lewis squinted through the rain – which hadn't stopped all day – at the tiny figure at the far end of the road, and then looked at Rachel. 'How on earth can you see that's Sadie?'

Rachel grinned. 'She walks in a very identifiable manner,' she said, not mentioning that she had known Sadie would be at that very spot at this very time. 'SADIE!'

She took Lewis's hand. 'Come on,' she said. 'Let's catch her.'

Dragging him along, she ran towards her sister, even though her legs were aching after football and a whole day in the factory.

'Sadie!'

Finally, Sadie heard and turned round, looking slightly

nervous to see Rachel thundering towards her pulling a man by his arm.

'Rach?' she said. 'What's going on? Who's this?'

Rachel stopped in front of her sister, trying to catch her breath. 'I saw you,' she panted. 'And I wanted . . .' She paused, still out of puff. 'I wanted you to meet Lewis.'

She pushed him towards Sadie. 'Here he is.'

Sadie gave her a curious glance. 'Hello, Lewis,' she said. 'Nice to meet you. I'm Rachel's sister, Sadie Spark.'

Lewis shook Sadie's hand firmly. 'How do you do,' he said.

Rachel felt a swell of pride. He was so handsome and had such lovely manners, even though his hat was dripping with raindrops, pulled down over his eyes against the weather, and his cheeks were red because she'd made him run.

'Lewis is my . . . erm . . .' She shut her mouth, not knowing what to say. For all her planning, she'd not thought about this part. But luckily, Lewis stepped in.

'I'd like to take Rachel out one evening,' he said. 'With your permission, Mrs Spark, that is.'

Sadie smiled. 'Call me Sadie,' she said. 'If Rachel would like to go out with you one evening, then you have my permission.'

Rachel nodded. 'Yes please,' she said, even though she and Lewis had been out several times already. 'That would be lovely.'

'Then I will see you soon,' Lewis said. He nodded to Sadie. 'Nice to meet you, Mrs Spark . . . Sadie.'

And he turned on his heel and walked away briskly, through the rain.

'Well,' said Sadie in delight. 'He is wonderful, Rachel. Where on earth did you find him?'

'Work,' Rachel muttered. 'He works at Wentworth.'

'In the factory?'

'Aye.' She shrugged. 'But in clerical.' She was almost sure that was where he worked.

Sadie was frowning. 'Christina said you had a young man.' She prodded Rachel affectionately. 'She told me and I didn't even pay attention.'

'Well, there was a lot going on,' Rachel muttered.

Sadie tapped her lips with her forefinger. 'She said there was something he wasn't telling you.'

'She did say that,' Rachel said with a sigh. 'But I think she just made it up. And he's not actually my young man.'

'But he wants to be,' said Sadie. 'That's obvious.'

Rachel felt a bit more hopeful. 'Do you really think so?'

'I saw the way he looked at you,' Sadie said.

'And you think Christina was just being nasty?'

'I do.' Sadie gave Rachel an affectionate glance. 'You're so grown up.'

'Och, get away.'

'I'm going to see Bridget,' Sadie said. 'Want to come?'

'Yes.' Rachel nodded. 'I feel bad for her.'

Sadie rubbed her nose. 'Do you mind? About her and Ida?'

'Not at all.' Rachel shrugged. 'I think I knew.' She smiled at her sister. 'Just the other day, I thought that the pair of them reminded me of you and Noah, you know? How they are with each other. It's just the same. So I wasn't surprised, not really.'

'Goodness.' Sadie blinked.

'I think perhaps it's all just love,' Rachel said. 'Och, look at Ellen and James – her a Catholic and him Protestant. Who are we to say who anyone falls in love with? Rich, poor, Jewish, Catholic, men or women.'

Sadie was staring at her.

'What?' Rachel said, feeling self-conscious. 'I just think life's too short to stop people being happy.' She gave Sadie a small smile. 'There is a war on, you know.'

'You young ones are very modern in your thinking.'

Rachel nudged her with her shoulder. 'You're not old.'

'Sometimes I feel it.'

'Do you mind? About Bridget and Ida?'

'A wee bit,' Sadie admitted. 'At first. It just seemed so strange to me. But then I saw them and they were the same as always and I found I didn't mind as much as I thought I did.'

Rachel nodded. 'Aye.'

'Ellen minds though.'

'I know.' Rachel groaned.

'I think she'll come round. Eventually.'

'I really hope so.'

A thought struck Sadie. 'Oh, while we're on the subject of Ellen – did you drop off the parcel?'

'Aye. Left it on the doorstep.'

'Grand,' said Sadie. She lowered her voice, though Rachel wasn't sure why, because the Clothing Exchange was all shut up and even if Ellen was inside, she'd not have been able to hear them. 'I've ordered some milk from the milkman for her too.'

'That's kind.' Rachel was touched. 'Wouldn't it be easier just to apologise, though?'

'Maybe,' said Sadie. She gave Rachel a sudden grin. 'I'm not ready for that yet, mind you.'

Rachel laughed, feeling lighter. Perhaps the women would all be friends again, and perhaps Lewis wasn't hiding anything after all – he'd been so charming to Sadie. She smiled at her sister.

'Let me know if you need any help,' she said. 'But please don't make me knit any more socks.'

Chapter Twenty-Nine

Ellen had been awake half the night, listening to the rain lashing against the windows and gushing down from the gutter. She hoped the repairs James had made to the frame would hold and she'd not have to deal with a leak by herself. Her da would know what to do but he and her mother were away in Fort William. Ellen felt more alone than ever knowing they weren't round the corner.

'I feel bad leaving you just when you need us both,' her ma had said when they were planning the trip weeks ago. But Ellen's da was feeling off. He'd been ill and he wasn't happy not to be working at the shipyard anymore, doing his bit. He felt old and tired and he was awfully crabbit the whole time, and her ma had decided it was best to take him away for a wee while.

'I'll be fine,' Ellen had said with a smile. 'Bridget's right round the corner and she never leaves me alone.'

Her ma had pushed Ellen's hair back off her forehead and looked at her closely. 'You look tired,' she'd said. Ellen hadn't known for sure then that she was pregnant, though she'd suspected, and it seemed Ma did too. 'Anything to tell me?'

Ellen, not wanting to say anything until she was certain, had shaken her head. 'Naw,' she'd lied. 'Nothing.'

Of course now her parents knew she was having another baby. But she hadn't told them about falling out with Bridget and Sadie. More secrets. More lies. More worries.

She rolled over onto her side in bed, and put her hand on her abdomen. The baby was growing and she had a fair tummy on her now. Though it didn't matter anymore – she didn't have to hide it now she wasn't going to Wentworth. She felt fluttering inside and smiled. Things were hard, but she was still pleased to be having another wean.

'Hello,' she whispered. 'Hello, baby.'

She knew she wouldn't go back to sleep now, and Annie was bound to wake up any minute. So she got out of bed, pushed her feet into her slippers, and went to put the kettle on. She looked out of the window. It was dark and gloomy outside, with the rain still teeming down, but in the street she could see a man. Waiting for someone, she thought. He was hunched into his jacket, his hat pulled down over his eyes.

Out in the hallway, she heard footsteps as people started going to work, and felt a moment of envy that they were off to earn a day's pay.

'Mama?' Annie appeared next to her, rubbing sleep from her eyes. Ellen scooped her up and kissed her.

'Good morning,' she said. 'Good morning, my sleepy wee girl.'

'Raining,' said Annie, wriggling to be put down.

Ellen plonked her back on the floor. 'It's not nice weather today,' she said. 'We'll be stuck inside all day.' She felt a flash of bleak concern, wondering what on earth she and Annie would do to fill the hours. Perhaps it would clear up in a while, she thought hopefully, looking out at the leaden clouds. Or perhaps not.

The day stretched ahead of her. She should go to the Clothing Exchange and do some alterations, or there were bags of donations that needed sorting. The Clothing Exchange was her only source of income now she wasn't working at Wentworth and she'd thrown all the other women out of it so it was just her. The need for it was so great, and the job of running it alone it made her head spin.

'Shall we do some sewing?' she asked Annie, making up her mind. 'We'll go to the shop and do some mending.'

'Yes.' Annie nodded. 'With Tida and Biscuit.'

'Auntie Ida and Auntie Bridget are busy today,' Ellen lied. 'But we'll have some fun anyway.'

Annie didn't look convinced, but thankfully she didn't argue. Ellen wasn't sure she could cope with her daughter being stubborn today.

'Milk?' asked Annie hopefully, and Ellen remembered that she had none in.

'Oh for heaven's sake,' she muttered. 'Annie, doll, we need to go out.'

'No.' Annie shook her head. 'Raining.'

The clatter of the milk cart outside lifted Ellen's spirits.

'We'll just run down and catch the milkman,' she said, hoping she had enough pennies in her purse to pay for a bottle. 'We won't go out in the rain. Quick, quick.'

She scooped Annie up and opened the front door, and there on the mat was a brown parcel with her name scrawled on the top.

'What's this?' she said to Annie. A bit awkwardly, she bent down and picked it up, almost dropping it because it was heavier than she'd expected.

The milk forgotten, she went back inside and put the parcel on the table. Annie clambered up onto a chair so she could see better as Ellen unwrapped it.

Inside, there was a bottle of milk – still cold – some potted meat, jam, a loaf of bread that smelled so delicious Ellen's stomach rumbled as soon as the scent hit her nostrils, and six eggs. There was a copy of the newspaper – strange, thought Ellen – and a little knitted hat in Wentworth football-team colours but the perfect size for Annie. It was the most thoughtful, considered, perfect parcel and Ellen felt like someone had peeked inside her head to see what she needed the most.

She sat down next to where Annie was perched on the table and kissed her daughter's little plump knees making her giggle.

'Would you like a piece and jam, and some milk?' she said. The relief of knowing she had food that would stretch for a few days was huge.

'Jam,' said Annie, looking pleased. 'Thank you.'

'We should really thank whoever sent this lovely present,' said Ellen, pleased at Annie's manners. 'I don't know who left it for us.' But even as she said the words she realised she did know – of course she did. There was only one person who would be so thoughtful, who knew her and Annie inside and out and knew what they would want in a parcel, and who was bold enough not to be fazed by Ellen's bad temper.

It was Sadie.

Ellen felt warm inside, like she'd had a hot drink on a cold day. Sadie was furious with her for working at Wentworth and Ellen was just as angry at Sadie for sticking her beak in and interfering. They'd both said awful, sharp, horrible things, but it wasn't all broken between them. That knowledge made her feel comforted, and much less desperate, suddenly.

She picked up the woolly hat and put it on Annie's head, making her giggle.

'Oh that looks very smart,' she said. 'We'll have to sign you up for the football team.'

Annie screwed her nose up. 'No,' she said firmly. 'No football.'

Ellen laughed. 'Well, that told me,' she said. 'Right you, let's get some food.'

She bustled around the kitchen, making bread and jam, and boiling the kettle for tea, singing nursery rhymes to Annie as she did so. Then they both sat down to eat and Ellen flicked through the newspaper, thinking that her ma would give her a row for reading at the table. It was an old edition and she couldn't quite understand why it had been inside the parcel, until she came across a page that had a grainy photograph of footballers and saw, to her surprise, it was a match report from the football game against the other factory.

'Ellen McCallum is an asset to the team,' she read aloud. Annie ignored her, more interested in her bread and jam, but Ellen was glowing with pride anyway. 'An asset,' she murmured. Then she was hit with a wave of sadness. Now she wasn't at Wentworth, she wasn't playing football. It had been three weeks since she last went to training, she'd missed more than one match and she knew there was another happening in a couple of days. In fact, it was the first round of the Munitionettes' Cup – Hilda had entered them in a moment of what Ellen believed to be over-ambitious madness. But it didn't matter now anyway.

Feeling prickly again, though not as badly because it was hard to feel prickly with a belly full of bread and jam, Ellen cleared away the plates.

'Shall we go for a walk to the Clothing Exchange and do our sewing?' she asked Annie, even though the rain was still lashing down. 'But we need to wrap up.' It wasn't a long walk to the shop but they'd still be soaked if they went out without proper coats.

A ring at the doorbell made Ellen pause as she was pulling on Annie's boots. 'Who's that?'

'Biscuit,' said Annie.

'No,' Ellen said with genuine regret. 'It won't be Bridget.'

With Annie on her hip, she went down the stairs to open the main door and there, to her surprise, stood Hilda from Wentworth.

'Oh,' Ellen said.

'I met the postman,' Hilda said, handing Ellen a few letters.

'Right.'

'Nice hat.' Hilda reached out and wobbled the bobble on the top of Annie's woolly hat, which she'd been wearing since they opened the parcel. 'Wentworth colours.'

'Yes,' said Ellen uncertainly. 'It was a present.'

'Wentworth is what I'm here to talk about,' said Hilda. 'Can I come in?'

Ellen, still a little unsure about why Hilda was there, led the way back upstairs to the flat, hung up Hilda's wet coat, dropped the post on the table, and put the kettle on again.

'We need you back on the team,' Hilda said, sitting down at the table. 'We miss you.'

'I don't work at Wentworth anymore.'

'Aye, I know that,' Hilda said. She rolled her eyes. 'More's the pity.'

'I'm pregnant.'

'I know that, too.' Hilda eyed Ellen with a focus that made her slightly self-conscious, so she turned away to fill the teapot and escape her gaze. 'But you're not due yet, are you?'

'No,' Ellen admitted. 'Not for a few more months.'

'And you feel well?'

'Aye, better than I did at the start.'

'Well, then.'

'But how can I play for the factory if I don't work there?'

'They can keep you on the payroll.' Hilda looked pleased with herself. 'I asked Lucinda and she said they can keep you on and just not pay you because you're not working.'

'I'd rather they paid me not to work,' Ellen grumbled. But only mildly, because she was actually quite keen on this idea.

'That way we're not breaking any rules,' Hilda went on. 'In case anyone checks.'

Ellen blinked at her. 'There are rules?'

'Oh aye, for the Munitionettes' Cup there are. There's a rule book.'

'Goodness.'

'So, what do you say?'

'You really think I can play for Wentworth?'

'Lucinda's going to check with her father, but she says it won't be a problem.'

'You've got it all worked out, haven't you?'

Hilda nodded. 'You're an important part of the team, Ellen. Ginny's the star, and Rachel's great in defence, but you hold it all together. We need you.'

Ellen felt warm inside again. It was nice to be needed. But the thought of going back to Wentworth – not working, just playing – was too much. She shook her head.

'I can't,' she said. 'It's just not possible.'

'But . . .'

'It's too raw,' Ellen said. 'And too difficult.'

Hilda looked at her for a long moment, then she shrugged. 'All right,' she said. 'But if you change your mind, you know where I am.'

'I do.'

'I'll see myself out.'

Hilda took her coat from the hook and went out the door, while Ellen sat at the table, feeling wretched. Then she remembered the letters, so she reached out for them and noticed, to her delight, that there was one from James. Just when she needed to hear from him.

'A letter from Da,' she told Annie, who wasn't interested.

It was quite a fat envelope, which was unusual. James wasn't one for long letters. She slid her finger along and pulled out the paper. As she unfolded it lots of smaller pages fell out, scattering over the table.

'What on earth . . .?'

She smoothed out James's letter, smiling at his messy handwriting, and read:

'The boys are all so excited about your football. Every time I get a letter from you they want to know more. There's not much room to play on board the ship, and they're all missing it. So they've been discussing tactics for your team. It's become a bit of a game between us all. Hardy and Boyd think you need to make more use of Ginny, but I reckon – and Smith and Watson all agree – that you could do with another striker to give her support. If she's injured, and you're relying on her to score goals, you could be in trouble.'

Ellen stared at the letter, amused and more than a little moved that these men – hundreds or possibly thousands of miles away

– were so invested in a team of amateur women playing football.

She read on: 'The messages are from the lads. They've all got so many ideas, it was quicker for them to write them themselves than get me to do it. They want you to pass them on to Hilda.'

Ellen grinned at the idea of Hilda taking advice on tactics from a bunch of men she didn't know. But she put down James's letter and turned to the other notes. There were a lot of them, ten perhaps, maybe more. Scrawled on torn-out pages from notebooks, or on the back of cigarette boxes. There were little diagrams of how to play certain moves, with dots symbolising players taking free kicks or corners. There were suggestions, tips, anecdotes about games the men had played or watched – all sorts. Ellen was laughing out loud now, and picturing Hilda's face if she showed her this unsolicited advice.

She turned back to James's letter.

'One thing we all agree on is we're cheering you on in the Munitionettes' Cup. Could you send us a list of matches, and let us know when you'll be playing? Watson said there are write-ups in the papers about women's games. Are the Wentworth matches being written about? Can you send us cuttings? Anyway, play well, and bring that cup home to Clydebank for us.'

Ellen sat at the table, holding the letter tightly.

'Oh, bugger,' she breathed.

'Bugger,' said Annie cheerfully.

'Bring that cup home to Clydebank for us,' Ellen said out loud. She pushed her chair away from the table and jumped to her feet, dashing to the window. She lifted the sash and, wincing as the cold and rain hit her face, peered out to see if Hilda was still in sight.

And what luck! There she was, just a little way along the road, chatting to a woman in a rain bonnet.

'HILDA!' Ellen bellowed. 'HIIIIIILLLLDAAAAA!'

Hilda looked round and then up at the window where Ellen was waving madly. 'Stay there!' she shouted. 'I'm coming down!'

She dropped the window back into place, thinking that James would tut at her for being heavy-handed. 'Come on, Annie,' she said. 'We need to catch Hilda.'

Annie looked thrilled. 'Come on,' she said. 'Come on.'

They pulled on coats and with Annie in her arms, Ellen raced down the stairs, out of the main door and along the street to where Hilda was still standing with the lady in the rain bonnet, both of them looking rather confused.

'Hilda,' Ellen gasped. 'Hilda!'

'Are you all right?'

'Yes.' Ellen caught her breath, marvelling at how much healthier all the football training had made her. 'I'm fine. I'll do it.'

'You'll come back to football?'

'Yes,' Ellen said with a grin. 'I have to bring the Munitionettes' Cup home to Clydebank.'

'Well, wouldn't that be something,' said the woman in the rain bonnet.

'Wouldn't it just,' said Hilda. 'Are you sure?'

'Positive.' Ellen paused. 'But I have a couple of requests.'

'Go on.'

'I'll need someone to look after Annie,' Ellen said. 'Ma's away and Bridget's . . .' She paused. 'Otherwise engaged.'

'My daughter is fourteen and a sensible lass. She could help?'

'All right,' Ellen said. 'That sounds good.'

'What else?'

'I want to make the kits. All of them. That way we'll all look the same. It'll be smarter than if everyone makes their own.'

'Done.'

'Good.' Ellen took a deep breath. 'Then I'll do it.'

Hilda let out a very un-Hilda-like squeal. 'Thank goodness,' she said.

Ellen grinned. 'When is the next training session?'

'This evening.'

'So soon?'

'First cup match is a week on Wednesday.'
'Oh, heavens.'
'We'll be grand,' Hilda said. 'Better than grand now you're back.'
'I'll try not to let you down,' Ellen said.

Chapter Thirty

Sadie had an idea but she wasn't sure it would work, so she went to the cleverest person she knew – Noah – to see what he thought.

'Bessie's awake,' she told him, almost as soon as he'd walked through the door after work. 'She's talking, though not much, and her ma's not getting much food into her.'

Noah took off his hat and hung it on the peg.

'That is good news,' he said, giving Sadie a kiss. He looked at her. 'Feeling happier?'

Sadie shrugged. 'Yes and no.'

Noah bent down to unlace his shoes and put on his slippers. 'Yes?'

'I'm glad Bessie is showing signs of getting better.'

'But no?'

'I really miss Ellen. And the Clothing Exchange.'

Noah frowned.

'Then go and see her and say sorry and put things right.'

'I don't want to.'

'Then don't complain.'

Sadie rolled her eyes. She and Noah had discussed this over and over in the weeks since the dreadful row, and he always told her to apologise.

But just when Sadie thought he might be right, and she should go and see Ellen, swallow her pride and make things right, she remembered the awful things they'd said to one another, and she couldn't bring herself to do it.

Noah was settling himself down beside the fire with his newspaper.

'What's for tea?' he asked.

'Pie,' said Sadie vaguely.

'I'm not eating,' Rachel said, appearing in the doorway.

'Again?' Sadie was a bit put out, which she really had no right to be because she'd bought the pie, and it wasn't yet warming up. 'Where are you going?'

'Just for a walk with Lewis.'

Despite her irritation, Sadie smiled. It was nice to see Rachel happy. 'Him again, eh?'

Rachel's cheeks flushed. 'He's nice.'

'And handsome.'

'Aye,' said Rachel, looking at her feet. 'But . . .'

'But what?'

'I'm still not sure he likes me.'

'What did I say the other day? He obviously likes you. He looks at you with those big puppy-dog eyes.'

'We haven't, you know . . .' Rachel looked embarrassed. 'We've not kissed or anything.'

'Maybe that's because you've not been in the right place at the right time?'

'We have,' Rachel said, sounding glum. 'In fact, more than once I've thought he was going to kiss me, and then he's pulled away.'

Sadie frowned. 'Why would he do that?'

'I don't know,' Rachel wailed. 'I even thought he might be married.'

Sadie gave her sister a hug. 'Och away, he's not married. He's a child.'

Rachel tutted and Sadie grinned at her, wanting to make her feel better. 'Perhaps he's just shy.'

'Perhaps.' Rachel didn't sound very sure.

'You could kiss him,' Noah suggested from behind his newspaper.

'Noah!' Rachel sounded horrified.

'You could,' said Sadie. 'There's nothing to lose.'

'My pride?' said Rachel, beginning to laugh.

'Do you have any?' Sadie laughed too.

'I'm going now,' Rachel said, pretending to be annoyed. She put her coat on. 'I'll see you both in a wee while.'

'It's awful weather,' Sadie said, nodding at the window where the rain was pattering. 'Not good for walking.'

'I've got an umbrella.'

'Maybe you could shelter somewhere,' Sadie teased. 'Somewhere quiet. Under a tree on the green, maybe? And if you're cold, maybe Lewis will have to put his arms round you to warm you up . . .'

'I'm going,' Rachel said. 'I can't even hear you.'

She hurried out of the door.

'Good luck!' called Sadie. 'Hope he kisses you!'

'Can't hear you!' Rachel shouted back.

Sadie chuckled as she heard her sister's footsteps disappearing downstairs.

'So sweet,' she said to Noah. 'Shall I put the pie on?'

'Tell me about your big idea first?'

'Oh yes.' Sadie sat down on the other chair beside the fire, opposite Noah and leaned forward. 'It's about Bessie.'

'What about her?'

'I don't think being at home is going to help her get better.'

'Really?'

'No, it's too . . . just too much.'

Noah frowned. 'Lots of folk around?'

'She's got umpteen brothers and sisters, and she worries about them constantly. Though I have to say her ma seems to have really stepped up. But it's cramped and cold and I just think it's going to take forever for her to recover.' Sadie took a breath, picturing Bessie's tiny living space. 'If at all.'

'Do you want to bring her here?' Noah said, pushing his glasses up his nose. 'We could maybe find space for Rachel in here. He looked around the kitchen, which doubled as their living area, and Sadie and Noah's bedroom. 'Then she could have Rachel's room.'

'Och, no,' Sadie said, her heart swelling with love that he'd even suggested it. 'That would be almost as bad.'

'Then what?'

'A convalescent home.'

'Are there any?' Noah looked thoughtful. 'I thought they're all being used for soldiers?'

'Most of them are, but Lil said there's one down in Peebles. Her aunt was there for a while last year.'

'Expensive?'

'Not ridiculous but of course far outside anything Bessie's family could afford.'

'So how would that work?'

'I think Wentworth should pay.'

'Right.' Noah nodded and Sadie was pleased he'd not dismissed the idea out of hand. 'And do you think that's a possibility?'

'Well, that's the question.'

'So what are you going to do?'

'I'm going to speak to Lucinda. I'll go to the factory tomorrow – I know she helps her father out on a Tuesday.'

'What about the football?' Noah said.

'What about it?'

'Rachel says they've entered this Munitionettes' Cup, right?'

'Yes, I think so.'

'And the games are proving popular?'

'Rachel says they're getting bigger crowds each time.'

'So perhaps you could do a collection, or charge folk to get in to watch?' Noah said. 'I've read about teams doing that and raising a lot of money for soldiers and sailors.'

'Yes, I've heard about that.'

'But there's nothing to say the donations have to be for soldiers.'

'So what would we use them for?'

'Munitionettes,' said Noah, sounding slightly triumphant.

Sadie was delighted. 'Do you think we could?'

'I don't see why not,' Noah said. 'It's two sides of the same coin, isn't it? They're doing vital war work, too, and they need help.'

'We could use the football matches to raise money for women like Bessie. And Rita, and the others.'

'A benevolent fund,' Noah said. 'Exactly.'

Sadie was thinking.

'We could help Bessie go to the convalescent home. Maybe pay for medicine, if anyone needs it. Or for a doctor's visit?'

'Yes,' said Noah, nodding.

'And, depending on how much we raise, we could use some of it to fund care packages for the pregnant women who have lost their jobs, or even just give them some money.' She felt a wee bit of the sadness that had enveloped her for weeks start to lift, just a little, like a chink of light in the dark. 'We could help to make up for them being out of work.'

'Write this all down,' Noah said. 'Before you forget. There's a notebook on the table.'

Sadie put her hands on her husband's knees and kissed him. 'Noah Spark, I think you are brilliant.'

'Why, thank you,' he said with a grin. 'You'll have to run it past Lucinda though, before you get too excited.'

'I will,' Sadie said. 'I'll speak to her tomorrow.'

Looking pleased with himself, Noah lifted his newspaper again.

'Rachel says Ellen's back playing football, you know?'

'Is she?' Sadie tried to sound casual.

'Aye, apparently.' He turned the page. 'Maybe you could wander past the pitch? See if she's there? Have a chat?'

'Say sorry, you mean?'

'If that's what it takes to put a smile on your face again, then yes, I mean say sorry,' said Noah.

Sadie thought about Ellen and the possibility of raising money to help munitionettes, and for the first time since their argument, she thought that perhaps she might manage an apology.

'Maybe I will,' she said.

The next day, Sadie set off to the factory feeling full of beans. She'd written a whole plan for the munitionettes' benevolent fund, with ideas of how they could use the money – Bessie's convalescence being top of the list, of course – and how they could charge folk for entry at the football matches.

Rachel had come home while she and Noah were bent over their notes, looking half exhilarated, half despairing.

'Nothing?' Sadie had said.

'Not even a kiss on the cheek.'

Sadie had given her a hug.

'How do you feel?'

'Tortured,' said Rachel dramatically. 'Like I never want to see him again, but also as if I can't live without him.'

'You know what that is?'

'What?'

'First love.'

Rachel screwed her nose up. 'Shut up.'

'I'm just saying what I see.' Sadie had chuckled, but Rachel had looked so distraught she'd realised it was time to stop teasing and leave her alone. And so in order to distract her sister, she'd recruited her to come up with some ideas too, and Rachel had been a wee bit grumpy at first, but then she'd actually been very helpful and written out a list of all the matches that were coming up, and how she thought they could arrange paying for entry.

Now, with those notes in her bag, Sadie was off to see Lucinda.

She thought if she could get her on board then Lucinda could pass the idea on to her father. But deep down, Sadie thought Hamilton Blyth seemed to be a good man. She thought he'd be pleased to help the munitionettes. Or, at the very least, to be seen to be helping them.

She spoke to the man at the factory gate, who let her through, and then headed towards the clerical offices.

Of course, she had no idea where Lucinda was – or even if she was there – but she knew a woman who would. Dilys.

She stuck her head round the office door, pleased to see Dilys there, putting papers into a cabinet.

'Hiya,' Sadie said.

Dilys grinned. 'He's not here.'

'I don't want Hamilton Blyth,' Sadie said, rolling her eyes. 'I wondered if you've seen Lucinda today?'

'Aye, she's here,' Dilys said.

'Where?'

'She's doing something with her brother,' Dilys said. 'I think they're in accounts. Down the corridor, second on the left.'

'Righto,' said Sadie. 'Thanks, Dil.'

She headed off down the corridor, and found accounts. It was a large office, with several suited men sitting at desks. In the corner was Lucinda, perched on the edge of one of the desks talking animatedly to the man who sat there.

'Lucinda?' Sadie said. 'Sorry to interrupt.'

Lucinda looked up. 'Hello,' she said, sounding pleased to see her. 'What's brought you here?'

'I wanted to have a chat with you, if you've time? About an idea I've had.'

'Of course.' Lucinda slid off the table and turned to the man she'd been talking to. 'I'll see you later?'

'I'll be here,' he said. Lucinda stepped aside, and for the first time, Sadie saw the man at the desk. Their eyes met and he looked horrified. She suspected she looked the same.

'Oh Sadie, how rude of me,' Lucinda said. 'This is my brother, Lewis. Lewis, this is Sadie Spark.'

Sadie stared at him in disgust. 'We've met,' she said.

Chapter Thirty-One

Rachel was a little grumpy. She was tired and sweaty after her shift and a very vigorous training session. And she'd hoped to see Lewis but there had been no sign of him, and then Hilda had been annoyed with her for being distracted and all in all it had been quite a disappointing, exhausting day.

So it was with a scowl on her face that she greeted Sadie, who'd unexpectedly been waiting for her as she left the factory.

'What do you want?' she asked ungraciously.

'Well, isn't that nice?' Sadie said. 'I just came to walk home with my wee sister.'

'Really?' Rachel eyed her suspiciously. 'You don't usually do things like that.'

'Do you want company on the way home or not?' Sadie said.

'Fine.'

Rachel began walking in the direction of home, but Sadie tugged her arm.

'I just need to pop into McKinley's,' she said.

'Oh, Sadie, I'm tired.'

'Please.'

'Why?'

Sadie stopped walking. 'Because,' she said, making a face, 'I've got something to tell you and I don't think you'll like it, and I thought Bridget and Ida might give me moral support.'

Rachel stared at her, worry overtaking her tiredness. 'What is it? Are you ill? Is it Noah? What's happened?'

'No,' Sadie said. 'Nothing like that.'

'Then what?' Rachel demanded. 'Come on, Sadie. You can't just announce you've something to tell me then not tell me.'

Sadie sighed. 'Fine. But let's walk while I talk.'

Rachel, annoyed at her sister, marched off. 'Speak,' she said over her shoulder, watching Sadie scuttling after her. 'Well?'

'I saw Lewis today,' Sadie began, slightly out of breath because Rachel had longer legs than she did.

Rachel's heart did the little jump it always did when Lewis's name was mentioned. 'What about him?'

Sadie rubbed her nose. 'He was at the factory.'

'Right.' Rachel had no idea where this was going.

In a slightly exasperated way, Sadie groaned. 'Let me start again,' she said. 'I went to the factory to see Lucinda, about my idea for the benevolent fund.'

'What did she say?' asked Rachel, a little sulkily.

'That doesn't matter for now,' said Sadie. 'What matters is that I found Dilys and she said Lucinda was in her brother's office.'

'And?' Rachel's patience had totally deserted her now.

'And I found her with Lewis.'

They waited for a cart to pass then crossed the road.

'So?' said Rachel.

Sadie sighed again. 'So, Lucinda's brother is Lewis.'

Rachel laughed. 'No he isn't,' she said. 'Lewis has two sisters and a brother.'

'A sister who's pregnant?' said Sadie. 'And a brother who's serving?'

'Yessss,' Rachel said slowly. 'But sure everyone has a brother who's serving. We do.'

'Aye we do,' Sadie agreed. 'But not everyone has a pregnant sister, and another sister who's just married, too.'

'But . . .' Rachel trailed off, thinking about the times she'd asked about Lewis's family and he'd changed the subject.

'What's Lewis's surname?' Sadie asked.

Hanging her head, Rachel said: 'I don't know.'

Sadie put her arm through Rachel's and squeezed her gently. 'I'm not making it up, doll,' she said. 'He's Hamilton Blyth's son. His father is in charge of Wentworth. I don't know why he's not told you the truth, but I'm worried he's using you in some way.'

Rachel shook her head. 'This makes no sense, Sadie,' she said. 'None at all.'

They'd reached McKinley's now. Sadie paused with her hand on the door. 'I know,' she said. 'But it's true. He is Lewis Blyth. His sister is Lucinda, and his father is Hamilton Blyth. He's been lying this whole time.'

'He's not been lying,' Rachel said.

'Well he's certainly not been truthful.'

Rachel felt dizzy suddenly. She pushed past Sadie and shoved the door to the shop open. 'Just give me a minute, Sadie,' she snapped. 'Let me think.'

Inside the shop, Ida and Bridget were behind the counter, dropping little screws into boxes. They both looked up as Rachel entered.

'Are you all right?' Bridget said. 'You look a bit odd.'

'I need to sit down,' Rachel said. She couldn't catch her breath and it was scaring her, reminding her of the nights when she was wee when she had struggled for air. 'I need to sit down.'

Bridget came round the counter and guided Rachel to a chair. Rachel could hear her pulse pounding in her ears, faster and faster.

'I can't . . . I can't breathe,' she gasped, clutching Bridget's hand. 'I can't . . .'

Then suddenly Sadie was there in front of her. She crouched down and put her hands on Rachel's knees.

'You're panicking,' she said. 'Look right at me. That's it.'

With an effort, Rachel lifted her gaze to her big sister's.

'That's right,' Sadie said. 'Now, you can breathe, don't worry. You just got a wee bit of a fright. Follow me, come on. Breathe in, and out . . . That's it, well done.'

Feeling relieved that Sadie had taken charge, Rachel did as she told her, mimicking her sister's breaths with her own. And gradually, her heart rate slowed down and her head stopped spinning.

'Better?' asked Sadie. Rachel nodded.

'Sorry.'

'I'm sorry,' Sadie said. 'I shouldn't have just blurted it out like that.'

Ida handed Rachel a mug. 'Sweet tea,' she said. 'It's good for shock.'

Bridget was looking worried.

'What is it?' she said. 'What's the shock?'

Rachel sipped the tea, letting Sadie fill them in.

'I went to the factory today,' Sadie began. 'And I saw Lewis. The chap Rachel's sweet on.'

'Oh, aye?' said Bridget. 'And?'

'And as it turns out, he's Lucinda's brother.'

Bridget and Ida both looked startled.

'Our Lucinda?' Ida said.

'Yes.' Sadie nodded.

'But that means he's Hamilton Blyth's son.' Bridget looked bewildered. 'And he never mentioned it before now?'

'Not once,' Rachel said, feeling more like herself.

'But why wouldn't he tell you?' Ida asked.

'Because it's wrong, isn't it?' said Sadie. 'He's the boss. He's management. He shouldn't be having a romance with a munitionette.'

Rachel felt a little annoyed at that. 'Why not?'

'Well, it's all squint. You're not . . .'

'Not what?'

'Not equal.'

Rachel glared at her sister. 'I thought you believed we were all equal.'

'Well, yes, ideally,' Sadie said. 'But that's just not how it is. Not really. I'm worried he has an ulterior motive for him courting you. He's management.'

'So, he's better than me?'

'No. Not better.' Sadie looked at the ceiling. 'It's just . . . well, you hear stories, don't you? About maids and their masters.'

'Oh, for the love of God,' said Rachel. 'That's not it at all.'

'Well, you never know,' Sadie said darkly.

'I do know.' Rachel put her mug on the counter. 'I know Lewis. He's not using me for some sort of unpleasant plan and he's certainly not taking advantage of me.'

'Right,' said Sadie. 'But it's just . . .'

'That's why he didn't kiss me,' Rachel said, suddenly realising. 'Because he didn't want to put me in a difficult situation.' She felt a rush of happiness. 'It wasn't because he didn't like me.'

'That is commendable,' said Sadie. 'But even so . . .'

Rachel rolled her eyes.

'You're not the same,' Sadie finished, a little weakly. 'You come from very different places.'

'I am not pleased that Lewis felt he couldn't tell me the truth,' Rachel said. 'But surely if we want to be together, we can?'

'I'm not sure it's that easy,' said Sadie.

'Of course it is.' Rachel smiled at Bridget and Ida. 'Isn't it?'

'Oh Rachel,' Bridget said. 'I don't know.'

'You two love each other,' Rachel said. She felt a little bit daring saying it out loud. 'You love each other, and you are together.'

Bridget and Ida shared a look. Then they both pulled up chairs and sat down. Sadie followed, more reluctantly.

Bridget took a deep breath and Ida gave her an encouraging nod, which Rachel noticed and liked.

'We do love each other,' said Bridget. 'We do. And we are very fortunate that we can live together quietly . . .'

'See!' said Rachel. 'Love is all that matters.'

'It's not been easy,' Ida said. 'We've never spoken of it before. Heavens, we've never even shared it with you, and we're all in each other's pockets all the time.'

'But . . .' Rachel began. Bridget silenced her with a look.

'It's important this goes no further,' she said firmly. 'No further. Malcolm and I are still married and just see how Ellen reacted when she found out.'

'I'd lose my job,' Ida said. 'I love my job.'

Rachel nodded. Then she allowed herself a small smile. 'I could put in a word with Lewis for you.'

'Rachel,' Sadie said, disapprovingly. But Bridget laughed. And then Ida laughed too.

'Listen, doll,' she said. 'Your sister is right to be cautious. Lewis is nice to look at it, and he seems charming – and Lucinda's obviously a good person – but there's no getting away from the fact that he's not been telling you everything.'

'No,' said Rachel. 'He's not.'

'But,' Ida went on, 'if you really like him, then talk to him. Don't just walk away.'

'Oh, Ida . . .' Sadie began. 'I'm not sure that's a good idea.'

Bridget put her hand on Sadie's arm. 'I know you're protective of Rachel,' she said. 'And that's understandable, isn't it? After all her illnesses when she was wee. But sometimes you have to let the weans make their own mistakes.'

'I'm not a wean and it's not a mistake,' said Rachel, bristling.

'Maybe not,' said Bridget with a shrug. 'But you won't know unless you try.'

Sadie looked bullish for a second, but then she sighed. 'You're right,' she said to Bridget. 'Talk to him, Rachel. But don't let that pretty face of his turn your head.'

'I won't,' Rachel said, with the very thought of Lewis's face making her cheeks burn once more. 'I am quite annoyed about him not being honest.'

'Aye, well, you hang on to that feeling,' Sadie said. 'Don't be too soft on him.'

Bridget cupped Rachel's face in her hands. 'You were right,' she said. 'What you said before.'

'What did I say?'

'Love is all that matters.'

'Love and common sense,' Ida added.

'And a clear head,' Sadie put in.

'Well, that doesn't sound nearly so romantic,' Rachel said, but she was smiling. Perhaps this would all be all right after all.

'It's getting late,' Ida said. 'Time for you to go home. Come on, Bridget, let's shut up shop.'

'Righto,' said Bridget, getting to her feet.

They all headed to the door of McKinley's and out into the chilly evening air.

'Thank you for being so kind,' Rachel said.

Ida winked at her. 'Any time, doll.'

'Come on, then,' Sadie said, looping her arm through Rachel's. 'Let's get home.'

'Bye, Bridget,' Rachel said. But Bridget didn't reply. She'd gone very still next to them. Rachel followed her gaze to where Rab, the messenger boy from the post office, was cycling down the street. He was looking straight at Bridget, but as she put her hand to her mouth and stepped forward, he lowered his gaze and cycled on by, faster than before.

'It's James,' Bridget said.

'Oh, doll, you don't know that.' Ida went to Bridget's side. 'You can't know that.'

'You saw the way he looked at me,' Bridget said. 'Like he was trying to tell me something.'

Rachel felt an awful, thumping heaviness in the pit of her stomach and she knew, she absolutely knew without a shadow of a doubt, that Bridget was right.

'We have to go,' Sadie said, tugging at her arm. 'Bridget, Ida?

Come on. We have to go to be with Ellen. Right now.'

In a swift movement, Ida shut the shop door and pulled down the grill.

'We're right behind you,' she said.

Chapter Thirty-Two

Ellen was singing silly songs to Annie and making her laugh. Playing football had raised her spirits, and Hilda's daughter, Fiona, was very sweet with the weans and had looked after Annie so well. And yesterday, there had been another parcel on the doorstep, so she didn't have that gnawing hunger in her belly, or the worries that she wasn't giving the baby inside her what he needed.

And yes, she was tired, and a little mud-splattered, but she was planning to get Annie to bed, then to have a good wash and an early night herself.

So when there was a knock on the door, she picked Annie up and danced over to open it.

'Who's at the door,' she said to her daughter, rubbing her nose on her soft cheek. 'Is it Mrs Adams from up the stairs? Have her boys been playing up again? Or is it another parcel?'

She opened the door and there, on the doorstep was Rab from the post office. Without any warning, Ellen's legs buckled and she leaned against the doorframe for support.

'Mama,' Annie said, wriggling. 'Too tight.'

Ellen realised she was gripping Annie's little body and she let her get down to run off and play.

'Rab,' she managed to say.

He took off his cap respectfully, and held out an envelope.

'Mrs McCallum.'

It was as though the whole world had shrunk to a tiny pinprick. Ellen couldn't see the walls, or the door, or the tiles on the floor anymore. All she could see was the envelope and her shaking hand reaching for it.

Her fingers touched the rough paper and she took the telegram, clutching it to her chest.

'No reply,' she whispered.

Rab nodded once. Then he turned and went down the stairs. Ellen watched him go, feeling like she was falling, tumbling down into unknown depths.

She felt cold underneath her, and understood she was somehow sitting on the floor, half in the flat, half in the hallway. But she couldn't stand up, couldn't get her legs to work. She could hear Annie laughing behind her, but she couldn't go to her. All she could think about was the telegram she still held to her heart.

And then suddenly, she was surrounded, and someone was helping her to her feet, and she had arms around her, and she realised Bridget was there, her big sister. And Sadie, her best friend. And Ida and Rachel. And she let them pick her up off the floor, and help her inside, and shut the door on the world, and sit her down on a chair. And Bridget put her arms round her and Ellen clung to her. Sadie took the telegram from Ellen's stiff fingers. Rachel took Annie and gave her some milk, and Ida boiled the kettle for tea. Ellen watched this all happening from the safety of her big sister's arms and felt that her world was ending, and how odd it was that things carried on.

When the tea was made and Annie was settled, the women sat around the table, Ellen shivery and pale with shock.

'Shall I open it?' Sadie asked. She put her fingertips on the telegram, where it still sat on the table.

Ellen shrugged, wearily. She didn't want to read the words, but she knew someone should.

Sadie tore the envelope open and with pinched lips, scanned

the words. Ellen watched her expression change from sadness to confusion, and her heart lurched.

'What?' she said. 'What?'

She snatched the telegram from Sadie.

Deeply regret to inform you Able Seaman James McCallum missing at sea, presumed drowned. Council of the Royal Navy sends their sympathy.

'Missing,' she said in a small voice.

'Well, yes,' said Sadie. 'But, Ellen . . .'

'If it was a mine,' Ida said, leaning over and putting her hand on Ellen's arm. 'If it was a mine, then . . .' She swallowed. 'And the water is cold . . .'

Until that moment, Ellen hadn't cried. She'd been frozen, as though this was happening to someone else, and she was just watching.

But now, with the mention of a mine, and the icy waters, and seeing her James's name written down in black and white, so harsh and matter-of-fact, the tears came. She buried her face in her hands and sobbed so hard she thought her heart had broken.

Bridget and the others sat there, quietly, letting her cry. They handed over hankies, and Bridget stroked Ellen's hair, and Sadie held her hand, and they didn't talk. They just let her sob.

When eventually she caught her breath and the tears began to slow, it was dark outside, and the tea in the pot was stone cold. Ellen felt the teapot with the palm of her hand and then she looked at the women sitting around her table and said: 'James hates being cold.'

Sadie squeezed her fingers. 'I know.'

'I don't know what to do.' Ellen took a breath. 'I don't know how to feel. I thought he was dead.' The word hung heavily in the air. 'But he's missing . . .'

'Chances are,' Ida began, then she stopped, and Ellen was glad.

'I write to him,' she said. 'I write most days.'

'Keep going,' Bridget urged. 'You absolutely must keep writing to him.'

Ellen nodded.

'Tell him about football,' Rachel said. 'You told me he liked that.'

'He does.' Ellen managed to smile. 'He and the others have sent me lots of ideas about where we're going wrong.'

Rachel winced dramatically. 'Did you tell Hilda?'

'Not yet.'

'Make sure I'm there when you do, I'd like to see her face.' She reached across the table and gave Ellen's arm a squeeze. 'Write about all the training Hilda's making us do, and the Munitionettes' Cup.'

Ellen nodded. 'Yes, I will.'

A knock on the flat door made them all jump. Ellen had almost forgotten there was a world outside.

'I'll go,' Sadie said. She got up from the table and went to answer the door. And there, in her police uniform, was Christina.

She didn't wait to be asked in, she simply swept past Sadie and headed for the centre of the room.

Sadie, one step behind her, caught her arm. 'Christina,' she said in a low voice. 'Now's not the time.'

'I won't stay long,' Christina said. 'I've actually . . .' She paused and then her words all came out in a hurry. 'I've actually come to apologise. I was interfering and sticking my nose in where it wasn't . . .'

She trailed off as she looked at Ellen's tear-stained face, the open telegram on the kitchen table and the pile of soggy handkerchiefs.

'Good heavens,' she said, putting her hand to her mouth. 'Ellen, I'm so sorry.'

Ellen pinched her lips together, unable to speak, and simply nodded.

But Christina wasn't finished.

‘This is sad news,’ she said. ‘But Ellen, I’m sure you will take comfort in knowing that your Jim . . .’

‘James,’ Bridget said. ‘His name is James.’

‘James,’ said Christina. She put her hand to her heart. ‘James has died a glorious death. As they say, it is sweet and fitting to die for one’s country.’

Ellen looked at Christina, standing there in her uniform, her fingers splayed on her chest, and felt nothing but hatred towards her.

She pushed her chair back and stood up.

‘James is not dead,’ she said, quite calmly but with ice in her voice. ‘And there is nothing sweet or glorious about this awful war.’

Around her, the other women stood up too.

‘I think you should leave,’ Sadie said.

‘I came to apologise,’ Christina said, affronted.

‘Aye,’ Ida said, taking a step towards her. ‘You apologised, and now you should leave.’

‘But . . .’ Christina began.

Ellen felt the blood pounding in her head. James was missing and this woman would not leave her alone. She put her hands up in front of her, palms facing forward.

‘Stop,’ she said to Christina. ‘Stop it.’

‘It’s important to remember the sacrifice made by the fallen and honour them as they deserve,’ Christina said. ‘Especially at a time when there are men refusing to fight.’

‘Shut. Up,’ said Ellen.

And then with as much force as she could muster, she shoved Christina hard in the chest. ‘Stop it,’ she said again.

Christina stumbled backwards and fell against the wall in a very ungainly fashion. With her balance off, she slid down to the floor, unhurt but humiliated. Her skirt got caught on the heel of her boot so when she tried to get up again, she dropped back on to her behind and had to spend a few seconds trying to get herself unhooked.

When eventually she got to her feet, her cheeks were red and her eyes dark with anger.

'I came to apologise,' she said again.

'Goodbye, Christina,' Ellen said firmly. She marched to the door and opened it. 'Don't let us keep you.'

Christina lifted her chin.

'I'm very sorry about your husband,' she said. She walked past Ellen and out into the hall. Ellen watched her go from the doorway.

'He's not dead,' she called as Christina stamped her way down the stairs. 'He's not dead.'

She slammed the door shut, making the flat shake. Bridget was standing by the window, looking out into the street as Christina left.

'She's furious, Ellen,' she said. 'She's marching along the road like she's on a mission. You really shouldn't have pushed her like that.'

'No,' Sadie said. 'But I'm glad you did.'

'Me too,' Ida added.

Ellen went to the window and saw Christina stamping round the corner.

'Oh, God,' she said. 'What have I done?'

'It'll be fine,' Sadie said, soothingly. 'Don't fret.'

'But what if she tells Hilda?' Ellen said, feeling wretched. 'What if she says I can't play football anymore?' She felt cold fear dripping down her spine. 'What if she goes to the police? The actual police?' She felt panic rising up in her. 'What if I go to jail?'

'Well,' said Rachel. The corners of her mouth lifted, just a tiny bit. 'It's a shame none of us saw it happen, isn't it? We're all right here, and not one of us saw anything.'

'Not a thing,' agreed Bridget, shaking her head. 'How odd. Sadie? Did you see anything?'

Sadie shrugged. 'No. How about you, Ida?'

Ida was wearing her own clothes – not her police uniform – but all the same she drew herself up taller and saluted. 'I am myself a policewoman, so of course I would notice a crime being committed.' She looked straight at Ellen, her eyes wide and innocent. 'And I saw nothing at all.'

Ellen looked at the women all standing in her kitchen.

'Thank you,' she said. 'I don't know what I'd do without you.'

Chapter Thirty-Three

Clydebank

7 June 1916

My dear James,

I wait for news and all the time, I keep thinking that surely I would know if you were dead. I would have felt it somewhere deep inside. Something would have shifted and the world would have been changed. But I don't feel that. Ida says if your ship was hit by a mine, then there is no chance. But I would have felt it. I know. And so I wait for news.

Rachel says I should tell you about football. She's here with me now. So are Bridget and Ida, and Sadie, of course. They're all here.

We hadn't spoken for weeks. Not properly. I'd seen Rachel at football of course, and I was fairly sure that Sadie was the one sending Annie and me parcels of food and milk. But Bridget, well. I'd not even set eyes on her. I'd been walking to Wentworth the long way round for football so I didn't catch a glimpse of her. And when I'd been at the Clothing Exchange, I scurried in and out the back door. I just felt so awfully embarrassed about it all. Like I might somehow wither up and crumble if our eyes met. Her and Ida! I couldn't understand it at all.

But now I do. Now I've felt the horror that would be losing you, somehow I see that you have to take happiness wherever you find it.

Last night, after I got the telegram and everyone arrived, we had a visit from Christina. I won't give you the details. All I will say is that she was awful, as usual, and I didn't react well. But the others, they all gave me strength. I don't know what I'd have done if I had been alone. So, later, as we were all getting ready for bed, I sat with Bridget for a minute and I said sorry for treating her so badly. And, of course she was calm and practical. She said that she and Ida love one another but they do so quietly and without attracting attention and she rather firmly said that was the way it had to stay. I promised her I'd never breathe a word.

So yes, now they're all here with me. They refused to go home and leave me alone with Annie.

Somehow they've all managed to find somewhere to sleep. Sadie's in the chair by the fire. Bridget is curled up with Annie, and Ida and Rachel are on our bed. I was there too, but I couldn't sleep. So now I'm sitting at the kitchen table drinking tea and watching the sky lighten outside.

What should I tell you about football? I got all your advice, and all the notes from the lads. James, I laughed so hard when I opened the paper and they all fell out. I've not given the advice to Hilda, yet. I'm not sure how she'll take it! But let me tell you, she really doesn't need any help. She has taken us from a ragtag group of beginners to something that really works. Ginny is our star, of course, but Rachel is wonderful. I told her what you said about needing another goal scorer and she agreed, so we thought we'd mention that to Hilda first. And I've been making the kits so we'll all look the same. Until now we've all made our own. And while everyone's been enthusiastic, well. Let's just say that as far as sewing goes, some of those lassies are lucky they're good at football.

One thing I have told Hilda is that we need to bring the Munitionettes' Cup home and it feels even more important now.

If we do it, James. If we bring the Munitionettes' Cup to Clydebank. Will you come home to see it?

Your ever hopeful, loving wife,

Ellen

X

Chapter Thirty-Four

Noah's face was white as he came through the door.

'Look,' he said, waving the newspaper at Rachel and Sadie. 'Look at this.'

Rachel couldn't see anything because he wasn't keeping still. 'What is it?'

Sadie got up from the table, where they'd been sitting playing cards, and took the paper from her husband. Rachel watched impatiently as her sister scanned the front page.

'Sadie,' she prompted. 'What?'

Sadie looked up. 'This must be the ship James was on – HMS *Hampshire*. The dates tally.'

'What does it say?' Rachel felt a little sick. 'Does it say there were any survivors?'

Slowly, Sadie shook her head. Rachel put her hand to her mouth. 'Read it,' she said, wanting to know, but also not wanting to know.

'It was Lord Kitchener,' Noah said. 'Lord Kitchener was on board.'

'From the posters?' Rachel was astonished. 'Why was he on board?'

'The crew were in good spirits,' Sadie read aloud. 'They had been informed they were sailing Lord Kitchener and his staff to an unknown Russian port.'

'Russia?' Rachel's head was spinning. 'Where was the ship when it sank?'

'Orkney.'

'Orkney? But that's no distance away.'

'Far enough,' Noah said.

'Less than three hours into the voyage, the ship is thought to have hit a mine. A massive explosion tore the vessel from stern to stern and the ship sank in fifteen minutes,' Sadie continued reading.

'Oh, lord,' Rachel stood up, then sat down again. She wasn't sure what to do.

'Wait,' Sadie said. 'More than seven hundred men are believed to have perished. Though the search for survivors is continuing.'

'So there could be survivors?' Rachel jumped on the tiny piece of good news.

Noah sat down heavily in one of the chairs next to the fire. 'I suppose so, if they're looking, but it mentions the wind blew a rescue vessel off course, and there's no denying how cold the water would be.'

'Should we tell Ellen?' Rachel looked to her sister for guidance, as always. 'Should we tell her about this?'

'I'm not sure . . .' Sadie began.

'She's not going to be able to avoid it.' Noah looked wretched. 'The news about Kitchener is everywhere. She'll hear every detail.'

'This is awful,' Sadie said. 'Awful.'

'We're playing football this afternoon.'

'On a Sunday?'

'We've got another round of the cup on Wednesday, remember? We're going to raise money for your benevolent fund.'

Sadie sighed. 'Lord, I'd forgotten. Maybe I should come with you. Make sure everything's in place. And then I can speak to Ellen, too.'

'All right.' Rachel checked the time on the clock on the

mantelpiece. 'But we need to go soon. I just need to get changed.'
'Let's go.'

Rachel got ready for practice and together, she and Sadie walked towards Wentworth. Rachel noticed that every newspaper board had the news about Kitchener and the ship going down. Noah was right – there was no way Ellen could avoid this. And the reports were so detailed about the explosion and the aftermath, it made Rachel shudder.

When they arrived at the football pitch, Ellen was there.

'Did you read the newspaper?' she said, dashing over to them. 'Did you read it?'

'I'm so sorry,' Sadie said.

'NO,' Ellen said firmly. 'No, don't be sorry. Because it said they are looking for survivors.'

'Oh Ellen, I'm not sure . . .'

'It said they are looking,' she said again. 'Why would they look if they thought it was hopeless?'

Rachel looked at Sadie who gave a tiny shrug, and then at Ellen.

'We need to get onto the pitch,' Rachel said. 'Hilda's got her serious face on.'

Ellen grimaced. 'I showed her all the notes from James and his friends.'

'You did?' Rachel was horrified.

'Aye,' Ellen laughed. 'And she thought some of it was nonsense, but she liked a few of the ideas.'

'Goodness.'

'And Lucinda said she is going to tell her father, because knowing we've been given advice from the men of the HMS *Hampshire* will encourage more folk to come and watch on Wednesday and it'll mean even more money raised.'

'That would be marvellous,' Sadie said. 'A fitting tribute.'

Ellen looked at her. 'Aye,' she said. 'To them that have died.'

Rachel felt her stomach twist with worry. Ellen didn't seem to be acknowledging that James could be among them. Was more than likely to be among them. She tugged her sleeve. 'Come on.'

'Righto, ladies,' Hilda boomed as they jogged across the grass. 'I've been doing some tinkering.'

'Oh Hilda, there's a toilet block just beside the changing rooms,' said Ginny with a cheeky smile. 'No need to do it on the pitch.'

The women all laughed and Hilda gave Ginny a mock stern look, before she chuckled too.

'We're doing well, but we could do better,' she said. 'Ginny, you're carrying all the responsibility for scoring goals, and it's not the best use of our talents. So I want Hetty to come alongside you. You're good together – you work well.'

She carried on outlining the changes she'd made, which all made total sense to Rachel, but didn't involve her directly. She felt her mind drift off, as Hilda talked. She'd not seen Lewis since she found out who he was. She desperately wanted to see him so she could ask him exactly what he was playing at, lying to her all this time. But she also thought her heart might break if he turned out to have been lying about other things too. Like the lovely things he said to her, and the way he looked at her.

'Rachel?' said Hilda, making her jump. 'You're quick and clever at reading the game. I want to see if you could do more if you come forward a little. Let Nell hang back to support Joan.'

Nell and Joan, who were standing beside Hilda, both nodded.

Rachel felt a little shiver of pleasure. 'Right,' she said. 'I can do that.'

'Let's go, ladies,' Hilda said, clapping her hands. 'Let's go.'

As always, Hilda worked them hard, so Rachel's legs were wobbling and her face was bright red when they finished. She flopped onto the grass to catch her breath, exhilarated from all the running about and the way Hilda's changes had really improved their game. Across the other side of the pitch, where Hamilton had built a wooden stand for spectators, she could see Sadie and Lucinda deep in conversation, their heads – Sadie so dark and Lucinda blond – bent over some notes.

'Lucinda's going to install a booth where folk can buy tickets.'

Rachel jumped in surprise and delight and alarm all at once as Lewis sat down next to her. She sat up, resting her elbows on her knees and fixed him with a stern glare.

'Oh,' she said. 'Hello, Lewis Blyth.'

Lewis looked shocked and then dismayed.

'I meant to tell you.'

'But you didn't.'

'No.'

'Why not?'

'Because I thought you'd think I was up to no good.'

'Are you?' Rachel stared at him. 'Are you up to no good?'

'Of course not.' Lewis sounded a bit cross. 'How could you think that?'

She shrugged. 'It's not unreasonable. You've been lying to me for ages.'

'Not lying,' Lewis said. 'Just not being completely honest.'

'Is there a difference?'

He opened his mouth and then shut it again.

'Your da is the manager of Wentworth,' Rachel said. 'My sister was the leader of the striking workers. And now she's campaigning to make the factory safer.'

'They're not enemies,' Lewis protested. 'My father wants the factory to be safe, too.'

'No,' Rachel said. 'Not enemies, but different. We are different.'

'I really like you.'

'I like you too,' she said. 'And really, love is all that matters. Ellen and James are Catholic and Protestant.'

The look of hope on Lewis's face almost broke her heart.

'But,' she added. 'I don't know if I can trust you. I don't know if you're the person I thought you were.'

'What can I do to prove it to you?'

Rachel shook her head. 'I don't know,' she said. 'I don't know if you can.'

Lewis put his hand on her shoulder. 'Let me try.'

'I have to go,' Rachel said. 'We're meeting at Ellen's to sew football kits for the match.'

Lewis looked eager. 'How about if I make a donation?' he said. 'I could give some money to the benevolent fund. Would that show you that you can trust me?'

Rachel looked at him. 'No,' she said bluntly. She raised an eyebrow. 'In fact, it just reminds me of the differences between you and me.'

Lewis groaned. 'You're right. Of course you're right.'

'I am,' Rachel said. She began to walk away, then paused and looked back. 'But you should make a donation anyway.'

Chapter Thirty-Five

Ellen had never been one for reading the newspaper. Not really. James hadn't either. Ellen thought they had so much to do with work and Annie and whatnot that they were too busy to be worrying about what everyone else was doing.

But not now. In the couple of days since she'd got the telegram and seen the reports of poor Lord Kitchener dying when the ship sank, it was as though she couldn't read enough about the tragedy. Every day she bought two or even three papers and carefully read every line, checking for any news of survivors.

There were rumours some seamen had made it onto rafts, but no one knew where they'd gone. When Ellen thought about James clinging on to a tiny vessel as it scaled the waves near Orkney it made her feel a bit seasick herself. But that was far better than thinking about him never coming home.

And now it was the day of the match and they were ready, pretty much, on the pitch, but every surface of the Clothing Exchange was covered in blue jerseys and socks, and she, Sadie, Rachel and Bridget were busy finishing off the final kits. The sewing machines were humming and it felt like old times. Before the war. Before James went away. Before munitions and mines and that constant knot of worry in her stomach.

'Nearly there,' Rachel said. She was counting the jerseys, and putting them into piles with a pair of shorts, socks and a cap. 'We've got thirteen here.'

'Fourteen,' said Bridget, flicking up the needle on the machine, and tying off a thread. She held out the jersey to Rachel. 'That's it.'

'Eleven and three extras,' Ellen said with satisfaction. 'Gosh, I didn't think we'd do it.' She added a pair of socks, shorts and a cap to the final pile. And then sat down quickly as tiredness overwhelmed her.

'Are you all right?' Sadie was right there, as she'd been ever since they'd heard the news. Ellen was so glad to have her by her side. And when Sadie wasn't there, Bridget was, keeping Ellen calm with her peaceful presence.

'Tired,' Ellen said. 'I've not been sleeping very well, thinking about James, and being kicked by this wee one.' She put her hand on her bulging abdomen. 'I think my football days are coming to an end.'

Sadie stroked Ellen's head. 'Aye,' she said. 'For now. But you can play again when the wean arrives.'

'I will.' Ellen nodded. 'I can't imagine not playing.'

'Maybe you could help Hilda, instead of pelting up and down the pitch,' suggested Rachel. 'You could be her assistant.'

Ellen made a face. 'The men on James's ship would love that,' she joked. 'They'd all be queuing up to join me.' Then with an awful, icy cold start she remembered that those men were undoubtedly among those who'd died, and she felt her face twist in pain.

Sadie – astute, caring Sadie – sat down next to her and took her hand. 'It just sneaks up on you, sometimes, doesn't it?' she said. 'I remember when Da died, and I'd be walking home from work thinking about something funny I'd tell him when I got in, and then there it was – the understanding that he wouldn't be there.'

Ellen gripped on to her friend's fingers, unable to speak for a moment. She didn't want to let the dark thoughts crowd into her mind – the thoughts that taunted her, saying James could be one of the dead. That the talk of survivors was outlandish and unlikely. She tried to think of good things. Positive things. Annie's wee smile, and the feeling of her baby squirming inside her. She pushed away the idea that James might never see his little girl laugh again, or meet his new baby.

She felt the concerned eyes of the others on her and with huge effort she managed to gather herself.

'Right then, girls,' she said, in a voice that quavered just the tiniest bit. 'We'd best pack these bundles up and get going.'

'All right?' Sadie asked her.

Ellen nodded. 'For now,' she said. 'Let's just focus on the game. If we lose this one, then the Munitionettes' Cup won't be coming to Clydebank.'

They tied up each of the new kits with string, then together they carried them downstairs. Ellen put Annie into her pram, which Annie was furious about, but which made life much easier, then they piled the bundles in around her, and set off towards the factory.

As they drew close, they could see folk everywhere, gathering by the far gate in a queue that snaked round the factory wall.

'Oh heavens,' said Rachel. 'Are they . . . are they waiting to get in to watch?'

'I think so.' Ellen felt half excited, half absolutely terrified. 'Didn't Lucinda say they would take the money at that gate?'

Rachel nodded. 'She's got them to build a wee booth and everything.'

'My goodness.'

'This is big.' Rachel stopped walking for a second and Ellen stopped too. 'It's really big, Ellen.'

'Too big?' Ellen said, feeling nervous.

But Rachel bounced on her toes, her eyes gleaming. 'No. Not at all. It's . . .' She looked up at the sky, finding the word. 'It's magnificent.'

Ellen looked at Rachel, jigging about on the spot and thought how young and eager she looked. She wished she was the same – she had felt very old since the telegram had arrived. Like she was dealing with things she wasn't ready for. But then Rachel threw her arms in the air delightedly and spun round, and said: 'We're going to win, I can feel it!' And Annie clapped her little hands, and the other women all laughed, and Ellen suddenly felt less worried and more ready for anything.

'Ida said she was going to try to find us,' Bridget said in wonder. 'But I can't see how she'll manage. There are so many people and she'll be so busy making sure everyone behaves.'

'Are the police service going to try to stop the game?' Ellen said, worriedly. 'I know they weren't keen on football at first.'

'Not at all,' Bridget reassured her. 'Ida said there were just a few of them who didn't approve, but generally they all see the benefits of the munitionettes keeping healthy. They're just here in case anything goes wrong, I think.'

'Is Christina working?' Ellen asked.

'Ida says she's not seen her for days.'

'Let's hope she doesn't show up, eh?'

Up ahead, a man in a Wentworth blue cap waved to them. 'Hiya, Rachel.'

'Hiya, Robert,' Rachel said. 'Are you making sure everyone goes the right way?'

'Aye,' Robert said. 'There are a lot of folk come to watch and the game doesn't start for another hour.'

'How many is a lot?' Sadie asked.

Robert shrugged. 'Too many to count,' he said. 'Thousands.'

'Thousands?' Sadie said. 'Thousands of people coming to Wentworth?'

'Oh, aye,' said Robert matter-of-factly. 'And some came all the way from Carlisle, where the other team's from. But there's not enough room for everyone. They've started turning folk away already.'

Ellen and Rachel exchanged an astonished glance. Sadie

nodded in satisfaction. 'We're going to make so much money for the benevolent fund,' she said.

'You're players, right?' Robert said.

'We are,' Rachel said. 'Me and Ellen. And we have the kit for everyone.'

'You need to go in the front gate,' Robert said. 'Mackie's down there. He'll let you through.'

Ellen thought it felt like the night before her birthday when she was wee. That shivery anticipation that something fun was about to happen.

Inside the factory gates there was a lively atmosphere. Somewhere someone was playing a fiddle, and there were shouts in the distance, and voices, and laughter.

'Shall I take Annie over to Hilda's daughter?' Bridget asked. 'Then you girls can go and get changed.'

'I'll help with the kits then come and meet you,' Sadie said to Bridget. 'See you outside the dressing rooms?'

Ellen, Rachel and Sadie took the parcels out of the pram and waved goodbye to Annie, who was looking a little pink in the face with excitement.

As they were making their way into the dressing room, Lucinda appeared, looking just as pink and excited as wee Annie had done.

'Ohmygoodness, ohmygoodness, have you seen?' she said, taking some of the parcels from Sadie and hugging them to her chest. 'Have you seen?'

'The people?' Sadie said, with a grin. 'Oh yes we have.'

'We'll have made so much money,' Lucinda said. 'Hundreds of pounds.'

The women all stared at her, stunned into silence. 'Bessie can go to the convalescent home straight way,' Lucinda added. 'And we can pay for doctors and food bills and all sorts.'

Sadie looked a bit teary. 'Really?'

'Really.' Lucinda nodded. 'And this is just the beginning. There will be more matches, and more money.'

Ellen felt a surge of pride in her friend. 'This was all your doing,' she said. 'Sadie, you're wonderful.'

Sadie ducked her head modestly, but Ellen knew she was pleased.

'I need to go and find my father,' Lucinda said. 'He's so chuffed about this. He says he's had other factory managers writing to him to ask for tips on how to start a football team.'

'And has he written back?'

Lucinda laughed. 'He's passed all the letters on to Hilda,' she said.

'Good for Hamilton.'

'Is Lewis here?' Rachel asked Lucinda quietly. 'Is he coming to watch?'

'He said he wouldn't miss it for the world.'

Rachel nodded, her face expressionless, but when she turned away, Ellen saw her smiling.

'Gosh, you need to go and get ready,' Sadie said, looking up at the factory clock. 'Hilda will be stewing.'

As they headed towards the changing room, raised voices made them look up. 'You're not on the rota,' someone was saying. 'You can't be here.'

Ellen rolled her eyes as Christina marched round the corner, in her police uniform, with Ida following closely behind.

'Christina,' Ida was saying, 'you're not working today.'

'You'll need help,' Christina said over her shoulder, not pausing in her swift walk towards the pitch. 'These women are out of control.'

'Christina!' Ida shouted.

This time Christina stopped. She turned and glared at Ida. 'Please stop telling me what to do, Ida McKinley,' she said. 'You're not in charge.'

Ida lifted her chin. 'Actually,' she said. 'I am. I'm a sergeant now, and it was me who put together the team to police today's event.'

Christina looked bullish. 'Don't talk nonsense.'

'It's true,' Ida said. 'I need you to leave.'

'Or pay the entrance fee,' Ellen called, unable to resist.

Christina glanced round and saw them all watching. Her eyes narrowed. 'Ellen Kelly,' she said in disgust. 'You'd think you'd know better than to get on the wrong side of me.' She gave Lucinda a sideways glance. 'After what you did.'

'It's a penny,' Lucinda said. 'You can pay at the booth.'

'Aren't you curious about what your employees have been doing?' Christina said.

Lucinda shrugged. 'They're not my employees,' she said. 'And as far as I can see, they've just been trying to get through the days as best they can. Like all of us.'

Christina snorted. 'You watch yourselves,' she said, pointing at each of them in turn, but lingering longest on Ellen. 'All of you. Be careful. Pride always comes before a fall.'

'That's enough, Christina,' Ida said deliberately. 'Come on now. I'll walk you to the gate.'

Ellen watched as Christina and Ida marched off.

'What did she mean by that?' she said to Sadie. 'Why did she say "be careful"?'

'Och, she's full of nonsense, that one,' Sadie said. 'Just ignore her.'

'My father always says that some folk put on a uniform and it changes them,' Lucinda said. 'The authority has gone to that one's head and no mistake.'

'Nope,' Ellen said, with a hint of devilment. 'Christina's not changed. She's always been a terribly annoying woman.'

They all laughed.

'What on earth are you doing out here chatting?' Hilda stuck her head out of the dressing-room door. 'I heard voices and I thought to myself that sounds like Ellen, but it couldn't possibly be her, could it? Because Ellen knows we've got our most important game of football yet, in . . .' She looked at the clock. 'In three quarters of an hour. She'll be changed already and getting warmed up.'

Ellen chuckled. 'We're coming,' she said to Hilda. 'With the kit.'

'And a hunger for victory?' Hilda said, slapping Ellen on the back as she walked past her into the changing room.

'Oh most definitely,' Ellen said. 'That too.'

Chapter Thirty-Six

Clydebank

15 June 1916

My dear James,

It was the hardest match we'd played. The other team, Hepburn & Sons, were from Carlisle and they were very well trained. Hilda said they'd been playing together since before the war, so they really knew what they were doing.

And they were used to the crowd. We were all a little overwhelmed at first because, James, there were so many people. They'd come from all over Clydebank to watch the match and we were astonished. They piled into the new seats Hamilton Blyth had built. They lined the sides of the pitch. Someone said folk were being turned away because there were too many of them! Fancy that!

The noise they made was something else. Like a roar. We could hardly hear ourselves think. We definitely couldn't hear what Hilda was shouting to us from the sidelines, so she ended up doing strange gestures and pointing a lot, which made us all laugh.

Not surprisingly, we were all a little taken aback. And it took us a while to find our feet. The other team scored a goal quickly. Joan, our goalkeeper, was furious. But then, she always is, and we couldn't hear what she was shouting anyway!

After your advice, Hilda moved Hetty up front alongside Ginny to support her and it was a great idea. Because she's wee, but she's quick. And she told Rachel to come forward too. So just before half time, Hepburn were attacking, but Nell – she's a big lass, sturdy and bold, she stepped up and got the ball back. She thumped it to Rachel, and she was off, running up the wing. I'm not so quick now, but I knew what Rachel was planning – we'd practised it a hundred times. As the other team went to her, she passed the ball to me, I waited for her to be free, and passed it back. And there was Hetty running forward. Rachel got the ball to her and BAM! Into the net. Honestly, James, my ears are still ringing from the noise. Hilda was beside herself at the break. I thought she was going to cry.

And then, James, straight after half time, Ginny went and scored a goal that I think people will be talking about for years. The other team just stood still and watched in amazement. Nell said she'll be playing for Scotland soon. Is that even possible?

But the other team weren't happy and they threw everything at us to try to get another goal themselves. Hilda took me off and I was pleased about that, because by then I was exhausted. I think this could have been my last game for a while. I'm nervous about running too fast in case I trip and fall and hurt the wean, and I get breathless too quickly to be much use. I told Hilda and she said I can help her with the management and training. I'm glad of that because football has become so important to me.

Anyway, we were 2–1 up and Nell and Rachel were doing so good, and Joan made some brilliant saves, but I could tell everyone was tired. So Hilda swapped a couple more players, and Hetty was dashing about all over the place, and then Nell walloped one of the Hepburn players and she got sent off!? I was surprised because no one had ever been sent off in one of our matches before. But Nell was, and I must admit, she probably deserved it. But then it seemed even less likely we could hang on. And Hilda and

I were screaming at the team from the sidelines, and the crowd were cheering, and then the whistle blew and that was it! We'd won! Just one more match to go and we'll be bringing the Munitionettes' Cup home. Will you come home, too, James? Please come. I miss you so much. Annie draws you pictures every day – she misses you too.

Come home.

Your loving wife,
Ellen.

Chapter Thirty-Seven

Sadie had woken up feeling quite odd. Her head was spinning and if she stood up too quickly, she thought she might faint. She was tired, she decided. She'd been so busy since last week's football match – and before that, too, getting the kits together. They had made a staggering amount of money for the benevolent fund. Sadie had cried when Lucinda told her that they'd got £196 and her father was going to top it up to make £200. She'd sent a telegram to the convalescent home immediately to see if they had a space for Bessie and they'd replied to say they had. So Sadie was going over there now to see if she could help her pack. Bessie's mother was taking her down to Peebles on the train, and the benevolent fund was paying for all their travel.

It was a lovely day outside – the sun shining brightly – so Sadie decided not to take a coat. She was feeling quite warm anyway, and hoped she wasn't feverish or coming down with something.

Picking up a parcel of sandwiches she'd made for Bessie and her ma for the trip, she went out into the street.

'Great game, wasn't it?' said the postman as he passed.

'Aye, terrific,' Sadie agreed with a grin. It was astonishing how interested everyone was in the football. Noah said football brought folk together and with the men's game stopped, it was a good way to give everyone a shared interest. Sadie thought he was right because, jings, wasn't it just all everyone was talking about.

Up ahead, she saw Ellen's and Bridget's ma, Gert. Ellen's parents had heard the news about James and had come home from Fort William, though Sadie hadn't seen them yet. She hurried over to say hello.

'Sadie, you're looking tired,' Gert said after giving her a hug. 'Are you doing too much?'

'Och, aren't we all doing too much?' Sadie said with a smile. 'All the football and the Clothing Exchange and now the benevolent fund. But folk need our help and we're not going to say no.'

'Glad that spirit is still strong,' Gert said. 'You're an honorary Kelly sister, you. Running towards a fight.'

Sadie beamed with pride. But then Gert looked serious. 'How's my Ellen doing?'

Not sure what to say, Sadie paused.

'Tell me the truth,' Gert said.

'She's still refusing to believe that James is gone,' Sadie said, biting her lip. 'She says she'd know if he was dead, and she's not feeling it.'

Gert looked worried. 'She's in denial.'

'It seems that way.' Sadie sighed. 'When anyone says they're sorry to hear the news, Ellen glares and says he isn't dead.'

'Oh my goodness.'

'And at the moment, football is giving her a good distraction, but there's just that one match left, and I'm worried what will happen when it's just her and her thoughts, and a new baby to care for.' Sadie's voice cracked. 'A baby who won't know his da.'

Gert's eyes filled with tears. 'We'll find a way to get her through it,' she said. 'But it won't be easy.'

'I'm pleased you're back,' said Sadie. 'She'll be glad to have you around.'

'Aye,' Gert said. 'And she's lucky to have you, too.'

Feeling relieved that Ellen had more support, Sadie gave Gert another hug, said her goodbyes and hurried off to see Bessie.

She was just in time. Bessie and her mother were ready to go.

Bessie looked thin and pale, wrapped in her winter coat – even though it wasn't cold at all and even the breeze was pleasant.

'We've got ages until our train,' she said with a narrow smile. 'But I'm slow on my feet.'

'I've come to help with your bags,' Sadie told her. 'We'll get there.'

Very slowly, the three women made their way towards the station. Sadie was alarmed by how frail Bessie was. More than once she had to sit down for a rest along the way and at one point she swayed so alarmingly that Sadie thought she might faint and miss the train altogether.

But eventually they made it. Sadie carried their bags up the stairs while Bessie's ma took her daughter by the arm and very patiently helped her climb the steps to the platform. From the top, Sadie watched them and thought how a mother was always a mother, no matter how grown-up her children were. The enormity of that idea made her reel with the sense of responsibility, and the sadness that she didn't have it.

Once Bessie was settled on the platform, her breathing shallow and her eyes closed, Sadie sat down next to her and exchanged a worried glance with Bessie's mother.

'She'll be all right,' her mother said. 'She just needs a rest. Once we're on the train she can sleep.'

'I hope so,' Sadie said.

Bessie opened her eyes and looked at Sadie without moving her head. 'Sadie, you've been marvellous,' she said. 'I don't know what we'd have done without you, eh, Ma?'

Her ma looked a bit tearful. 'I do know,' she said, patting her daughter's bony knees. 'I do know, but I don't want to think about it.'

Sadie felt a lump in her throat. 'It was nothing,' she muttered.

'Och, it was something,' Bessie said. 'Let's not pretend and do that thing women do when they make out something wonderful is of no consequence.'

Sadie flushed. 'Well, I wanted to help.'

'You saved my life.'

Too choked to speak, Sadie took Bessie's hand – gently, because she was so fragile – and nodded.

Bessie wasn't done. 'If I don't recover . . .' she began.

'Oh, Bess,' said her ma. But Bessie ignored her. 'I know I'm not well,' she said. 'And I know I might not get better. And if I don't, Sadie, I want you to know that you gave me my best chance.'

Again, Sadie nodded, pinching her lips together.

'And carry on,' Bessie said. 'Carry on raising money and helping more women. Because there are a lot of sick munitionettes who need help.'

'Aye,' Sadie managed. 'We will.'

Along the track, they could see the smoke that meant the train was on its way. Sadie helped Bessie to her feet and gave her a hug, feeling her shoulder blades through her coat.

When the train arrived, she and Bessie's ma made sure she got up the step all right, and then the porter helped Sadie with the bags. She watched them through the window, with Bessie's ma fussing over her daughter, putting a blanket over her legs and getting her settled in her seat, and felt once more that bleak longing for motherhood. But she pushed it away and waved to the women through the glass.

'Good luck!' she called. 'Write to me!'

Bessie waved back and the train pulled away.

Sadie waited on the platform until the smoke faded into the distance and then she headed back down the stairs, intending to call on Ellen and check on her before she went home.

She was walking along the main road, when she saw – up ahead – Christina coming towards her, with a face like thunder.

Not in the mood for a row, Sadie went to cross the street, but Christina had spotted her and she followed, looking furious.

'Spark!' she bellowed. 'Spark!'

Sadie stopped and turned to face the other woman. 'It's Mrs Spark.'

Christina looked as though she didn't much care.

'Are you happy now? You and your coven of witches?'

'Lord, you're always so dramatic, Christina.' Sadie rolled her eyes. 'By coven, I'm assuming you mean my friends? And I have no idea if they're happy – I've not seen them today.'

'So you've not heard the news?'

'What news?'

'I've been asked to leave the police service,' Christina said. She looked genuinely upset and for a moment, Sadie felt sorry for her. 'Apparently, my conduct is below what is expected.'

'That's a shame,' Sadie said, honestly. 'It seems harsh.'

'Harsh?' Christina growled. 'It's outrageous.'

Sadie wasn't sure what to say, so she just made a face that could have been agreement or disagreement.

'My conduct has been fine,' Christina went on. 'It's those around me who have made my position so difficult to maintain.'

'Those around you?' Sadie asked.

'Ellen McCallum,' Christina said, ticking the names off on her fingers. 'And her disgusting sister and her morally repugnant "friend".'

Sadie went to walk away, not wanting to be subjected to another rant.

'I told the inspector about Ida McKinley's behaviour,' Christina said, raising her voice a little so Sadie could hear her. 'I told her everything.'

Sadie froze.

'And what did she say?' she asked, over her shoulder.

Christina stared at her, the dislike in her eyes clear to see. And then she dropped her gaze. 'She said it was nasty gossip and it was none of my business.'

Sadie turned to face Christina properly, and decided she rather liked the sound of the inspector.

'And then she said that my personal opinions were interfering with my work, and that it would be better if I left my uniform in the changing room and went home. She said my ideas about the women's football were . . .' She took a breath. 'My ideas were outdated and unhelpful. And she said they've had complaints about me.' Her eyes bored into Sadie, who sighed.

'I've not complained about you,' she said, with a touch of weariness. 'Honestly, Christina, I've not got the time to worry about what you're up to. You're so low down on my list of problems you barely feature.'

It was the wrong thing to say. Christina's face darkened.

'This is all because of you, and those other women,' she hissed. 'You have been making my life a misery for years. I lost the respect of the suffragettes because of Bridget Kelly; her hot-headed sister assaulted me when I was trying to apologise, and now Bridget's despicable bidie-in has clearly manipulated the inspector into turning on me.'

'Oh for heaven's sake, get a grip,' said Sadie. 'The only person responsible for the misfortune in your life is you.'

But Christina wasn't interested. 'Someone is to blame for making me lose my job and I will find out who.'

Sadie shrugged. 'Do your worst,' she said. 'Now if you'll excuse me, I have a lot to be getting on with, and I don't have time to listen to your ramblings. Oh and by the way, you forgot to leave your uniform behind.' She gestured at Christina's black dress and tie. 'You're still wearing it.'

Chapter Thirty-Eight

Ellen was walking home from her parents' flat. On her own. Her ma and Annie had been so delighted to see one another that Gert had asked to keep Annie for the day, and Ellen had gladly obliged. She'd decided to spend the day at the Clothing Exchange, checking through donations and mending any items that needed attention before they could be passed on.

Her ma had told her to go home and rest, but the truth was, Ellen was a little afraid to be alone with her thoughts. When she stopped for a moment, the horrible worries about James crowded into her mind again, and she felt herself spiralling down and down into terror and grief. So she didn't want to rest. She wanted to keep busy. She needed to keep busy.

As she skirted the edge of the factory, she could hear the noises of the munitionettes working. The clanging of shells, the shouts, the hiss of the machinery. She could smell the cordite in the air and feel the heat from the equipment. She wished she could be there with them, but then, as the baby turned in her belly, she was glad she wasn't.

She turned the corner towards the Clothing Exchange and saw, beside one of the side gates to the factory, Christina. *Urgh.* Keen not to engage in conversation, she crossed the road and pulled her hat down over her eyes, pretending not to have seen her. But Christina wasn't paying attention anyway. She was focused on the doorman – a friendly, if a wee bit dozy chap called Paulie, who was always put on that gate because no one used it much. Ellen carried on walking, her steps slowing just a bit as she tried to see what Christina was up to. She was in her uniform, so it had to be official business, and she was carrying a large bag.

Paulie laughed at something Christina had said, which surprised Ellen. Christina was not the funny sort. And then he opened the gate and Christina went through.

Ellen carried on, her curiosity about what Christina was up to soon replaced by thoughts of what she had to do today, and what Annie might be getting up to with her doting grandparents.

'Ellen!' A shout made her look round, just as she got close to the Clothing Exchange, and there was Sadie hurrying towards her.

The women embraced and Ellen eyed her friend. 'You look pale,' she said. 'Are you all right?'

'I'm fine, a wee bit tired, I think. I've just got Bessie off to the convalescent place in Peebles.'

'Well done,' Ellen said, impressed. 'Do you have to be somewhere now or do you have time for a cup of tea?' She tilted her head towards the Clothing Exchange. 'I'm just going to go through donations and do some mending. Fancy helping me out?'

Sadie grinned. 'Love to.'

Ellen unlocked the door and they went inside, chatting about Bessie and Gert and wee Annie. Ellen filled the kettle and put it on the little stove, and they made tea and sat together, drinking and talking, and Ellen thought how very lucky she was to have Sadie back in her life. Impulsively, she gave her friend a hug.

'What was that for?' Sadie asked with a chuckle.

'Just because.'

'Well, that's nice.' Sadie put her mug down. 'Now I can hug you back properly.'

Ellen squeezed her friend tightly, trying to tell her without words that she was glad she was there and that living with this constant dread about James would be much harder without her. She thought Sadie would understand.

'Right, then,' she said eventually, letting Sadie go. 'Shall we get stuck into these breeks?'

'Lead the way,' Sadie said good-naturedly.

They sat side by side, ready to start hemming trousers and patching tears.

'You'll never guess who I saw earlier?' Sadie said. 'Ranting and raving as usual.'

'Who?' Ellen pushed her needle through the knee of a pair of school trousers.

'Christina.'

'Did you speak to her?' Ellen laughed. 'I saw her a while ago too, but I managed to sneak by without her seeing me.'

'Oh, I spoke to her,' Sadie groaned. 'Or at least, she spoke to me. She was up to high doh about us. Called us a coven of witches.'

'I wish we were a coven of witches,' Ellen said, tying off a stitch. 'It would make things much easier if we could cast spells all the time.'

Sadie chuckled. 'Aye, wouldn't it just?'

'What else did she say?' Ellen said, despite herself.

'Oh God, she was awful,' Sadie said, rubbing her nose. 'Said awful stuff, about Bridget and Ida and all of us. She said she'd told her boss about Ida.'

'No!' Ellen was horrified.

'Och, it's fine. Sounds like the inspector sent her packing with a flea in her ear.'

'That's a relief.'

'And the best bit is, Christina's been asked to leave her job with the police service,' said Sadie. 'So she won't be bothering us any-more. And obviously that's all our fault. She was swearing she'd get her revenge on us all. Making threats left, right and centre.'

Ellen frowned. 'She's left the police service?'

'Aye, she's been kicked out because her conduct wasn't up to standard,' Sadie giggled. 'I'm surprised they let her join in the first place, to be honest.'

But Ellen wasn't laughing. 'I saw her,' she said. 'Just five minutes before I saw you. And she was wearing her uniform.'

'I know. She was asked to leave it behind, but she didn't.'

'She was going into the factory,' Ellen said. 'I saw her at Paulie's gate.'

Sadie's brow knotted. 'What was she doing there?'

'I don't know.' Ellen put down the trousers she'd been mending and stood up. 'I don't like it, Sadie.'

With a worried look, Sadie stood up too. 'She's got no reason to go to the factory.'

'None whatsoever.'

'And she went through Paulie's gate?'

'Aye,' said Ellen. 'And we know Paulie is the one to go to if you want to get your own way without any awkward questions. He'd never say no to someone in uniform. Not in a million years.'

Sadie's eyes widened. 'Oh, Ellen. What is she up to?'

'Maybe she's going to try to speak to Hamilton Blyth?' Ellen said. 'Or cause trouble for Hilda – we know she hates the football team.' She had a sudden thought. 'She had a big bag with her, Sadie. I think she's going to do something to make sure we can't play the next football match.'

'Like what?' Sadie sounded doubtful.

'Cut the nets down?' Ellen said. 'Dig a hole in the pitch? Steal all the kit? Puncture the balls? It could be anything.'

Sadie threw her head back in despair. 'Lord, I think you're right,' she said. 'Stupid bloody woman.'

'We need to go and stop her,' Ellen said. 'And we need to hurry, because it's at least an hour since I saw her.'

Sadie was already getting her jacket on.

'We should fetch Ida, too.'

'You do that, I'll lock up,' Sadie said. 'Go.'

Ellen didn't wait. She raced next door and into McKinley's

where, to her relief, Ida was sitting behind the counter. 'Christina's up to something,' she said. 'I've just seen her going into the factory in her police uniform, but she told Sadie she'd lost her job.'

Ida took off her specs. 'Aye, she's been asked to leave,' she said. 'She most definitely shouldn't be wearing her uniform anymore.'

'We need to go and stop her,' Ellen urged. 'I'm worried she's going to try to ruin the football pitch or do something else to prevent us playing.'

Ida got up. 'Let's go,' she said.

'Where's Bridget?' Ellen asked.

'Rolling bandages.'

Ellen was relieved that her sister was out of the way.

'Come on.' She tugged Ida's sleeve. 'Hurry.'

'Right behind you, doll,' said Ida.

Together the three women raced along the street towards the factory. Ida was fastest because Ellen was slower now thanks to the baby, and Sadie – who was normally quite quick on her feet – lagged behind.

'Come on, Sadie,' Ellen said. 'Hurry up.'

Sadie picked up the pace and without speaking, they headed to Paulie's gate.

'Let me talk,' Ellen said as they drew near. 'You've not got your uniform on, Ida, and he doesn't know you so well, Sadie.'

'Good idea,' said Ida.

Ellen went forwards to the gate. 'Hiya, Paulie,' she said.

'Ellen Kelly,' he said. 'As I live and breathe.'

'Och, Paulie, you're a one,' said Ellen with a laugh. 'Don't you know I've been married to my James for years. I'm Ellen McCallum now.'

'I know,' Paulie said with a wink. 'How's your da?'

'Same as ever,' said Ellen. 'Back from Fort William, mind. He'll be wanting to see you.'

'I'll track him down,' Paulie said. 'Probably in the pub.'

'Aye, you're right there.' Ellen paused. 'Do us a favour, Paulie?

My pal Sadie here is needing to see her wee sister – Rachel. She's a munitionette. Family emergency.'

Paulie looked worried. 'Oh no.'

'I said I'd help her find her, as I used to work there. And this is Ida, she's erm . . .' Ellen's mind went blank. 'She's here too.' She breathed in. 'Is that all right?'

'Of course,' Paulie said. 'Go right through. I hope you find her, doll.'

He got out of his little box and unlocked the gate. Ellen, Sadie and Ida all trooped through, thanking him as they passed, and then when he'd shut the gate behind them, they looked at one another.

'Where now?'

'Football pitch?' said Ellen, pointing. 'It's right over the other side of the factory. And there's a changing room there, with a cupboard where Hilda's put all the balls and the spare kit and everything we need to play, just about.'

'We'll follow you,' Ida said. 'But we should hurry.' She looked up at the sky. 'I should have put my uniform on.'

'There was no time,' Ellen pointed out. 'We may have missed Christina already.'

'Which way should we go?' Sadie asked. 'Which is quickest?'

'Through the munitions hall actually, but we should go round the side because it's not safe to go through,' said Ellen. 'We've not got the right protection on. Follow me.'

She led the women across the back of the factory, and round towards the part where she had once worked. Twice worked, she thought to herself with a wry smile. The noise was so loud now that she, Ida and Sadie had to shout to make themselves heard.

'This way,' she called, heading past the edge of the huge brick building so they could cut across to the football pitch.

'Oh lord, there she is,' said Ida. 'Over there!'

Ellen looked in the direction Ida was pointing – which was back the way they'd come – and saw to her horror, Christina marching towards the munitions hall as bold as brass with what looked like a spade over her shoulder.

'No,' she breathed. 'No.'

'She's going to dig up the pitch,' said Sadie, sounding disgusted. 'She'll ruin the grass and stop you all playing and she doesn't even care if anyone sees her doing it. How dare she?'

'She can't have metal,' Ellen said. 'She shouldn't have metal. Not here.'

Sadie looked confused. 'What?'

But Ellen was off, running towards Christina, who was heading right to the door of the munitions hall. 'Christina!' she bellowed, but it was too loud. 'Don't go through there!'

Her heart was thumping in her chest. 'CHRISTINA!'

Christina walked into the entrance to the hall as Ida and Sadie caught up with Ellen who was gasping for air.

She clutched Ida's arm. 'Stop her,' she begged. 'She can't go in there.'

Ida nodded, understanding, even if she couldn't hear the words. She darted off towards the munitions hall.

And then, there was a huge whooshing sound, as though the whole factory had breathed in, and the loudest booming, ear-shattering noise Ellen had ever heard. She and Sadie both staggered backwards, covering their heads with their arms. And when Ellen looked up, her ears ringing, Ida had vanished, engulfed in a huge plume of smoke.

She and Sadie looked at one another in sheer panic and disbelief.

Ellen went to run towards where the munitions hall should be, but Sadie grabbed her and held her tight.

'No,' she screamed into Ellen's thumping ear. 'NO! It's not safe.'

'Ida,' Ellen shouted. 'We have to help Ida!' She felt tears streaming down her face, even though she hadn't known she was crying. 'She needs our help.'

Sadie pulled her into a hug. She was crying too. 'She's gone,' she said, her lips so close to Ellen's ear that she could feel them. 'Ida's gone.'

Chapter Thirty-Nine

Rachel was in the canteen when the explosion happened. Hamilton Blyth had decided that twelve-hour shifts were hard on the munitionettes and he'd introduced a rota where they changed tasks after four hours, with a break in between. It was much better, and the women were all finding work less of a slog. Still tougher than anything Rachel had ever done, but less bone-crushingly wearisome.

That morning, Rachel had been finishing shells, then she'd moved to weighing powder, and now she was going back to finishing. It was a relief to move to a different role, because each job took its toll on a different part of her body, and swapping round made it easier.

So she was in the canteen on her break, gulping down a cup of tea and discussing tactics with the footballers who worked in her department. Later she understood that she'd been lucky to be at the back of the munitions hall, but it didn't feel that way at first.

When the explosion happened, she thought it had to have been a zeppelin raid, like the one that had attacked Edinburgh. It was so loud, Rachel felt the noise deep within her and the ground beneath her shook.

Without thinking, she dropped to the floor and lay there, feeling her heart thump against her boiler suit.

'Oh no,' she whispered over and over. 'Oh no.'

The room filled with smoke and she felt panic rising in her chest as it crept into her lungs and her breathing grew shallow. It was dark in the canteen anyway, as it only had a few windows, high up on its walls, but now it was pitch-black.

Slowly, Rachel got to her feet, feeling her way. The factory, which was always full of noise and clanging and clattering and shouts was silent, for a second. And then the crying started from within the room they were in, and from outside, too. There was wailing and calling for help and just simply sobbing.

Rachel wanted to help – she wanted to move – but her feet were frozen to the floor, her breathing coming faster.

And then, oh thank goodness, she heard Hilda. Lovely, strident Hilda.

'Listen!' she shouted. 'LISTEN!'

Rachel listened, and the room quietened.

'Is everyone all right?' Hilda shouted. 'Anyone hurt?'

No one replied. Rachel breathed out in relief.

'We have to get out of the building,' Hilda said, her voice cutting over the now muffled sobs. 'We're going to go towards the back door. I'll lead the way and I'll keep talking as I go. Find the wall to keep your bearings, then follow the sound of my voice. This way.'

Rachel reached out and touched the cool wall of the canteen. Then, with her hand flat on the bumpy surface, she gingerly walked towards where Hilda was still talking.

'That's the way, come on ladies,' she was saying. 'Almost there.'

There was a banging and a thump and then daylight shone into the room – the back door was open.

'DON'T RUSH!' Hilda yelled. 'Steady pace, and we'll get you all out.'

The women carried on shuffling forwards. Rachel could hear her own breathing and feel the closeness of whoever was in front of her and whoever was behind. Knowing she wasn't alone gave her comfort. And then suddenly she was outside in the open air, where the smoke wasn't so thick and where she could see. Her knees buckled and she thought she might fall but someone – now she could see it was Nell – grabbed her and kept her upright.

'AWAY FROM THE BUILDING!' Hilda was saying. 'GET AWAY!'

Now the women all rushed, haring round the side of the building and into the courtyard. The factory bell was clanging madly, asking for help from whoever could provide it.

Rachel gasped as she saw the front of the munitions hall where flames licked the pile of rubble that had once been the entrance.

'There's folk in there!' she panted at Nell. 'There are people in there. We need to get in!'

Nell held on to her tightly. 'Let them do their bit first,' she said. She nodded to where the volunteer fire service had already arrived with their cart and their pump, ready to take water from the canal and douse the flames. They were all women, of course, from various parts of the factory. Hetty – the wee woman who played in the football team – was at the front, unrolling the hose, and Rachel recognised a woman who worked in clerical, her neat blouse stained black with dirt, helping.

'Stand back!' Hetty shouted.

The water began flowing and, not sure where to go, Rachel staggered a little further away.

'Rachel!'

It was Sadie! Why was she here? Rachel had no idea, but she'd never been so pleased to see her sister in all her days. She ran to her, and held her tightly, feeling Sadie's tears on her neck.

'Ida,' Sadie sobbed. 'Ida was here.'

'What?' Rachel's heart lurched. 'Where?'

'She ran into the munitions hall.' For the first time, Rachel realised Ellen was there too. 'She ran that way and then she just wasn't there anymore.'

Rachel thought she might vomit with the horror of it all. She clung on to Sadie, and then realised that, for once, her big sister was looking to her to take charge. The realisation made her giddy, but she forced herself to stand up straight. She looked around at the chaos unfolding everywhere. The firefighters were directing water onto the flames, which were dying down, but all over the courtyard were women, blackened with smoke, dazed, afraid, bleeding, moaning in pain, or – worst of all – lying on the cobbles, very still.

'Stay here,' she said firmly, turning back to Sadie and Ellen. 'Stay out of the way for now. People will want help and you might be needed but for now, stay here. I'm going to find Ida.'

She guided the trembling, frightened women to a corner and made them sit down, then she looked at the munitions hall, no longer burning but clearly unsafe.

'I'll be back soon,' she said.

Keeping her breathing regular she made her way through the smoke, towards the hall. Someone grabbed her arm and she turned to see Hilda and Nell and fell on them like they were old friends.

'It's awful,' Rachel said, squeezing them both tight. 'It's awful.'

'It's chaos,' said Hilda looking around. 'No one knows what to do.'

'Someone said ambulances were coming but I'm not sure if they'll make it through these people.'

Rachel felt a clarity and clear-headedness that she'd never had before. She'd been to the infirmary many times as a little girl. She'd watched the nurses organising the folk who came in. She knew what to do.

'We need a space where everyone can go, away from the building,' she said. 'There's so many shells in there, what if there's another explosion? And we need to separate out the walking wounded and the more badly injured.' She swallowed. 'And the dead.'

'The football field,' said Hilda. 'We'll take them there.'

'Perfect,' Rachel said. 'Good. Hilda, you go to the field. Use the kits to keep people warm. Use anything you've got. I'll send the patients over.' She looked over to where Sadie and Ellen were huddled together. 'No, I won't,' she said. 'They will.'

'I can do the dead,' Nell said matter-of-factly. 'My da's an undertaker. I'm no scared.'

Rachel looked at her in awe. 'All right,' she said. 'Good.'

'At least we're not short of stretchers,' Hilda said. 'Can we get to them?'

'Aye,' said Rachel. 'I think so. I'll find some others to go over that way.'

The women all looked at one another and nodded, united in this strange chore. And then Rachel turned and ran back to where Sadie and Ellen were.

'On your feet,' she said briskly, knowing the only way to snap them out of their bewilderment and fear was to be stern. 'I've got a job for you.'

'What do you need?' asked Sadie.

'I need organisation.'

'We can do that,' Ellen said, getting up slowly.

Rachel patted her on the arm. 'I'm putting you both in charge of the walking wounded,' she said. 'Send them to the football field. Hilda's over there.' She thought for a moment. 'Mark them. Mark their foreheads if they're hurt. Find some chalk in the football cupboard. Then the ambulances will know who to look after. But get everyone over there. We can't risk folk being here if there's another explosion.'

'Righto,' Ellen said, as though Rachel had simply asked them to make a cup of tea.

Sadie gripped Rachel's fingers. 'Ida?' she said.

'I'm going to find her.'

She left Sadie and Ellen and headed back towards the munitions hall, hoping some stretchers would arrive soon. It would be hard to get the more injured folk away from danger without them.

'Lucinda!' she yelled, seeing her ahead through the smoke. 'LUCINDA!'

Lucinda turned. 'Rachel!'

'I need stretchers,' Rachel said. 'Ellen and Sadie are organising folk to get to the football field, away from the building.'

'I'll sort it out,' Lucinda said, without hesitation. 'My father is here too. And Lewis.'

With a trickle of icy fear, Rachel said: 'Lewis? He's not . . . He didn't? He's not inside the building?'

'I don't think so,' Lucinda said. 'He was trying to find doctors and nurses to help. I think the ambulances are here.'

'Oh thank goodness,' Rachel said. 'Thank goodness.'

Lucinda gave her a quick hug. 'I'll get stretchers,' she said. 'You carry on.'

Rachel walked further forward then stopped, thinking hard. Ida had been running towards the munitions hall, Ellen had said. Not into it. Perhaps she'd been thrown backwards by the blast?

Carefully she turned and surveyed the area, which wasn't easy as there were people everywhere. She thought she saw Ida lying on the cobbles, but it was another woman, bleeding from her stomach, where a shard of metal had speared her. 'Help,' she gasped as Rachel went to her. 'It hurts.'

'I know,' Rachel said. 'Don't try to move.'

The woman ignored her, and tried to sit up. A gush of blood flooded onto the ground and Rachel pushed her back down.

'Don't!' she said. But the woman had fainted. Rachel stood up and waved at a nurse who was hurrying over. 'Here!' she cried.

She carried on with her search, tripping over discarded shoes and hunched people, until she saw, slumped beside a pile of planks, Ida. She was completely still. Her face was grey. Rachel closed her eyes briefly, hoping that when she opened them again, this would all have been a bad dream. But it wasn't.

'Please don't be dead,' she said, her heart thumping. She dashed over to where Ida half sat, half lay, against the wood.

Just as the nurses had done to her all those times in the hospital, Rachel picked up Ida's wrist to check her pulse and felt dizzy with relief to feel it pumping away, faintly, but evenly.

'IDA!' she said loudly in her ear. 'Ida McKinley, you listen to me, you great big goose. You wake up, right now.'

Ida opened her eyes. 'No need to shout,' she croaked.

Rachel went to throw her arms round her, but Ida cried out loudly in pain.

'Are you hurt?' Rachel said.

'I think my arm is broken,' Ida said. 'And maybe my ankle too?'

'I'll get someone to help,' Rachel said. 'Hiya! Over here!'

'Have you seen Christina? Is she all right?'

'Christina?' Rachel was confused. 'Was she here?'

'She went into the munitions hall, just as the explosion happened,' Ida said, her voice weak and rasping. 'I tried to stop her.'

'Everyone who can walk is out of the building.' Lewis was there, standing tall and beautiful like an angel among the hellishness of what was happening. Rachel looked at him in wonder. 'But there are injured folk still in there. My father has a list of who's safe and . . .' He looked stricken for a second. 'And who's not been found.'

'No one will be looking for Christina,' said Rachel. 'She won't be on a list.' She looked at the munitions hall. 'We need to go and get her.'

'Rachel . . .' Lewis said. 'I'm not sure—'

'No one will know she's there,' Rachel said firmly. 'We can't leave her in there.'

'It's not safe.'

'We can't leave her,' Rachel said again.

'We should tell someone.'

'There isn't time.'

Beside her Ida moaned and she saw with relief that a nurse was heading their way. 'Look, Ida, someone's coming to help,' she reassured her.

Then she turned to the nurse. 'This is Ida,' she told her. 'She thinks she's broken her arm and her ankle.'

'I'll take it from here, doll,' the nurse said.

Rachel bent down and kissed Ida on the forehead. 'You do as this nurse tells you,' she said.

Ida nodded, her face twisted in pain.

'Right, then,' Rachel said to Lewis, her mind made up. 'I'm going to get Christina. Are you coming?'

Chapter Forty

Ellen and Sadie were shepherding people from the chaos of the munitions hall, round the building to where Hilda had somehow made the football pitch look like a hospital. At one end were the folks who were hurt, but not dangerously so. Some were lying on stretchers, others were sitting, with Lucinda walking among them, keeping their spirits up.

And at the other end were the ones who weren't hurt, but who were wide-eyed with shock, covered in dirt and dust and, in some cases, other people's blood. With the noise of the blast and the ringing of the factory bell, local people had rushed to help and Sadie, with her brilliant talent for getting everyone to join in, had commandeered some women who lived nearby to make tea for anyone who wanted one. Now those women were bringing mugs and cups and even jam jars of tea and handing them out, as they chatted to anyone who looked tearful or scared, and Ellen thought for the hundredth time how clever and thoughtful Sadie was.

She looked along the lines of people, checking again if Ida was among them, but she wasn't. Should she go and fetch Bridget, she wondered? But surely she'd have heard the explosion? Maybe she was even on her way. Ellen wasn't sure what she'd say to her sister if she arrived.

'No Ida?' Sadie said, coming over. 'No sign of her.'

'Rachel said she was going to look for her,' Ellen reminded her. 'Maybe she's found her.'

'Maybe,' said Sadie, but she didn't sound very sure.

'I'm going to see if there are any more people to bring round,' Ellen said to her friend. 'I'll check where Rachel is, too.'

Sadie nodded. 'Lucinda says Hamilton has a list of everyone who would have been in the munitions hall when the explosion happened.'

'Except Ida,' Ellen said. 'Are they looking for Ida?'

'Lucinda got her da to put her on the list.'

'Thank goodness.' A thought struck Ellen. 'But how about Christina?'

Sadie stared at her. 'Oh heavens,' she said. 'No one is looking for Christina.'

'I'll go,' said Ellen, starting to hurry away. 'I'll tell them.'

She dashed round the side of the building, hoicking up her skirt as she ran so she wouldn't trip, because it was hard to see with all the smoke.

The courtyard was still busy with people, but now there were more nurses and injured folk being carried to ambulances. Ellen averted her eyes from the side of the cobbles where there was a row of three people covered completely in sheets. Nell was there, speaking to an older gentleman in a dust-covered suit.

'Nell!' Ellen called.

To her relief, Nell came over, so she didn't have to go and stand beside those sheet-covered people.

'Ellen. How are you doing?'

'We're all right,' said Ellen. 'Sadie's doing a great job.' She bit her lip. 'Who's that?' She tilted her head towards the bodies on the ground.

Nell breathed in. 'Two women from shell painting,' she said. 'Betty Collins and Franny Abraham.'

Ellen felt a wave of sadness. She knew Franny had small children, and Betty was only a young woman.'

'And the other one?' she asked, blinking back tears.

'Dilys Reilly from clerical. Hamilton Blyth's devastated. She worked directly with him and he'd sent her down to the munitions hall to do something for him.'

'Lord, she was friendly with Sadie,' Ellen said. 'This is so horrible, Nell. I can't bear it.'

'More casualties of war, I suppose,' Nell said. 'Tragedy after tragedy.'

'Is this . . .' Ellen swallowed. 'Are these the only folk who have died?'

'So far.'

Ellen nodded, relieved that Ida wasn't among them, but guilty for feeling that way.

Nell clearly knew what she was thinking. She took Ellen's arm. 'I heard you were looking for your sister's friend? The policewoman?'

'Aye.' Ellen felt a tiny prickle of hope. 'Have you seen her?'

'Not myself, but I heard a nurse talking about her. I think they took her to hospital.'

Ellen felt light-headed for a second. 'Are you sure?' she said.

'As sure as I can be. You can check with Hamilton if you need to – I know Lucinda put her on his list. Her name's Ida McKinley, right?'

'Right.' Ellen nodded vigorously, and then – to her surprise – burst into tears. 'Is she . . . was she?'

'She's fine, Well, she's broken an arm and a leg, so she's not going to be doing much marching for a while, but she was talking, that's what the nurse said.'

'Oh, thank goodness,' said Ellen, throwing her own arms round a startled Nell. 'Thank goodness.'

Nell gave Ellen a quick hug in return then untangled herself. 'Didn't do anything,' she said, offering Ellen a rather grubby handkerchief, which Ellen took gratefully.

She wiped her tears away, held the hanky – now soggy and even dirtier than before – out to Nell, and then thought better of it. 'I'll keep this,' she said, stuffing it into the pocket of her skirt.

Shouts from the munitions hall made them both look over. There were more firefighters there now – not just Hetty and the factory volunteers, but actual firefighters from the station in town. They were mostly men, big and brave and with proper equipment that made Ellen – feeling a wee bit disloyal to Hetty – relieved that they were there.

But now they were pulling folk back from the hall. 'It's going to collapse,' they were shouting. 'Stand away! Stand back!'

Nell and Ellen watched as the rescuers all stood away from the hall, hearts in their mouths. 'Is anyone still in there?' Ellen said.

Nell, white-faced, simply nodded.

Across the courtyard, more shouts caught her attention. There was Rachel, racing towards the hall, with Lewis in pursuit.

'Rachel, no!' he was shouting. 'It's not safe.'

'Ginny's in there,' Rachel shouted. 'Ginny and Christina!'

'It's too late,' Lewis shouted. 'It's too late!'

Just as she did on the football pitch, Rachel darted round one of the firefighters who tried to stop her, and sent another the wrong way. She skirted the edge of the fire wagon and without any hesitation, she clambered over the rubble at the entrance of the hall and went inside.

One of the firemen went to follow and was stopped by another.

Ellen gasped, realising just how foolish Rachel was being. Leaving Nell staring in horror she dashed across the courtyard and grabbed Lewis.

'Why has she gone in there?' she demanded. 'What is she doing?'

'She wanted to look for Christina,' Lewis said, his breathing ragged. 'Bloody stupid Christina. And I persuaded her to put her name on the list instead, but when she did, she noticed that Ginny was still missing.'

'Oh no,' Ellen breathed.

'And when the firemen told everyone to stay back, she said she couldn't leave them.' Lewis choked on a sob. 'I tried to stop her, Ellen. I did.'

Around them, everyone had fallen silent, their eyes fixed on the entrance to the munitions hall.

Ellen could feel her heart thumping. She found she was holding Lewis's hand, gripping his fingers tightly.

Then were was a shout from inside, and the fireman who'd tried to go in before, darted forward inside the entrance, then reappeared with someone in his arms. Ellen and Lewis both gasped, but then there was Rachel behind, her hair wild and her face completely black with soot and dust.

'It's Ginny,' Ellen said, seeing the red hair. 'It's Ginny, oh lord.'

Lewis was pale. 'Look at her leg.'

Ginny's leg, held carefully by the fireman, was bloodied and hanging limply. Ellen felt faint and she was glad Lewis was there by her side.

'No!' he shouted suddenly, and she looked up just in time to see Rachel heading back into the building.

'She's gone to get Christina,' Ellen said.

And then there was huge cracking sound, a groaning and a creaking, and the part of the building that was still standing swayed from side to side. Ellen had never seen anything like it; a solid, brick-built structure, waving like it was made from straw. Next to her, Lewis made an odd sound, and then he was gone – weaving past the firemen, just as Rachel had done, and into the building.

Ellen realised she was crying as she watched, begging God and the heavens and anyone who might be listening to watch over them,

Another huge crack split the air and slowly the building began to list to one side so dramatically, Ellen's stomach lurched.

'GET BACK!' one of the firemen shouted. But Ellen blinked, because through the dust and the falling debris, she could see a figure. She held her breath. And yes! It was a figure. Two of them, in fact. As they drew closer she could see it was Lewis and Rachel – thank God. Oh thank God. And between them they were carrying Christina. Her face was black with dust and her clothes were burned and soaked in blood. Her body hung between them and it was clear there was nothing to be done to help her.

They clambered over the rubble and two firemen went forward – one took Christina over his shoulder and one helped Rachel and Lewis. Then they urged them back – further away from the building. Ellen rushed to Rachel, who staggered a few paces and then sank to the ground, sobbing.

'I couldn't reach her,' she said. 'I couldn't save her.'

Lewis dropped to the ground next to her, gathering her into his arms. 'No one could have saved her,' he said, stroking Rachel's hair. 'You rescued Ginny. You saved her life.'

'I should have been faster,' Rachel cried. 'I could have got to Christina.'

Ellen cleared her dry throat. 'She was right at the heart of the explosion,' she said. 'She'd have been killed immediately.' She put her hand on Rachel's shoulder. 'You're a heroine, Rachel. Ginny is alive because of you, and Christina can have a proper burial.'

More frantic shouts started up and people began rushing past them. 'Away!' someone called. 'It's going to go up!'

Around them folk were running in all directions. Ellen dragged Rachel to her feet. 'We have to go,' she urged. 'Come on.'

And that was when the whole building exploded once more.

Chapter Forty-One

When Ellen opened her eyes she didn't know where she was. She spread her hands out and felt smooth sheets under her fingers – very different to the bedspread she slept under each night – and for a moment she felt disorientated. Then she blinked and saw Bridget sitting beside her bed.

'Why are you here?' she said.

'Well, that's nice, isn't it?' Bridget smiled. 'I've been here all night waiting for you to wake up.'

'Here?'

'You're in the infirmary,' Bridget said. She put her hand out as Ellen, shocked, tried to sit up. 'You're fine. The baby's fine. Everything's fine. You just banged your head.'

'Where's Annie?'

'With Ma. She's fine too. You've just been here since yesterday.' Bridget looked at the clock on the wall. 'It's still morning.'

Ellen closed her eyes again as memories crowded into her mind. The explosion. Ida. Christina . . .

'Ida?' she said, without opening her eyes. 'How is Ida?'

'She's just along the corridor here and she's doing well,' Bridget said. 'Very battered and bruised and she has a broken ankle and a broken arm, but she'll be fine. Rachel was the one who found her. She's a real heroine.'

'She found Ginny,' Ellen said. 'Oh gosh, her leg. Ginny's leg.'

Bridget made a face. 'She's in a bad way.'

A tear trickled down Ellen's face and she wiped it before it dripped onto the pillow. 'Poor Ginny.'

'It would have been a lot worse if Rachel hadn't been so brave.'

'And Christina?'

Bridget shook her head.

'I'm afraid she didn't make it.'

Ellen nodded, pinching her lips together.

Bridget took a breath. 'Ten folk killed altogether. Christina, and that lass from clerical that Sadie was friendly with.'

'Dilys.'

'Aye, that's the one. Seven women from the factory. Mostly from shell painting, I think. And one fireman who was too close when the second explosion happened.'

'Awful.' Ellen looked up at the ceiling, thinking about what Nell had said. 'More victims of the war.'

'That's right.' Bridget nodded. 'The whole munitions hall is gone. Hamilton's gone to pieces. Lucinda's really worried about him.'

A nurse bustled into the room. 'Oh good, you're awake,' she said. 'Headache?'

'A bit,' said Ellen. 'When can I go home?'

'Once the doctor has checked you over,' the nurse said. 'Won't be long. You're doing grand. And that baby of yours is in fine fettle. We felt him kicking away in there.'

Ellen relaxed back against the pillows, relieved. 'He's going to be a footballer,' she said. 'Like his ma.'

When Ellen was allowed home later that same day, she was pleased to discover Sadie, Rachel and Lewis all waiting for her. Bridget helped her up the stairs and Ma brought Annie round and soon her wee flat was full of people.

At first, Annie pottered around and cheered everyone up, but once she went to bed, the atmosphere was sad and muted. Ma went home to get Da's tea, and Bridget went to visit Ida, who was going to be in the infirmary for a good while yet. Then Ellen, Sadie, Rachel and Lewis – who, according to Sadie, hadn't left Rachel's side for a minute since the explosion – sat down at the table and talked.

'Was it Christina?' Ellen asked, finally putting into words what they all knew. 'Was it her that caused the explosion?'

Lewis looked shocked. 'Christina?'

Sadie and Ellen glanced at one another. 'We saw her,' Sadie said. 'She was going to the factory with a spade – we thought she was going to dig up the pitch.'

'Why?' Rachel looked pale and tired.

Sadie shrugged. 'She was a sad woman who blamed others for mistakes she'd made.'

'Blamed us,' Ellen pointed out. 'You and me and Bridget and Ida.'

'Well, whatever the reason, she went to walk through the munitions hall.'

'With a spade?' said Rachel in disbelief. 'A metal spade?'

'Aye.' Ellen nodded. 'Ida ran after her. And then the whole place exploded.'

'She didn't know that metal wasn't allowed?' Lewis was bewildered.

'Didn't know?' Ellen thought about it. 'Perhaps. She'd never worked in munitions. Or maybe she forgot.'

'We don't know for sure that it was Christina,' Rachel said slowly. 'No one will ever know for sure.'

'I suppose,' said Ellen doubtfully.

'There was an explosion in that factory in Cumbria,' Rachel said. 'Explosions happen all the time, but the newspapers don't report it.'

'We need to keep morale high,' Lewis said through gritted teeth.

'So what I'm saying is, Christina may have caused that explosion or maybe she didn't.' She took a breath. 'She's paid a terrible price for her mistake, and I don't think we should sully her memory by pointing fingers.'

Ellen stared at Rachel, who just five minutes ago, it seemed, had been a sickly wee girl. Now here she was all grown up and so very wise and brave. She looked at Sadie, who gave a tiny nod, and then back to Rachel.

'You're right,' she said. 'There's nothing to be gained by telling everyone. I'll speak to Bridget and Ida but I'm sure they'll agree.'

Rachel nodded. 'Thank you.'

Sadie, who also looked pale, with dark smudges under her eyes, sighed. 'What about the families of the folk who died?' she said. 'Dilys's husband, and that fireman's weans? Don't they deserve to know the truth?'

'The truth is, we don't know how the explosion happened,' Rachel said.

'But if Christina was still here then we'd want her to face justice . . .'

'Aye, but she's not,' Rachel said. 'She's faced the ultimate justice.'

There was a pause. 'Right,' said Sadie. 'Fair enough.

'And I think we should go to the funeral,' said Rachel.

'Oh come on,' Ellen said. 'I agree we shouldn't tell everyone she could have caused the explosion, but going to the funeral?'

'Well, I'm going to go,' Rachel said. Ellen watched as Lewis squeezed Rachel's hand and gave her a look of pride and love that made Ellen ache inside with sadness for James.

'I'll come too,' he said.

'I'll think about it,' said Ellen. 'But I'm not making any promises.'

'In the meantime, we need to get back to the Clothing Exchange,' said Sadie. 'Folk will need us now more than ever.'

'And the benevolent fund,' Rachel added.

'Aye, that's right,' said Sadie. She looked slightly weary at the prospect, Ellen thought. 'There's going to be so many people who'll need our help.'

'Just like in the strike,' Ellen reassured her. 'We helped them then.'

'Yes,' said Sadie uncertainly. 'I suppose we did.'

'Let's get to the Clothing Exchange first thing in the morning and start getting everything sorted, shall we?' Ellen said.

Rachel nodded. 'All right,' she said. 'It's not like we'll have anything else to do.'

It was a dishevelled, subdued group that met at the door of the Clothing Exchange the next day. Ellen was still a bit sore, with an egg on her head where she'd banged it. Sadie was so wan and tired-looking that Ellen thought she might keel over, right there and then. Rachel was tearful and wrung out, and Bridget was trying to help out with the Clothing Exchange, as well as visit Ida in the infirmary and somehow keep McKinley's store open at the same time.

But even so, they opened the doors, hung the sign outside, and felt pleased as locals came streaming in, either to donate clothes, shoes and bits to eat, or to make use of everything that was on offer.

By the late afternoon, everyone was exhausted, the clothes rails were almost empty and they had more bags of donations to sort out.

Sadie sat down heavily in a chair and Ellen watched her with concern.

'Sadie,' she said, 'do you think you should go and see that Dr Cohen?'

'Why?' Sadie asked. 'I wasn't hurt in the explosion.'

'I know. But you're so tired and pale and just not yourself.'

Sadie looked like she might argue, then she shrugged. 'I suppose so,' she said. 'I thought perhaps I'd been overdoing it, but maybe I need a tonic or something.'

'Can't hurt to get checked out,' Rachel said. She was putting donated shoes into pairs and checking the soles for wear. 'Look at these – the cheek of whoever gave us this pair.' She pushed her hands into the shoe and waggled her fingers through the hole in the sole.

'Bin,' said Ellen and Sadie together.

Lewis, who'd been in and out of the shop all day, making sure Rachel was all right, took the shoes and put them in a pile to throw away.

'How's your da?' asked Ellen. She'd become rather fond of Lewis, because of how devoted he clearly was to Rachel.

'Still upset of course,' Lewis said. 'Lucinda's said she'll take over at the factory to give him a break, and Da is determined he's going to pay for all the funerals.'

'Goodness,' said Ellen, impressed. 'That's very kind.'

Lewis nodded. 'He is kind, but I'm worried he's going to get himself into debt. He's comfortable but not rich, and he's offering to pay from his own pocket.'

'The factory should pay,' Sadie said, from her seat in the corner and without opening her eyes. 'Or better still, the Government.'

'Aye, but we'll be waiting a long time for that, eh?' said Lewis.

'What about the benevolent fund?' asked Ellen, who had very little idea how much a proper send-off cost. She pushed away the fact that she might need to organise something for James. 'Sadie, could the fund help pay for funerals?'

This time Sadie did open her eyes. 'Yes,' she said. 'There's enough in the bank for that. But it won't last forever.'

'I might be able to help with that,' said a voice. Hilda was standing by the door to the shop, looking – Ellen thought – absolutely marvellous.

She dashed to Hilda's side and gave her a hug.

'That's enough of that, McCallum,' Hilda said, but she didn't push Ellen away. Not at first anyway.

'I'm so pleased to see you,' Ellen said. 'Have you heard about Ginny's leg? Isn't it awful? But apparently the doctors say she'll be all right as long as it heals in the proper way. And Hetty got a load of dust in her eyes – did you hear? She's got a patch over one of them because it was all scratched and sore.'

Hilda put her hand on Ellen's arm, trying to calm the stream of chatter. Ellen understood and closed her mouth.

'What can we do for you, Hilda?' she asked.

Hilda took a breath. 'You can play football.'

Ellen laughed.

'It's sad that it's over, isn't it?'

'It's not over,' Hilda said. 'Not at all.'

'But the factory?'

'Is still up and running. Still making stretchers and horseshoes and the munitions will be back before we know it. And in the meantime, we've got a cup game to play and lots of money to make for the benevolent fund.'

Ellen stared at her.

'Are you serious?'

'I am serious.'

'You want us to carry on playing.'

'I do.'

'With this?' Ellen arched her back to make her swollen belly protrude and smoothed her skirt over it.

'Well, you might have to,' Hilda gave a small, grim smile. 'We've lost a few players. Ginny and Hetty, and Nell's helping her da with the funerals. We need more women to step up.'

'Oh, Hilda I'm really not sure this is a good idea,' said Ellen. 'The cup game is only supposed to be a week or so away. We can't find a new team now.'

'It won't be easy, but we'll try our best.'

'Sadie will play,' Rachel said. 'Won't you, Sadie?'

'Erm, I'm not sure of the rules,' said Sadie looking alarmed.

'Och, Sadie, it's not hard. Don't be such a baby.' Rachel put her hands on her hips and glared at her sister.

Sadie rolled her eyes. 'Fine, I'll play,' she said. 'But don't expect me to be like Rachel.'

'Lucinda will do it,' Lewis said. 'I'll talk her into it.'

'Great,' said Hilda. 'Who else?'

'Bridget might have a go. Oh and what about the suffragettes?' said Ellen. 'They're all bored of bandage rolling. Helen would definitely want to help. And maybe some of the others.'

'Can you speak to them?' Hilda said.

'I'll find them tomorrow.'

'Get them to come to the pitch in the afternoon,' Hilda said. 'We've got a week to get you all into some sort of a team and quite frankly, I think I'm on a hiding to nothing, but we'll see.'

Ellen nodded meekly. 'We'll do our best,' she promised.

Chapter Forty-Two

Christina's funeral was a sorry affair. Only the front three pews at St Andrew's were filled. The front row had a sour-faced elderly woman in a fur stole, even though it was June, alongside an equally stern-looking young man in an officer's uniform – Christina's mother and brother, Rachel assumed.

Behind were some of the suffragettes, a few women from the police service, Lucinda and Hamilton Blyth, then Rachel herself with Lewis, Ellen, Sadie and Bridget. Ida had wanted to come but she was to stay in hospital for a few more days.

So it was a small band of mourners that gathered. The eulogy was short, simply mentioning Christina being a daughter and sister, and a proud member of the Women's Police Service. When it became clear nothing was going to be said about her support of the suffragettes, the women in the second row whispered briefly to one another in disapproval. No one looked very sad, except for poor Hamilton, who was still struggling to come to terms with what had happened. He looked much older suddenly and leaned on Lucinda's arm when they stood to sing 'Abide With Me'.

After the ceremony, Christina's mother and brother walked down the aisle of the church, and Rachel heard the woman say: 'What would you like for supper? I was thinking of asking Cook to get some lamb chops?'

Aghast at such indifference from a bereaved mother, she

glanced at Lewis, who'd heard it too, and raised her eyebrows. No wonder Christina had been such a difficult woman, she thought, if that was the family she'd been raised in.

As if he read her mind, Lewis squeezed her arm. 'If we ever have children,' he said into her ear, 'let's give them so much love they grow up to be perfectly delightful, friendly, sweet-natured types.'

Rachel, thrilled at the very notion of having children with Lewis, squeezed his arm back in agreement.

Christina's mother and brother didn't stay for the burial, but the rest of the mourners did. It was one of those summer days where rain and sun alternated every few minutes and the breeze whipped hats from heads, so the vicar didn't spend too long over the words. And then it was done and Christina was gone, and Rachel felt so sad that her whole life had amounted to this quick, bleak ritual, with mourners who'd all clearly rather have been elsewhere.

But she didn't have long to fret about it, because they were all heading to the factory for football practice with the new members of the team.

'I'll meet you there,' Sadie said, coming over. 'I just have to pop to see Dr Cohen. See if he can give me a tonic.'

'Good luck,' said Rachel with a grin. 'Though I think you'll find the best tonic is putting on your football kit and running around. That's what Hilda would say.'

Sadie rolled her eyes. 'I'm not sure me running around in shorts is good for anyone,' she joked. 'But needs must. I'll be there in an hour.'

Rachel went to chivvy along the other players. 'Come on,' she urged. 'You need to learn that Hilda does not welcome latecomers.'

Lucinda was talking to Lewis, a worried look on her face. He beckoned Rachel over.

'I'm going to go back to the factory with my father, while Lucinda plays football,' he said. 'She doesn't want him to be alone.'

Rachel felt uncharitably annoyed that Lewis wouldn't be coming with her, but she knew that Hamilton was suffering, and she was proud that Lewis was supporting him.

'You're a good man, Lewis Blyth,' she said.

He smiled at her. 'Have I proved myself, then?'

'Diving into a collapsing building to save my life?' Rachel said. 'I think that's enough.'

Lewis glanced left and right, saw that everyone else was distracted with conversations, and gave her a quick kiss that left her legs feeling a little wobbly. 'I'll see you later,' he said.

With a rush of giddy pleasure, Rachel gathered the suffragettes – Helen, Agnes and Willa – who had volunteered to play football, as well as Lucinda, Bridget and Ellen, and hurried them all along the road to the factory, where Hilda was waiting, with papers in her hand and a whistle round her neck. She looked like she meant business.

'Right!' she bellowed. 'Three laps of the field.'

The women – all still wearing their funeral garb – looked alarmed.

'Hilda, we just need to get changed first,' Rachel said.

Hilda laughed. 'Course you do. I'm getting ahead of myself. Off you go, but be quick now.'

Sadie was staring at Dr Cohen in disbelief.

'I'm sorry,' she said. 'Can you repeat everything you just said?'

Noah, who was sitting beside her, took her hand and she was so glad he was there.

'From the beginning,' he added.

Dr Cohen looked at Sadie. 'You're pregnant,' he said. 'Quite far along by my estimate. I'd say four months.'

Sadie couldn't speak for a moment. She looked at Noah, who was as surprised as she was.

'Four months?'

'At least,' Dr Cohen said. 'I'm surprised you've not felt any movements.'

'Movements?' Sadie repeated, still in shock. 'What kind of movements?'

'From the baby. I believe most women describe it as a fluttering sensation.'

Sadie dropped her hand to her abdomen, which – now she thought about it – was firmer than usual and slightly rounded. 'I thought it was wind from something I'd eaten that disagreed with me,' she said, beginning to laugh. 'I thought I'd had too much cabbage.'

Noah started to chuckle too. 'It's not cabbage,' he said. 'It's a baby.'

'It most certainly is,' said Dr Cohen fondly. 'Congratulations.'

'Four months?' Sadie said again.

'Maybe five,' Dr Cohen said. 'I'll book you another appointment and we can have a proper look.'

'Last time . . .' Sadie began.

But Dr Cohen shook his head. 'There are no guarantees, as I'm sure you know,' he said. 'But you are a good deal further along than you were last time. I'm feeling optimistic. Just be careful, won't you? Lots of rest.' He looked at Noah. 'Don't let her do too much. No climbing up ladders or hanging out the washing. Best to keep your arms by your sides.'

Sadie raised an eyebrow, thinking of all the women she'd known over the years who'd hung out washing and more besides while they were expecting, but she didn't argue.

'What about football?' Noah asked. 'Sadie's just been recruited to play in the Wentworth team.'

'Absolutely not,' said Dr Cohen. 'I forbid it.' He made a note on his pad, tutting to himself. 'Now, I do have other patients to see so if you make an appointment with Miss Clark on your way out, we'll meet again in a couple of days.'

'All right,' said Sadie, slowly getting to her feet and realising as she did so that she'd not been bending properly at the waist for a while now. And that her skirt was digging into her skin because it was so tight. She felt a bit a silly that she'd not noticed all these changes happening. But, she reasoned, there had been a lot happening with the news about James, and worrying about Ellen, the benevolent fund, and Bessie, and then the explosion and the aftermath, and now preparations for the final of the Munitionettes' Cup . . .

'No football?' she said to Noah as they went down the steps outside Dr Cohen's surgery. 'Hilda's going to be furious.'

'Och, we'll name the baby after her,' said Noah gleefully. 'She'll get over it.'

'The baby,' said Sadie. 'Noah, we're having a baby!'

Noah picked her up and spun her round. 'WE'RE HAVING A BABY!' he shouted. A woman who was walking past, laden with shopping bags, glared at him.

'You're not the first and you won't be the last,' she said.

Noah put Sadie back on her feet, both collapsing into giggles. 'Well, that's us told,' he said.

Hand in hand they sauntered towards the station. 'Do you not have to go back to work?' Sadie asked Noah. He'd been given a break to come to the doctor with her.

'I asked for the whole day off,' he said. He bit his lip. 'I thought it might be bad news.'

'Well it's not,' Sadie sang. 'It's wonderful news!'

'Shall I come back to the factory with you and help you tell Hilda?' Noah asked.

'Yes please.'

Noah gave her a kiss. 'If we hurry, there's a train in ten minutes. I'll just buy a newspaper to read on the way.'

He walked across the pavement to where a young lad was selling that evening's first edition. But when he came back he was white-faced and trembling, staring at the front page as he walked.

'What?' Sadie asked. 'Noah, what is it?'

Slowly, he turned the paper round and held it up for her to see.

'Oh my goodness,' Sadie gasped. 'Oh my goodness!'

She grabbed the newspaper from Noah and examined it closely, Then she looked up at her astonished husband. 'We have to get back to Clydebank!' she said. 'Let's go.'

The football training was going very badly indeed. Ellen was working hard to stop Hilda from descending into complete despair.

'Are you sure you won't play?' Hilda kept saying to her, and Ellen kept shaking her head. 'I can't, Hilda. You know that.'

Hilda raked her fingers through her hair and looked at the women on the pitch. 'That Willa's quick and she's got a good right foot,' she said. 'We can put her up front and bring Rachel forward too.'

Ellen nodded, wondering what James and his shipmates would suggest. They had all said to be braver, bolder, more willing to take risks. 'Lucinda's dogged,' she said. 'She's not always accurate but she keeps going. We should put her behind the two forwards to help get the ball up the pitch.'

'Nice,' said Hilda, scribbling on her notes. 'Yes.'

'Then stick Agnes on the wing, because she's really fast,' said Ellen, thinking hard. 'Put Helen and Bridget either side in defence.'

Hilda sighed.

'I know,' Ellen said. 'But they're both willing to have a go, even if they're not brilliant.'

'Best we've got,' admitted Hilda. 'That'll do, then, and we'll put Sadie in the middle? That could work.'

'And maybe we can persuade Nell to play?' Ellen suggested. 'I know she's been helping her da but it's just one day and most of the funerals have taken place now.'

'It's worth a try,' said Hilda.

'I can play,' said a voice. They turned to see Hetty, still with one eye patched, but wearing her kit. 'The doctor said I'll be fine.' She gave a small smile. 'Just put me on the other side to usual, because I can't see.'

Hilda gave a very un-Hilda-like squeal. 'Thank goodness,' she said. 'We can drop Willa back to midfield, then,' she said to Ellen, who wrote it down. 'Go on,' she said to Hetty. 'Get cracking.'

'Nothing's changed, then,' Hetty said to Ellen with a grin.

'Nothing whatsoever,' said Ellen.

Out on the pitch, the women were clearly trying their absolute best, and failing completely. Ellen stifled a laugh as she watched Bridget try to kick the ball, get tangled in her own feet and tumble onto the grass on her behind.

Next to her, Hilda closed her eyes.

'We just have to play,' Ellen reassured her. 'We just have to turn up to get the money for the benevolent fund.'

She ignored the little voice inside her that reminded her she'd promised James she was going to bring the Munitionettes' Cup home to Clydebank for him. 'Sorry,' she said to him in her head. 'Maybe next year, eh?'

'FRANKLIN!' Hilda yelled at Rachel across the pitch. 'Go and help Bridget to her feet, for pity's sake. She's like a ladybird stuck on its back.'

'I heard that,' Bridget shouted back.

Ellen laughed.

'Hetty, I know you're blind in one eye, but surely you can see the goal?' Hilda was shouting now. Cheerfully, Hetty stuck her tongue out and carried on running.

'It's not about winning,' Ellen said.

'Are you trying to convince me or yourself,' Hilda said with a wry smile. 'AGNES! RUN FORWARDS!'

Across the way, Ellen saw two figures running full-pelt towards the football pitch. She narrowed her eyes. Was that Sadie? she wondered. And Noah? What was he doing here? Lewis appeared near them and Noah called something to him. There was a little pause, then he was running too.

'What's going on?' Ellen said to Hilda. 'Why is Sadie running to us?'

Hilda looked over. 'No idea,' she said. 'Is she crying?' She squinted. 'Or laughing?'

Ellen tried to make out Sadie's expression as she drew nearer. 'Both?' she suggested.

'ELLEN!' Sadie was calling. 'ELLEN!'

Now all the women on the pitch had stopped playing and were watching too. Sadie got close and stopped running, resting her elbows on her knees awkwardly and taking great gulps of air.

'Look,' she said. 'Look at this.' She held out the newspaper and Ellen took it.

'Front page,' Noah said.

Confused, Ellen shook out the paper and stared in amazement. The headline exclaimed 'Survivors!' and beneath the writing was a large photograph of about twelve men, all wearing life vests and all looking tired but happy. And there, right in the middle, with a broad grin, was James.

'What's this?' she said, not taking it in at first. 'What does this mean?'

All around her the women were gathering, trying to see what was happening. Ellen turned to Bridget. 'What does this mean?' she asked, thrusting the newspaper at her sister.

'The twelve survivors of HMS *Hampshire*, photographed for the first time since they arrived on Orkney on rafts,' Bridget read.

'Orkney?' Ellen repeated in wonder. 'Orkney?'

'The survivors drifted off course as they tried to make land and only reached Orkney on Friday, after the lighthouse keeper at Hoy Sound spotted their raft. An official from the War Office is journeying to Orkney to speak to the survivors.'

Ellen looked at Bridget, who was fighting tears. 'Then it lists the names,' Bridget carried on. 'And there . . .' She jabbed the paper. 'There it says Able Seaman James McCallum.'

Ellen sat down suddenly on the grass, because her legs couldn't hold her up.

'He's alive?' she said. 'My James is alive?'

Sadie sat down next to her, more slowly, then Bridget too, and Rachel.

'He's alive,' Bridget told her.

'Just like you said,' Sadie added.

'He's coming home?'

'He is,' said Rachel. She looked at the newspaper. 'Well, eventually.'

Ellen put her hand to her mouth. 'Gosh,' she muttered.

And then suddenly all four of them were crying and laughing and hugging and talking nineteen to the dozen about how Ellen could send a telegram to Orkney and how James would come home.

'I don't want to interrupt,' said Hilda after a while. 'But we do have a football match in just a few days and we really need to get on with training.'

Ellen wiped her face. 'You're right,' she said. 'Help me up, Bridget. I'm like a beached whale these days. We really do have to bring the Munitionettes' Cup home now.'

'No pressure,' said Rachel with a grimace, getting to her feet and holding a hand out to Sadie.

'Ah,' said Sadie, as she got up. 'About that.'

'About what?' replied Hilda icily. 'About football?'

'Yes,' Sadie said, looking sheepish. 'I can't play.'

Ellen's outraged squawk of 'Sadie!' was matched by the others' equally frustrated groans. But Sadie was smiling so broadly that Ellen was confused. 'What?' she said. 'Why can't you play?'

'Dr Cohen told me not to,' Sadie said. 'In fact, he said he would forbid me from playing.'

'Are you sick?' Rachel asked, worried.

'Not sick,' Sadie said. 'No.'

Ellen knew what her friend was about to say. She did a little bounce on her toes. 'Sadie . . .' she said. 'Are you . . .?'

'I'm pregnant!' Sadie announced. 'I'm having a baby!'

'Oh for heaven's sake,' said Hilda good-naturedly as the women all cheered and clapped and slapped Sadie on the back – gently. 'Not another one of you.'

Epilogue

They didn't win the final. The Munitionettes' Cup went home to Liverpool instead of Clydebank. But even though the Wentworth players were disappointed to have lost the match – and lost it convincingly, Ellen had to admit – they felt like they'd won.

The match was held at Wentworth, even though it had been planned for Liverpool. Hamilton had talked the organisers into moving it to Clydebank to boost morale, and as a way of raising more money for the benevolent fund. And so, once again, thousands of spectators piled into the seating. Ginny was there, in a wheelchair, alongside Ida, in her own chair. They were both joined by nurses from the infirmary who'd volunteered to look after them on their days off.

Bessie's ma came with news that Bessie was on the mend, and Nell arrived straight from the cemetery in the nick of time, throwing off her black funeral outfit and diving into her kit as the whistle blew.

The match itself was terrible. The Liverpool team – Nolan's Ironworks – were a goal up after two minutes and by half time it was four. Hetty managed to sneak one past their keeper early in the second half, and Rachel was given a penalty towards the end of the game that she fired into the net, but Nolan's weren't resting on their laurels, and they scored another three, making the final score a rather embarrassing seven-two.

But none of the Wentworth team cared. Not really. They whooped and cheered as Nolan's went up to lift the cup. They might not have been celebrating victory but they were celebrating life.

The money poured into the donation tins, a piper played, folk began dancing on the field as the Nolan's players passed around the cup, and the Wentworth women hugged. It was a celebration of hope, where just a couple of weeks ago there had been fear and danger and death.

There were so many people on the pitch, dancing and singing and laughing, that when Ellen saw a familiar figure through the crowd, she thought her eyes were deceiving her. She blinked a few times, tilting her head to see past a group of Nolan's girls who were singing a raucous victory chant. Annie was dancing round her legs, and now Ellen bent down to her daughter and picked her up.

'Annie,' she said. 'Look.'

She pointed through the gaps in the Nolan's women, needing someone else to confirm what she thought she saw, even though that someone was a two-year-old girl who was giddy with dancing.

'Can you see who that is?'

Annie looked at Ellen and then she smiled.

'It's Dada,' she said.

And then Ellen was off, gripping Annie tightly as she wove through the crowds on the pitch to get to James.

'You're here?' she said, as she stood in front of him. 'You're really, truly here?'

James smiled his lovely, familiar smile.

'Aye,' he said. 'I'm here.'

She went to him, and they embraced. She felt his face and his breath and the very realness of him and only then did she let herself believe he was actually there. Thinner and paler perhaps, but alive and well.

Little Annie was giggling in between them, putting her skinny arms round each of their necks and pulling them in close.

'You've got so big,' James said, nuzzling Annie's ear.

'I'm two,' she told him.

'Well I never,' he said.

'I didn't bring the cup home for you,' Ellen said. 'I'm sorry.'

'I came home to you instead.'

'That's better than any cup.'

They stood there for a long while, forehead to forehead, looking at one another, and laughing with Annie.

'So tell me,' said James eventually. 'What's been going on here?'

Ellen looked around at the blackened shell of the munitions hall, at Hetty's patched eye, at Ginny in her wheelchair, and Ida with her broken limbs, Bridget's hand protectively on her shoulder. She looked at Rachel and Lewis, arms entwined, at Lucinda sitting in the ticket booth counting donations. And she looked at Sadie and Noah, his hand on her belly. Then she looked back at James.

'Oh, you know,' she said. 'Nothing much.'

Acknowledgements

I've wanted to write about women's football for ages, so a big thank you to my brilliant editor Samantha Eades for giving me the opportunity! Also thanks to Snigdha Koirala for her support, and to my agent Amanda Preston, who's always got my back.

Thank you to the England women's team and the Scotland women's team, and all the women and girls playing football at every level, for making everyone more interested in the game.

And, of course, a big thank you to my readers. I hope you enjoy this one.

Credits

Posy Lovell and Orion Fiction would like to thank everyone at Orion who worked on the publication of *Last Witness* in the UK.

Editorial
Sam Eades
Snigdha Koirala

Copy editor
Sally Partington

Proof reader
Marian Reid

Audio
Paul Stark
Louise Richardson

Contracts
Dan Herron
Ellie Bowker
Oliver Chacón

Design
Rose Cooper

Editorial Management
Charlie Panayiotou
Jane Hughes
Bartley Shaw

Finance
Jasdip Nandra
Nick Gibson
Sue Baker

Production
Ruth Sharvell

Sales
Catherine Worsley
Esther Waters
Victoria Laws
Toluwalope Ayo-Ajala
Rachael Hum
Ellie Kyrke-Smith
Frances Doyle
Georgina Cutler

Operations
Jo Jacobs

If you loved *Victory for the Sewing Factory Girls*, then make sure to pick up *The Sewing Factory Girls* – the first in this uplifting series!

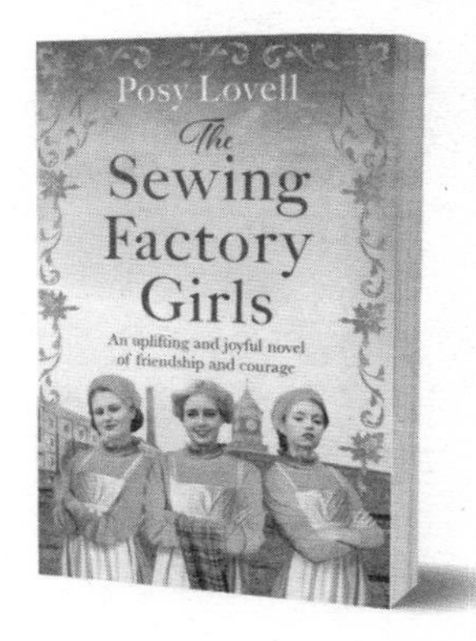

Like half of all the young women living in the Scottish town Clydebank in early 1911, Ellen works at the sewing machine factory. So does her big sister, Bridget, Bridget's fiancé Malcolm, and her new friend Sadie, who has come to work at the factory after the death of her father . . .

For Sadie, the factory is a way to make ends meet, but Ellen has sewing in her veins. She is even making Bridget's wedding dress on her beloved sewing machine. But after the excitement of the wedding dies down, everything changes. Ellen discovers that the work of the cabinet polishers – her job – is to be reorganised, and they will be doing more work for less pay.

Ellen feels betrayed – the sewing factory is her family and they've let her down. Sadie is more pragmatic. But the women aren't going to give in without a fight. They've been reading about strikes and they've got an idea – much to the disgust of manager Malcolm.

Meanwhile, Bridget, forced to choose between her husband and her sister, has made a new friend and is fighting her own battle, alongside the suffragettes.

The events of the strike will throw Ellen, Bridget and Sadie's lives into turmoil but also bring these women closer to each other than they could ever have imagined.

ORDER NOW!

Don't miss the heartwarming wartime tale from Posy Lovell, *The Kew Gardens Girls*!

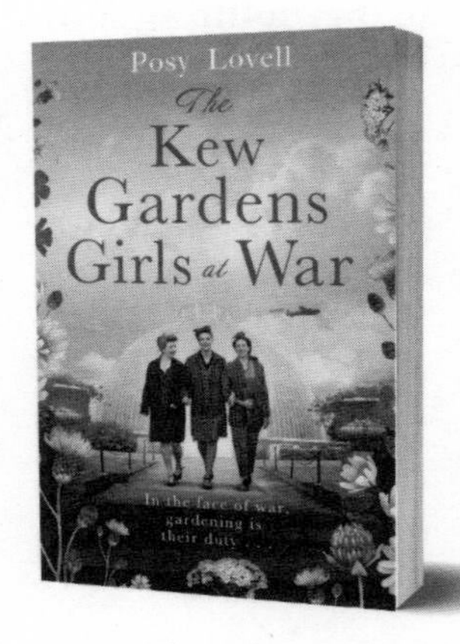

It's 1940 and for newlywed Daisy Turner, Kew Gardens is a haven away from the bombs that are falling nightly on her East End home. She grew up around plants – her parents met when they were gardeners at Kew in the last war. And her work on the Dig For Victory campaign at Kew keeps her occupied while her husband Rex, is away in the RAF.

Beth Sanderson works with Daisy at the gardens, but she dreams of being a doctor while juggling her gardening job with nursing shifts. And there's the added complication of her forbidden romance with her colleague, Gus Campbell. Gus is from Jamaica and it seems impossible for he and Beth to be together. But can they overcome the prejudice they're facing and build a life together?

Meanwhile Louisa Armitage, who worked at Kew Gardens during the First World War, is feeling old and useless, having retired to the countryside. So she jumps at the chance to work with Kew again and rally the WI to get them involved in growing plants for medicines.

With Daisy and Beth becoming minor celebrities and featuring in magazines and on newsreels, the Kew Gardens Girls are the talk of the town. But when tragedy strikes and Daisy's life is changed forever, it falls to her friends at Kew Gardens to step in and save her and her family. Before it's too late.

ORDER NOW!